The Proving

Thomas Szollosi

Doubleday

NEW YORK   LONDON   TORONTO   SYDNEY   AUCKLAND

Published by Doubleday, a division of Bantam Doubleday Dell Publishing Group, Inc., 666 Fifth Avenue, New York, N.Y. 10103

DOUBLEDAY and the portrayal of an anchor with a dolphin are trademarks of Doubleday, a division of Bantam Doubleday Dell Publishing Group, Inc.

Library of Congress Cataloging-in-Publication Data

Szollosi, Thomas.
    The proving/Thomas Szollosi.
    p.   cm.
    ISBN 0-385-24239-5
    I. Title
PS3569.Z6P76   1988   87-19711
813'.54—dc19

For Donna, Evan, my parents, and brother Jim.
For Richard C., Stephen J., for Dewey, and Chris.
And of course, for Fred.

Part One

One

HUSKY MARTIN's wide, friendly face showed none of the almost obsessive determination he'd been displaying for the last few months. Right now, it was creased in a smile as he buzzed his secretary, Marge Glass.

"You know what I want you to do, Marge?"

"Usually," came the answer over the intercom.

He could hear the smile in it. Smug, barely qualifying as double entendre.

"I want you to call Dr. Beerey and set me up for that root canal I've been threatening to have."

"He's not on the plane yet."

"He's as good as on the plane."

There was a moment's silence before Marge finally sighed. "Jesus, I thought you were a pro, Husky."

He grinned, turning his face away from the windowed wall of his lieutenant's office so she couldn't see her victory. On a whim he opened a desk drawer and pulled out a bottle of scotch. The Styrofoam cup that had held his last cup of coffee would do for a quick nip. Celebrational.

As she hung up, Marge looked up to see Husky coming out of his office. He was a couple years her senior, but they were *both* too old for the flirting banter that went on between them. Still, they looked forward to it.

"You know your car's gonna take at least another day," she told him. "Which means a total of four days from now."

He sighed. "I've still got the rental." Shook his head. "What's the new reason?"

"Mechanic won't settle for English connectors. He says the rubber's always bad in English connectors, so he's waiting for German connectors." She smiled as if she actually understood this.

"Connectors to what?"

She lit a menthol, giving him the look she normally reserved for the guys who hadn't been with the department as long as she had. Which was everybody here in Homicide except for Husky. She emitted a cloud of smoke.

"Your car, right? You should know."

"Never have before."

She put her chin on her palm, smiling at him. She allowed him, more than anybody else in this place, to see the way she genuinely liked him.

"I told you five years ago, Husky, English cars are the rolling dogshit of the world. When Marge tells you something like that, you listen, 'cause Marge's got a brother in the auto business. And he says English is dogshit."

"You're a poet, Marge."

Husky turned away on her smile and nod, still enjoying the slight peppery sensation of the scotch on his lips and tongue as he headed for the elevator.

"Gonna kiss him goodbye?"

Husky just nodded, looking back and sharing a smile.

4

Then he showed her his teeth and pointed to them as if to say: "Make the appointment." She nodded and gave him the okay sign. Already done.

"Beerey said come right over," she called out.

The elevator closed and he was gone.

Inside, descending, Husky stood comfortably, hands at his sides, staring at the numbers as they dropped.

Today he was shipping Edgar Lamp back to Dallas.

Husky drove from Parker Center to the impassive concrete of L.A. County Jail. He entered by the main doors, waving as he passed the desk, not bothering to see if he got a wave back. Sheriffs ran the jail, and though they didn't particularly worship LAPD, Husky had friends here. He'd bought enough lunches and drinks to ensure that.

His mind was on the logistics of transporting Edgar Lamp to Los Angeles International Airport. He wouldn't personally go along, but he'd won the point of having two of his own detectives, Stu Johnson and Clay Terrance, sitting on either side of Lamp for the whole flight. Sheriffs would sit in other, neighboring seats.

Husky's hard shoes sounded like a racquetball court as he went down the boomy hallway leading to PRISONER COUNSELING, as the sign said. He was the only man in the hallway. From behind a massive metal door ahead, the eye of a deputy Husky knew only as Charley watched him through the small wire-reinforced glass aperture. He held his badge aloft for inspection when he got there, even though Charley had let him pass a million times before. No exaggeration. A million, easy.

Edgar Lamp and Garth Cheesbro sat face to face in the small interrogation/counseling room when Husky came in. Garth was Husky's oldest friend, the two going back to UCLA about a century before, it seemed. They'd been

5

English majors together; only Garth had stayed with the written word. Now, thanks to his connection with Husky, he was doing the book on Edgar Lamp. Husky hated Lamp, but he could see where the fascination came from. Serial killers made brisk sales.

In Dallas, Lamp would be tried for the murders of twenty-eight young women. In Los Angeles, he had already been tried and convicted of the murders of twenty-eight young men. Husky would never understand why women in Dallas had changed to men in L.A.

Garth was doing the book and *he* didn't understand, at least not yet. But he kept vowing to "crack the code," as he put it. Husky would believe that when he saw it.

Right now it looked like Edgar was in one of his closed-off moods. Not hard to understand, considering he was about to get sent away for round two. He sat back in the plastic seat, avoiding Garth's eyes. His arms were folded in front of him, but the nerves he couldn't hide made his feet bouncy with agitation. Husky looked at the two men from the open doorway a moment, then entered and closed it behind him.

Edgar stared right at Husky. Their relationship was different. Garth might be the prober, but Husky had been the hunter. And he'd brought Edgar in, which always earned him the dead-on stare.

"Thought you were gettin' a haircut," Husky said.

Edgar tossed the unruly tangle he'd kept intact. He wasn't a massive guy, not somebody you'd imagine over-powering many people. He ran his fingers through his hair. Husky noticed for the hundredth time how bony the arms were. He'd stopped trying to figure where the strength . . . the violence . . . came from. Edgar just looked back, not saying a thing.

"You know those judges in Dallas're only gonna hate

you more with the hair. That's the only reason I'm saying what I'm saying."

Edgar smiled. "Yeah, you're losin' sleep nights worryin' 'bout how I'm gonna get a fair trial."

"Yes, I am." Husky didn't smile back. " 'Cause when you're through being nailed, I want you to stay that way."

"It won't hold. It's all gonna fall to shit, 'cause you got nothin.' "

"Not what the L.A. jury thought, was it?" Husky looked to Garth. "Any new revelations from our buddy?"

"We're reluctant today," Garth said.

"No last-minute tidbits of wisdom from the Emissary of the Dark Place?"

Edgar's face didn't change.

"You know, Edgar, the one thing nobody's ever been able to pin down is exactly why. Why *did* you kill all of 'em?"

Edgar leaned forward a little, looking confidential.

"I never *said* I killed anybody at all."

Husky couldn't let the moment pass.

"You're gone."

"Eat shit, Martin. I'm *never* gone. I'm *always* here."

"That what you used to tell Grandma and Grandpa?"

Edgar just laughed. Husky checked his watch. It was almost time. The little fleet of sheriff's cars would be in position to take Edgar to LAX, hand him over to Terrance and Johnson, and fly him out of here.

Husky and Garth watched them stuff Edgar Lamp into the back of an armor-plated sheriff's car, one of six in the convoy, which then took off for the airport.

"When you flying down?" Husky said after a few moments.

"I don't know, week or so." Garth would do back-

7

ground on the Dallas judge and attorneys before the trial began.

But he'd already been to Texas once, digging around for some sense of what really beat where Edgar Lamp's heart was supposed to be. The simple facts of it all were almost enough to shape a theory.

■ ■ ■ ■ ■

Lamp Luck

Edgar had lived with his mother and father on a small farm in East Texas. The farm itself was a flat, infertile square of hopeless land, though most of East Texas is lush, green, and great for growing almost anything.

Lamp luck, relatives called it.

In one awful winter, the place simply seemed to wear Edgar's parents down; sapping strength, energy, and optimism right out of two nice young people. After that the dry, dead soil might just as well have opened right up and swallowed both of them.

The truth was almost as simple, though hardly as romantic. First Edgar's mother, Carrie, caught pneumonia and died quickly over a single weekend.

That left Edgar's father, Stanley, who was unable to deal with the loss. He sank into a constant drunken state and simply withdrew.

Edgar's paternal grandparents, Harper and Alice Lamp, finally decided something had to be done after weeks of this, so Harper showed up and took Edgar away for his own sake.

Allowed to follow his own course, Stanley Lamp sank deeper, until one night he went for a drive at 4 A.M. With icy roads and falling sleet, the accident was probably no more than a drunken error in judgment.

Harper, however, became convinced his son had committed sui-

8

cide. A mortal sin. He decided that if the father could do such a thing, it was entirely possible such traits had been passed on to the boy. Harper would strive to fight such tendencies in his grandson with all his might.

He was, he believed, uniquely qualified to do so.

Harper Lamp was an old-fashioned, scorch-the-tent-with-the-heat-of-your-passion preacher.

Even Alice Lamp Corinth, Edgar's surviving grandmother, believed that her then husband, Harper, took the task of saving Edgar much too far. She believed, in fact, that he took it to the point of insanity.

■ ■ ■ ■ ■

Dr. Beerey, not a man to sugarcoat much, made a face and shook his head.

"You're a damn fool to wait six months to do something like this."

Husky glared at him from behind the cotton, water lines and hardware that Beerey had perched in his mouth at the moment.

"Look," he tried to say, "I came here right away. I finished the job I had to do fifteen minutes ago and this is the first thing I'm doing, all right?"

"You couldn't've taken one lousy afternoon in six months?"

Husky pulled some cotton out of his mouth to talk better.

"I couldn't take the chance. The guy was way too dangerous when he was out there running around. And then when we caught him we had to move fast or we'd lose witnesses. People don't like to stick around for a thing like Edgar Lamp's trial. He scares 'em."

Beerey plainly didn't give a shit.

9

"Well, you had your priorities. But now I'm gonna have to go deeper than I thought." He put the cotton back in.

"You shoulda been a fucking barber," Husky growled. "Dentists will *all* go to hell," he added. It felt like somebody was taking a jackhammer to the right side of his skull. Cold air, cold water, and that goddamned quasi-mint smell were all irritating the shit out of him. He'd have put this off longer if he'd imagined the pain. It had passed irritation, passed discomfort. It had become hell.

Beerey probed a bit more with one of his shiny silver pointed probers and Husky arched his back and gasped a little *ah* of pain, shutting his eyes and wincing.

"That's too much for one face to do, Husky," Beerey kidded.

Husky glared up. The comment hadn't felt much better than the probe.

"Do I pay you for banter?"

"For a man with a mouth like yours, I should charge just for acknowledging your existence on earth. Your entire dental picture is green . . . and not from the light in here. Your molars line up like the headstones in a very old cemetery. Just after an earthquake."

"I'm glad to hear all this." Husky looked past Beerey at the blinding reflector bulb that lit his face morgue style.

"I've seen prettier train wrecks," Beerey persisted.

"Keep working." Husky finally sighed.

"Just letting you recover from the last round of pain, if that's okay . . ."

"If he's in pain, I'm coming in from the waiting room," said Garth, a little louder and cheerier than Husky would've liked. Garth ambled around the corner and smiled down at Husky just as Beerey leaned between them and went on with his inquisitional practices.

Husky moaned. It really hurt. Garth winced, caught his

10

breath for just a moment, then went on to divert his buddy.

"You're luckier than you know, Husk. Really good guys like Beerey here are more skilled than your basic great sculptors. They drive their lab boys to the point of suicide getting just the right plates. They slave over mouths that reek of halitosis and onion-soup lunches . . ."

"They molest little boys . . ." Husky managed to get out.

Then he shuddered in pain again. Garth looked at the back of Beerey's head and wondered. Naw. Couldn't have done that just because . . .

Husky gasped again. Shuddered. Moaned.

"Root canals are not the most fun in the world, Husky," said Beerey through his own tightly clenched teeth, "but when they're over you're glad you had 'em."

"Jury's out . . ."

"I ever tell you I had a root canal once?" Garth asked, leaning his padded middle against the doorjamb as he watched.

"On the way over," Husky told him wearily. "In detail."

"It wasn't as bad as yours sounds," Garth said honestly.

"I know. I remember the details. You're fucking *good* at details."

Garth smiled.

Along with his burgeoning book career, Garth was radio columnist for the L.A. *Times,* a chore he'd looked after contentedly for the past fifteen years and would just as soon keep till retirement, whenever that might be. Garth listened to the radio a lot and batted out columns on the personal computer he kept at home. He phoned it in and showed up at the office nowadays to pick up checks and attend the odd staff meeting. It was his dream job.

It was also routine. Edgar Lamp wasn't. Edgar was

11

Garth's dream adventure, a Hitchcockian brain mangler of an investigation. And of course, writing about it put Garth unusually close to the goings-on of the case. In a sense it was sort of his property, so he wasn't above offering Husky the weight of his intellect. Husky had known that intellect from the UCLA days, which Husky said were "sometime before the dawning of the human consciousness and sometime after we both graduated from high school."

He might joke about it all, but Husky took Garth seriously. There was no other continuing relationship of such durability in Husky's life.

After UCLA, Husky became bored with substitute teaching jobs, advertising copy jobs, occasional inept magazine pieces, and the general grinding poverty and disillusionment that falls on ex-lit. majors like so many volumes of the Oxford English Dictionary.

He therefore did what he'd always, deep in his heart, longed to do. He became a cop.

His father laughed at him, his mother took to career nail biting, and his old friend Garth Cheesbro, by then entrenched in his family while working on a rag somewhere out in Riverside and closing fast on the L.A. market, envied the shit out of him.

Not that envy meant *complete* envy. Garth couldn't truly covet the lifestyle of a man who spent most of his time up there in that goddamn airless office in Parker Center, hovering over his desk, placating the little fascist called "Chief" while supervising a breathtakingly ghastly rainbow of murder investigations.

Of course, Husky didn't have a helluva lot to go running home to. He'd never married, choosing instead to live with three or four different women over the years. He referred to them as his "ladies."

Not with the arrogant, demeaning tone younger guys

12

used these days. He said "lady" as if it meant "woman of value," not "broad." Not some biker's "laaaady."

All that was past tense now. Husky hadn't lived with anyone in five years. When Garth asked him why, he laughed, pointed to the remains of his once burly, strong body, and shook his head.

"Molecules in constant flux. Mostly downward flux."

Garth tried to encourage Husky to join some kind of social organization. Maybe one with women in similar flux. Husky told him to butt out. Cops were the social organization he needed to fill his time with.

"Afraid you'll look pathetic, Husky?"

"No. I know I look pathetic. And I'm not gonna have some woman, young or old or otherwise, check me out and wish she'd stayed home to watch Dynasty.*"*

"I don't mean naked," Garth had kept up. "Naked we all look pathetic. There is nothing as ridiculously anticlimactic as a naked person. Particularly the male variety. I was referring to your fear of looking pathetic while trying to be a human with something to offer."

"Do you charge money for this, or do I just thank you profusely?"

Garth hadn't been dissuaded. He pressed on. He knew about the reality Husky wandered around in, filled with perpetrators and victims and angles of trajectory. Waking moments loaded with possible motives for why Person A might've pinched off the nipples of Person B with a pair of Craftsman pliers before using said pliers as a skull-bashing device. These things didn't put *anybody* in the mood for airy, fluffy cocktail chatter. Certainly, not Husky, who'd been dealing with them for a long succession of days and nights.

"It's made you a little weird, if you don't mind my saying."

"No shit," Husky had shot back. "Want me to grow a shell?"

13

"Admit it to yourself. Conscientiously. Actively. Think how you can deal with it so you don't shut out the entire world. I mean, look, do you have one single friend who doesn't get his check from the police department?"

"You, Garthie."

"Other than me? Other than somebody who you've known since before you put your frontal lobe in the garbage disposer?"

Husky just looked off. It took a moment, but he finally shook his head. No. There was nobody.

Well, there *was* somebody. But it wasn't exactly a verbal relationship. And Husky was a very verbal man.

He had a great dog. The dog's name was Fred, so dubbed after a former chief of the department. Husky had named him Fred so he could tell Fred what to do. Order him around, at least at home.

Fred was half shepherd and half collie. A great, deep-chested, bounding eternal puppy of a dog. He was a tawny light brown adorer of Husky Martin, and it was Fred who, after all, kept his master sane. Fred gave love; gave Husky something *to* love.

Fred often came into the office with Husky, but in the past few months, colored as Husky's life was by the stench of Edgar Lamp, Fred had been kept at home. Husky would assign the job of feeding him to a neighbor kid. He had a deal with the boy that if Husky's car wasn't parked in the driveway—he never put it in the garage since the garage was too full of disorganized junk—by seven at night, then the kid should go ahead and chow Fred down. Husky gave the kid a buck every time it happened.

"Kid's making half your salary," Garth had told him.

"Got that right."

But now that kid was looking at an economic down-trend. Edgar Lamp was finished in L.A., no doubt almost to the airport and his ride toward longhorn justice. Husky would have plenty of time for Fred, at least for the present. It would do his soul good.

Edgar Lamp could worry about his own damn soul.

■　■　■　■　■

Though he'd never let on, there had been many times in the last six months when Husky had wondered if he would ever get Edgar Lamp convicted at all, anywhere.

Of course he'd expressed only absolute confidence. But he'd obsessively haunted the courtroom; always ready to testify or send a coaching note if the DA overlooked even the slightest point of evidence or discrepancy in testimony.

Joey Tucker, the round-faced kid lawyer/gofer who'd hopped and jumped self-consciously when the DA sneezed, started calling Husky "the chess master" because he knew everybody's moves before they did.

Husky figured that was true. Nobody'd given as much time to the Lamp case as he had, and damn near nobody'd sat in as many courtroom hothouses for as many years as he had, either.

Including the DA.

During the Lamp trial, while the gawky, fidgety defendant with those unshamed eyes endured day after day of proof; mountain after mountain of evidence, Husky Martin became confronted . . . distracted . . . with another nemesis.

Julian "the Python" Katella had risen out of the past and sent Husky's concentration into splintered disarray.

He'd been after Katella, on and off, since 1975 . . . better than a decade. The evidence had always come up too thin, or the man himself had simply vanished. And now,

15

with this absolute marathon of a trial going on, Katella was back.

Husky railed inwardly; how the *hell* could he pursue Katella while the Lamp trial went on? Katella would have required his full concentration at any time; and that just wasn't available.

Husky knew it was hopeless, but when the chance came up, a good cop couldn't allow himself to let it go by. Not with this guy.

Katella killed people who didn't cooperate with his bosses, who manipulated one of the largest international cocaine organizations on earth. They did a lot of business in L.A., so intermittent chances at Katella were part of Husky's diet.

He was having coffee out of Styrofoam cups with Joey Tucker when a young uniformed cop approached in the courthouse cafeteria.

"Lieutenant Martin?"

Husky looked up at him. "What'd I do now?"

A piece of paper was held out for him. "Chief says give this to you."

Husky looked at the kid a moment longer. "One of the Chiefie's little lads, huh?"

The kid didn't know what to say. Joey was smirking. Husky finally smiled and took the note.

"Keep his ass wiped, son. You'll be givin' me orders in six months, right?"

Resentment replaced confusion in the kid's eyes; he turned and left.

"Fucking ace cadets," Husky grumbled.

The note said: KATELLA. It gave an address in West L.A.

Husky bit his lower lip, looked at his watch, and wondered what the hell to do.

16

"When do you think," he asked Joey, "your Imperial Leader's gonna drag my ass up on the stand?"

Joey checked his own watch, made a face, and apologetically said, "Tomorrow."

Husky didn't even comment on the fact that he'd been forced to waste much of yet another day in the stuffy hallways and cafeteria of the County Courthouse. He just sighed, gave Joey a little farewell wave as he got up, and headed for the door.

The bathtub was filled with a young Latin man of about twenty-five, a great deal of his blood, and a python. The snake slithered back and forth nervously across the guy's belly, which bore evidence of several deep knife wounds.

It was Julian Katella's signature.

Husky had seen plenty of these before.

"That's his handwriting," he said.

"We knew that, like I told you, right off the bat." The frequently smiling other guy in the bathroom with him was Gabe Schatzer, a narcotics investigator Husky liked even less than he liked either Katella or Edgar Lamp.

"But the procedure book on Katella says when he shows up, they want you to show up, too. So now you showed up. Good?"

Husky managed a nod. "Tell me about this guy."

"Mr. Tub? Rubén Echeverría. American-born. Sold a lotta crack, a little legitimate powder . . . and I would say he didn't pay his supplier as quick as he made his junkies pay him. Good?"

"Every time I see you, Schatzer, it's like I'm back in school." Husky's smile didn't hide the fact; he hated dealing with the narco boys.

"You know we didn't have to call you *right* away. . . ."

"*Thank* you for calling me, Schatzer." Husky sighed and

17

even bowed a little. "I *owe* you, okay? That what you wanna hear?"

Then he left Schatzer alone in the bathroom with the body and the snake, closing the door on them all.

It was old school, maybe even bush, but Husky detested working with any division other than Homicide. Call it ego; he didn't think anybody else worked as thoroughly.

When somebody transferred into his division, they got the shakedown cruise from Husky; nobody else.

He personally loved Homicide work because it was ultimate-stakes gamesmanship. Every case they got was literally as serious as a heart attack. Not some robbery nobody really gave a shit about. Not some white-collar embezzler pulling a scam.

The real world of Homicide was real death, real gain and loss; nothing artificial or arbitrary.

Every other division in the department envied Homicide. It had the best men, the goriest cases; headlines like nobody's fucking business.

And that's what it was *really* about to guys like Schatzer, Husky knew. That's where the attitude came from. This was Hollywood just as much as it was L.A., and nobody ever forgot about it. Schatzer and his legitimized glue sniffers sucked up plenty of the glory when they got to bust a starlet or somebody, but they positively shit bricks over the fact that when the strokes got short and final, it was time to call the boys from big H.

Husky had always felt much the same kind of disdain for partners he'd been saddled with . . . even *within* Homicide. His edges could get a little rough in the throes of an investigation, and there weren't many guys who could stand him. That was fine. It cut in both directions: if a guy didn't want to get the job done, as far as Husky was concerned he could collect unemployment.

18

Some people in the department didn't buy that. They said two of Husky's first partners, years before, collected more than unemployment. Husky's contention was if you got to be a cop, you had to accept that you could get killed in the line. A popular theory at Parker Center said even though that was true, Husky still liked to go a little harder than conventional wisdom considered prudent.

He got the job done for himself, but he tended to be the only guy standing when it was over. On either side.

Husky personally thought *that* little accusation was further evidence of a theory he called Crap Universality. Everywhere you looked, you could find crap. You could delve into the minds of the finest thinkers, the greatest intellectuals, and right there beside the original ideas and clever insights would be a fair amount of crap.

Sometimes, he believed, there was evidence to indicate that truly excellent criminals, the ones who were the hardest to catch, had less crap per pound of brain matter than honest people.

Edgar Lamp, capable of true savagery, was beyond cunning. He was a totally inhuman animal, Husky believed, but that was different from crap.

When he'd looked Edgar in the eye, trying to fathom what went on in that mind, Husky had felt no doubt whatever that *none* of his loyal, hardworking officers could match this man's brain power.

Similar conclusions had led Husky to dump the second two partners he'd been teamed with over the years. One had nearly gotten Husky killed by missing an obvious clue about an ambush. The other was so clearly unreliable . . . unable to show up on time, lax in the most basic arrest procedures . . . that Husky simply began hitting the streets without him.

After that, when it became clear Husky would *always* be

19

leaving that stunned partner lingering in the squad room with no place to go, he was officially "put on solo."

The entire division breathed a sigh of relief, but they still couldn't have imagined how pleased *he* was. Solo work let you protect . . . and run . . . your own life. Husky believed nobody else could do it better.

There was much evidence to indicate he was right.

No officer in the history of the LAPD had enjoyed the kind of solo success Husky racked up in Homicide.

The department would never officially admit the truth of that, of course, since it blew a great deal of fecal matter in the face of all their partner theories and teamwork propaganda. But *who* did the chief phone in the middle of the night when he had an Edgar Lamp on the streets? *Who* got what *no* other cop got: his own name entered, standard procedure, as the *only* person to notify when any other division encountered a Julian Katella?

It wasn't one of their teams.

It was the Old Guy, the Long Beard, the Single Shadow.

Even after he had become Homicide Badge One *after* beginning to work solo, he had been warned in no uncertain terms by Chief Nash that he was to support, encourage, and foster the continuance of *teams* among all the officers under his command.

Hassled all the way.

But that had been fine, too. It meant *he* assigned new teams and *he* rearranged old ones. It also meant no one, at any time, would have to be teamed with him.

Even before he left the scene of the Rubén Echeverría killing, just talking to the lab boys on hand, Husky had known there was something different about this hit. It had clear, reliable prints. They would prove the killer to be Katella.

That jarred him. Maybe the guy just forgot his rubber

20

gloves for once. Maybe he was in too much of a hurry. Maybe his girlfriend pissed him off and blew his focus.

The response to all of these explanations was the same: impossible. Husky was unable to believe such incredible gaffes by this man. This man was so careful, so clean, he had kept Husky shaking his head in admiration for ten years.

No, if Julian Katella had left *prints*, it was because he had fucking well meant to, wanted to, and had purposely decorated the place with them as a postcard to his old dance partner, Husky.

Katella'd been reading about the Lamp trial, Husky decided. He must have known they had Husky corralled down there, so he'd *known* Husky hadn't the time to shit or sing grand opera. So he'd done this taunt. That had to be it.

Husky had laughed to himself, but he hadn't stopped thinking.

With these prints, Katella was convictable if caught. For the first time Husky could remember, Katella perhaps *hadn't* been thinking down the road.

"Let's say we don't catch him right now," he'd told Marge Glass on the phone. "Let's say two years go by, he comes back to town, and we happen to nail his ass then. Prints from today still hold, this case isn't closed, and we bag him on the rebound."

He'd been talking to her from a gas-station booth near the crack dealer's apartment; thinking rapidly, talking nonstop.

"Now just in *case* we get his dick in the wringer this time, I'm jumpin' down to LAX. You call around, see about flights down to Colombia today . . . to Bogotá, in fact . . . then catch me on the band."

Before she could tell him okay, he'd hung up and was walking quickly to his car. Marge Glass had become used

21

to hearing Husky in such moments of job frenzy. She punched in another line and started calling international carriers. When she got the information, she walked down to the dispatcher's room and took one of the mikes from her friend Gwen.

"You're the rudest bastard who ever walked," she began.

In his car, hauling ass, Husky laughed and picked up his own mike.

"So what're his travel plans?"

Marge threw Gwen a look.

"Just one flight to Bogotá today. Japan Air, two o'clock."

"Two? That's comin' up fast." He thought a moment. "Japan Air?"

"Beats me, Husky."

"Yeah." He clicked off.

The counter girl at Japan Air was a blonde named Stephanie who talked like she was from the valley. She looked with wide eyes at Husky's badge and ID, shaking her head and frowning.

"You know, I'm afraid you're a little late, Detective."

He made a face. "The information I had said two o'clock. I just need to know the gate, then I can get on the plane with my ID."

"I'm sure you could, only that flight left for Bogotá at two o'clock this *morning*."

He stared.

Her smile was worthy of any airline ad; perky in the face of adversity. It remained fixed even when he slapped the counter and yelled, "Motherfucker!"

Katella had probably been *in* goddamn Bogotá by the time Husky'd reached the ticket counter at Japan Air.

It hadn't even been close.

When he'd returned to the office, a clean glass sat waiting.

Marge, who'd gone home, had known he'd be ready for a jolt of hooch whether he'd won or lost. Husky smiled and, thinking better of it, turned the glass upside down on his desk blotter. Pass for tonight.

Then he'd noticed the package. A small, neatly wrapped parcel on his chair. It was addressed to him, bearing the name JULIAN in the upper left corner where a return address would normally have been.

For a moment he'd wondered if there was a risk; if it could have been a letter bomb. But Katella was not a terrorist: not the Arabic variety, anyway. He might drive his victims through the limits of imaginable suffering as he killed them, but his relationship to Husky was a game to him.

A game. As the insult of that realization stung his consciousness, Husky ripped the paper, finding a book and a short note.

"While you wait to testify against that beast, enjoy," said the note. It was signed as the parcel had been: JULIAN.

But the audacity of Julian calling some other criminal a "beast" was quickly overshadowed. The book itself left Husky stunned at both the brazenness of Katella's taunting and the eerie perception the man possessed.

The book took Husky back to an unlikely auto ride four years before.

Husky and another cop had transported Katella to Santa Barbara for a hearing. As they'd driven up the rainy coast north of Los Angeles that glum day, the conversation had turned, out of boredom, to history.

Husky loved history, loved talking about it, but most of all loved one particularly obscure cranny dealing with the Indo-European culture of ancient times.

Indo-European was often claimed to be the "mother

tongue" that led to English, the Romance languages, German, even Sanskrit.

Julian Katella, as Husky discovered during their ride to Santa Barbara, had also been long fascinated with the Indo-European subject.

At first Husky couldn't believe it. This was one of his favorite hobbies; a thick vein of human brilliance in which he'd for years loved to immerse mind and imagination. When he'd craved something other than homicide to fill his thoughts, this had been his avenue of escape.

The other cop in the car had no idea what the hell they'd been talking about.

Just as Husky had no idea how a man capable of such lifelong violence could also have been well versed in a purely intellectual, abstract pursuit like the Indo-Europeans.

The book he held in his hands four years later was called *Our Indo-European Roots*.

Staring at its cover, Husky still remembered Katella, whose superb lawyers were paid for by his Colombian benefactors, as he had walked smiling out of court on a technicality. Even four years later, he remained more stunned at Katella's discordantly cerebral hobby than at his actual release.

Husky had lingered by his desk several moments, uncertain about whether to throw the book in the trash or keep it. Finally, he'd kept it; telling himself that good, healthy intellectual curiosity *should* overcome revulsion at a man who carved humans to death in bathtubs.

That settled, plunking the book down on his desk, he stretched and yawned. Husky let his mind go back to the case that still, after Julian Katella's quick entry and re-exit, demanded his energy and attention. The case he'd been haunting the courthouse on; the Edgar Lamp affair. A fucking Russian novel of multiple murder with crisscrossing stories and alibis, and witnesses who wanted to be anyplace on earth but on that stand.

He felt more certain than he'd ever felt about any case that questions and theories regarding *why* Edgar Lamp murdered people were a complete waste.

The irrefutable fact, to Husky, was that he *did* murder.

It was a relief to have a simple issue; one in which he had an utter absence of doubt.

Not that Edgar Lamp was simple; this man was surely brilliant, too. But his brilliance sprang from a different country of the mind. There was no surprise student of history and culture lurking in Edgar's secret self. There was only the capacity for a greater, more cunning monstrosity.

Edgar Lamp had been put where he belonged: in jail and on trial. No room for argument, no possible dissent.

And to that "cop's truth," Husky had turned his glass upright once more to pour himself a drink.

It would be an arduous half year before Edgar's L.A. trial would end in a conviction; before Husky and Garth Cheesbro watched the cluster of sheriff's cars pull away, taking his prisoner to Texas.

Then Edgar would find himself embroiled in another trial, but that would not be Husky's headache.

He took a long drink, and hoped the time would go quickly.

TWO

ONCE EDGAR HAD LEARNED to slip out of manacles as a kid, he'd never forgotten. His fascination with magic had come only after he'd been moved in with his grandparents, Harper and Alice Lamp. Since he rejected his surroundings on their farm so completely, he turned to a world that at first seemed like fantasy but soon involved him in the precise mechanics of the tricks that could be learned from books. Of course, he'd have to hide the books from Grandpa Harper Lamp or risk terrible sessions of hellfire and brimstone about the devil's work. But there was always the secrecy of the attic.

By the light from its window, Edgar had learned "slipping the manacle," as the author had called it.

In the fourth of the six sheriff's cars, sitting in the back seat between two burly officers, Edgar pretended he hadn't done a thing. They had no idea the plastic cuffs now dangled from just one wrist.

There were two more deputies in the front seat, but not one of these guys was paying the slightest attention to him. They were engrossed in a blonde driving an Alfa with the top down.

Edgar was figuring the time to act was just before they hit the off ramp at Century Boulevard. He'd heard them discuss whether to use that or La Tijera over the radio, and the decision had been Century. Most direct airport entry. Easier to just get it over with.

It couldn't have been easier. The off-ramp transition didn't go too smoothly for the sheriff's caravan, with a Fiat just zooming in and slipping between the third car and the one carrying Edgar.

"Fucking believe that?" said the deputy-driver.

"Goddamn Arabs in that car," said the one to Edgar's right. He was leaning forward to make sure he was right. "Yeah, that's what it is, bunch a Arabs. Drive worse than Chinese. Probably late for a flight to Bay-fucking-root."

As the deputy leaned forward, Edgar's right hand flashed out and grabbed the gun right out of his holster. The deputy on Edgar's left had no idea it had happened because the left arm remained motionless.

Edgar, lips pursed slightly with concentration, had discharged the first bullet into the left-hand side of the Arab-hating deputy's rib cage in less than two seconds. The man hadn't even known his gun was out. The bullet passed through internal organs and ricocheted off a rib on his right side, stopping in his right lung. He gasped as confusion rippled through the car.

The deputy on Edgar's left was going for his gun, having heard the deafening report, but Edgar backhanded him ferociously in the nose, breaking it and blinding him with pain for several seconds. During those seconds Edgar lifted the gun farther and shot the detective riding shotgun in front. This bullet went through the man's left tem-

27

ple as he was turning to see what had gone wrong. The right side of his face spattered across the dash and the inside of the windshield. As the driver looked over in shock, Edgar whipped the gun barrel around and planted it in the chest of the deputy with the broken nose. Expressionless, Edgar pulled the trigger.

The deputy at the wheel was by now braking and reaching for his gun, but Edgar had the drop on him.

"Get to the bottom of the ramp and go *right*."

This would take them away from the airport. The deputy wasn't about to argue, though he hoped the guys in the next car, which was right on his ass, would realize everything was now out of control.

They realized it when he gunned the car to the right at the bottom of the ramp.

Edgar rode in back, leaning over the seat amid the three dead deputies, keeping the point of the gun close to the driver's skull.

"I'm doin' the best I can," the deputy told him.

"Fuck you, you think you're gettin outta this alive if I don't get away, man."

The deputy drove faster. The radio sparked with questions and anxiety from the car behind them.

"Tell 'em to back off or I'll kill you." Edgar was grinning at the guy. "*Do* it now . . ."

The deputy grabbed the mike in a sweating hand and delivered the message. Edgar watched in the sideview while keeping an eye on the deputy constantly. The official cars behind them dropped away.

"All right. Tell 'em to *keep* away and don't send anybody in from up ahead." He nudged the guy's ear with the gun. "Your mama'd want her boy comin' home for dinner, right?"

As the deputy delivered the second message, Edgar pointed for him to make a turn into a side street. He did as he finished the message. They were moving down an alley a few moments and a couple directions later, coming up behind what Edgar recognized to be a car wash.

"Pull in for a hot wax."

The guy shot him a look in the rearview.

"You need a map? You're the fuckin' lucky strike in the pack here, and you're thinkin' what you can do to dick around? God*damn*, just drive into the *car* wash!"

The sheriff's cruiser pulled into the Kleen-Ko car wash, moving past the guy who asked you whether you wanted Carnauba, regular wax, or just the plain wash and dry. Everybody in the place was black. Edgar figured them for mostly veterans of county lockup at one point or another. They had the look. The eyes. They just froze and watched when they realized this white dude had a piece planted in a fucking sheriff's deputy's right ear.

The car came up to the start of the wash train. As the hook caught, Edgar climbed over the deputy on his left and got out, keeping the gun on the driver, whose window was rolled down.

"Told you. You're the lucky strike here, six-gun . . ." And Edgar whipped him across the face with the butt of a gun that had somehow appeared in his other hand. It was from the holster of the deputy with the broken nose. Edgar laughed at the guy's surprise, backing away, keeping the gun on him as he started through the car wash.

"Don't you get out now. Don't you do that or you get your ass cut right down."

He wagged the gun at the deputy, moving away, waiting until the sheriff's car was well into the wash and the deputy couldn't see what was happening.

Edgar turned to the man who'd been there to ask if they wanted it waxed. He'd be the assistant manager. He might own his own car.

"Gimme the keys to the king-dome."

29

"Any wheels you want, man . . ."

Edgar smiled at him. He jumped into a repainted Impala and it started up like somebody took good care of it. He backed it out of the custom wax bay it had been occupying, the power buffer falling off the hood to the ground as its cord ran out. Edgar looked out the window at the assistant manager.

"I believe I'll refer my friends," he said, and peeled ass out of the lot, fairly flying over the curb and onto the street.

He cut back under the freeway, right past one police car that had no idea what to look for. The deputy couldn't broadcast worth shit till he came out of the car wash, and even then he sounded pretty disjointed and rattled, sitting in that car with his three butchered buddies.

■ ■ ■ ■

Worry

Harper Lamp never worked harder to show anyone how God would deliver hope. Would deliver his followers from despair, from hate, from drink, from sin and envy and every other low-life variety of misstep and miscue.

But no matter how hard he tried, Alice Lamp Corinth would later remember, no matter what lengths Harper went to, he never got through to Edgar. The rift only became deeper.

Edgar ran away again and again, heading back toward his parents' farm, though he knew they were both dead and buried, and that the farm had been sold. He never told anyone what he expected to find there, or why he went. He didn't seem to care that his grandfather worried, or that Grandma Alice worried even more.

Each time Edgar was found and brought back, Harper's solution was the same.

Townspeople in Gullickson, Texas, where they lived, could hear Harper preaching thunderously to his grandson long into the night. He would shout dire warnings of eternal death and unbelievably ornate tortures that awaited them in hell. He would hold forth for hours on end, describing the nature of flesh-ripping, skin-burning, mind-searing trials that had no resolution.

Instead of being terrified, Edgar was impassive in the face of his grandfather's rantings. After he had heard them several times, he began a psychological war with the old man that went on for the remainder of Harper's life. Edgar would look him in the eye, and at a key moment in his descriptions, laugh in his face. There was not a trace of fear in the boy.

Harper countered by describing the very tortures that hell kept in reserve for none other than Edgar Lamp, personally. He recounted them every night, night after night.

Alice Lamp Corinth believed that she might go mad hearing it, but years later she told police officers that through it all, Edgar had shown no such feelings of stress. He could apparently just turn off his grandfather's endless verbal clubs. He could simply ignore.

Alice had always thought that remarkable. She had hoped it meant the boy had an iron will and a strong sense of himself.

She had come to believe in later years, however, that it was something else. There was a quality in Edgar that other people didn't have. Or perhaps it was the other way around. Maybe there was something in other people that Edgar didn't have. He was always different, always aloof. His performance in school was good enough when something caught his interest, but for the most part things bored him and he didn't even try.

The only thing he seemed to truly love as a boy was magic and magic tricks. Of course, Harper would not allow such things into his house, so Edgar was subjected to lectures on how the devil dwelt in mysteries like the ones that fascinated him. So that issue, too, arose between them. And like so many others, it wouldn't go away.

The fact that Edgar displayed a greater resolve than his own grandfather drove the old man to greater and greater heights of desperation. He would whip Edgar. He would lock him in his room. There were endless hours of chores, and of course the frequent "private sermons," as Grandma Alice came to call them.

As Harper became more rattled by his grandson's unflinching resistance and hatred, he seemed to become uncertain of almost everything in his life. He became sick often, missed more Sundays in his church than anyone could remember, and finally, in the dead of a winter night, Harper Lamp simply fled. He could not bear the cold presence of his grandson. He believed in his heart that the devil had beaten not only the boy but the preacher as well. Harper left home, church, congregation . . . everything.

Edgar seemed to be above it, as if unaware anything had changed, though Alice wrung her hands and the whole town went looking. Most people around the town knew he'd run from Edgar, and no one ever treated the boy quite the same after that.

■ ■ ■ ■ ■

Dr. Beerey's phone rang. The sound of it, emanating from the wall phone three feet from the chair Husky sat wincing in, sent a razor of pain from the tooth in question up to his brain.

"Get that . . ." he whispered.

"I was," Beerey answered. He grabbed the phone. "Dr. Beerey." He listened. "One second."

Husky looked up to see Beerey turn and extend the phone to him.

"Yours."

Husky took it, pulling a little cotton out of his mouth first.

32

"Martin."

The voice on the other end was another investigator, one of the guys working for Husky. Husky was sort of group commander and den mother all rolled into one. The guy's name was Patton, and he took a shitload of crap for it.

"Sorry to bother you, Husk. Chief says get right into the Lamp thing."

"What Lamp thing?"

Garth looked up.

"You didn't hear? Sonofabitch got away."

"How the fuck'd he do that?"

"Blew the shit out of three sheriff's deps and lost everybody in a car wash."

"Is this a fucking joke?"

"No way, Husk. Guy took off in some car they had in there for a custom wax and there wasn't a cop in the area knew what to look for."

"Jesus Christ. And he killed three deps?"

"Right in the car with him. Fourth was the driver, and Lamp leaves him goin' through the hot-wax nozzles. Spade runnin' the place said the guy looked crazy, so they let him take whatever the hell he wanted."

Husky sighed. His mouth came roaring back, a wall of pain that encompassed half his head. Finally, he could talk again.

"Smart move on their part."

"Excuse me? You got somethin' in your mouth, Husky?"

"You could say that. So he never got to the airport."

"Nope." Patton sighed. Husky could hear him shuffle a couple papers as he looked for some information. "Report says . . . happened starting at the Century Boulevard off ramp of the San Diego Freeway, whereupon the unit made a right turn instead of the customary left, after

33

which pursuing officers were warned off or else Lamp was gonna blow the driver's brains out, too."

"Where is this driver?"

"Hospital. Sedated. Chief's really pissed, Husk."

"Chief can eat my shorts, Patton. You can tell him that. I didn't blow this, the fuckin' five-pointers blew this."

"I think I'll hold off tellin' him that," Patton said.

"Yeah. Look, I'll be outta here in fifteen minutes, and then I'm on it."

He gave the phone back to Beerey, disgusted.

"No, you won't," Beerey warned, hanging up the phone.

"Gimme something temporary. I gotta go to work."

Husky looked at Beerey. The doctor just stared. Husky pointed at his mouth.

"Make magic."

■ ■ ■ ■ ■

They came out of Beerey's office at a fast pace. Husky had a prescription for Percodans in his pocket. When he'd seen what it was, he'd damn near climbed back into the chair and said finish it. But Lamp wasn't going to wait for anybody's root canal.

"Loan me your car," Husky said.

"I'd never see it again," Garth replied, not even looking at his friend.

"It's not the same thing, interviewing this guy and trying to deal with him on the street."

"I'd still never see it again. And you're in no damn shape to drive just yet."

Husky sighed. "I'll be worse if I take this Percodan he's prescribed."

"It's your head."

34

They were getting into Garth's car.

"That was my line." Husky groaned. "You go out after Edgar with me, it's *your* head."

"I can take care of myself pretty well, Husky. I've had classes in karate, you know."

The image made Husky laugh, which made him grab his face at the instantaneous electric current of pain. He gasped, finally catching his breath, eyes wide.

Finally Garth asked, "Where to?"

Seen in daylight, the Sixth Street underpass of the 10 Freeway was the essence of the "good old" L.A. architectural idea. It reminded locals of the city's former grace and ambitious western innocence.

The Sixth Street underpass was many other things, too.

As Husky and Garth headed for it, it was the scene of some quick-change artistry, Edgar Lamp style. The Impala he'd boosted from the car wash was by now a liability, so he left it there. Armed to the teeth, he began scouring the area for new wheels.

The underpass was one of several regular spots the city's bum community hit on a regular rotating basis. They drifted from this one to that, getting rousted and moved along by cops in the various neighborhoods. Nobody really got scared when squad cars showed; it was just time to pack meager belongings and shuffle. Then they'd relocate and be left alone till the next set of locals started to bitch, and in would come the protectors of civic decency once more.

For his part, Husky wasn't coming to move anybody along. He was coming because he *knew* Edgar Lamp would very likely stop by at Sixth. He also knew the guys who were to be found there hadn't cracked under his interrogation, so Edgar would consider them relatively safe ground now that he was loose again.

35

But Edgar was too smart to stay long. When he'd been captured, Husky had talked with him one-on-one about how he'd hung out at Sixth, about how everybody down there sure must've been scared shitless of him, 'cause those old boys just clammed right up when Husky started probing and quizzing. Edgar would remember the conversation and feel uneasy there. So it was timing. And Husky had no way of knowing just whom Edgar might single out for "help," or just what help he might be after. Another car? A weapon? A reload? He told Garth to hit the gas.

Edgar was glad the guys were here tonight. They were swinging east, and by tomorrow night or the next night they'd be into the barrio section. With the gangs out there it was almost as bad as their westernmost stopping point, the gazebo area at the head of Olvera Street. You couldn't feel protected or private in that place. No matter where they were, Bumtown never shifted more than one habitual hop on the long-established checkerboard. But the current stop was the one Edgar liked.

Some things were reliable; safe.

Just as Edgar was about to amble up to the fire, he stopped himself. These old guys sitting around it would probably freak if they saw him. Expecting them to shut up again when Martin showed was expecting too much. He would avoid them, after all.

He moved between burned-out, abandoned car shells that sat like huge roaches beneath the traffic that still lived high above, on the freeway.

He didn't know that amid those shells, shivering from the rush of Mexican Brown, a thin, dirty man watched him pass within three feet. The man's eyes widened, blinked, darted back and forth as he struggled to remember . . . and finally placed the face that had just passed him as he sat hunkered in the back seat of a dead red Caddy.

When Edgar had moved on, intent only on hooking up with something drivable, the man climbed out of the decaying Eldorado and hurried toward the fire.

Husky knew the majority of the tired, tense faces under the shadow of the freeway. They sat around their illegal fire, most of them passed out on what they'd been swilling all day. These guys managed to buy enough bad wine to dance with their demons every night, yet they couldn't put enough change together to sleep under a roof. It never made sense unless you knew they didn't want a roof. Nonconformists didn't necessarily mellow with wrinkles. Some hardened their resolve until it became a way of life, no matter how grueling.

The first one Husky recognized was a tall thin man with a bad case of shakes. When he'd been a fair to bad pickpocket, he'd earned the name Scooter, because one thing he could do real well was run. People always knew Scooter had copped their wallet, but catching him was a whole other issue. The way he'd get nailed was the victim would file a report, and then when Scooter had transformed the boosted wallet into a bottle or two of Thunderbird, he'd just hang around in a drunken haze and let the first cop who saw him make the collar. Husky figured Scooter had just never grown the brains to figure out the police had radios and put out wants on guys. Or maybe he'd simply wanted to get caught. You never knew. A lot of them wanted to.

"Hey, we got us a big one out tonight." Scooter's grape-roughened voice came out to greet them.

Husky smiled and extended his hand to shake. Garth hung back, fascinated.

" 'Nother bum killer running around?"

"Might do that next. So far it's just been working people." Husky went into a squat beside the smelly rail of a man. "I'm tryin' to find Edgar Lamp, Scooter."

The campfire tensed up. Eyes from all around were fixed on the burly cop.

"He *out?*"

"He got away from us. Killed some sheriffs to do it."

The men looked restless. They avoided eye contact and stared at the fire or the ground. This was fear, the fear of small animals when the smell of the wolf is on the air.

"Lamp don't take with Bumtown guys, Mr. Martin"

"That's what you've told me, guys. But to be honest, I'm having a little trouble swallowing it." Husky kept the threat out of his voice.

Another face around the eerie fire, a round and bearded one, spoke up. This was Baseball Jack, a codger who'd been known to turn over information in exchange for tickets to the ball game.

"I read where Lamp was convicted and being shipped back to Texas for his second trial."

"That's right." Husky's voice was calm. He couldn't just prod these boys. Explanations were in order. They liked to feel respected here. "But like I said, he managed to get around the deputies."

"Any idea how?"

Husky chose to answer indirectly. He said the whole thing had been pretty mysterious.

"Still don't change the fact he never hangs with guys like us."

"He might start 'cause we're looking. I was hoping he'd already come through, or maybe he'd run into somebody you know of."

"You're just about runnin' on empty, then, I'd say." Baseball Jack grinned and shook his head. "We're a long shot."

"I've used your grapevine more times than I care to admit." Husky smiled back.

"We can put the antennas up, but if I was Lamp I'd be in New Mexico by this time." Scooter shifted position to get a better look at Husky. As he did, he noticed Garth. "Who's your rookie?"

"Friend of mine. Garth Cheesbro, this is Scooter . . ."

Garth, wearing an uncomfortable smile and feeling completely awkward with these appraising eyes on him, reached over to shake hands. Scooter wasn't a brave man, but he gauged Garth for soft stuff and looked right through him.

"Since when you bring friends along?"

"Long story. Besides, you go after Lamp, you want your friends with you, huh?"

This got a laugh. Garth wasn't quite sure if they laughed at the observation about Lamp or the absurdity of Garth himself as anybody's idea of backup. Husky was laughing, too, so the confusion only deepened.

They drank strong coffee with the bums around the fire and listened to a lot of opinion about what Lamp would probably do now. Most of it ran to getting out of town and growing as much hair on his face as possible.

But everybody agreed he'd give himself away sooner or later just the same. They all read the papers carefully. Men who live under freeways and leave themselves in the open air know about full-time fear, know about watching their backs and looking over their shoulders. Too many bums had dropped face first onto hard ground with knives in their ribs over the years. Too many had died even while the clothes were being torn off their backs to warm their killers. Killers got their attention and held it. Edgar Lamp held it in a terrible grip.

"Lamp's your basic serial murderer, way I see it. Can't stop, doesn't want to stop." Scooter drew in the dirt with a stick as he spoke. "But he may not even know places like this exist, Mr. Martin. Least we hope not, huh?"

This got general agreement from the other boys around the fire.

"You can be sure we'll let you know," an old black man put in.

Husky nodded. Garth noticed something as Scooter took another sip of his coffee. The stick he'd been drawing in the dirt with . . .

Husky saw it too. Etched in the loose soil was a word. S-C-A-V.

Husky looked at Scooter, but Scooter wasn't looking back at him.

"Husky . . ." Garth started.

"We better take off now, Garthie, let these boys grab some zees before the uniforms show up and run 'em off, huh?"

His look said, *Shut up and just do what I'm saying.*

Garth hesitated, then realized there was more than he understood here. He nodded.

"See you later, boys." Husky gave them all a little wave. There were waves and goodbyes in return, along with a couple nice-meetin'-you's to Garth, who nodded back with his uneasy smile, and the two intruders made their exit, walking over the rough ground that led to Garth's car. When they were out of earshot, Garth had to ask.

"What did he write in the dirt?"

"Message."

Garth shot Husky a look.

"But why would he write it down?"

"Didn't want to make a big thing of it." Husky could see Garth still wasn't catching on. "There was probably somebody around that fire Scooter didn't know too well. He couldn't be sure if the guy was tight with Lamp."

"He's that scared?"

40

"They're all that scared, Garthie, believe me. So he wrote it where nobody but you and I could see it."

"But what'd it mean? What's Scav?"

"Who. Who's Scav."

"You know?"

Husky nodded. Scav was short for Skidrow Scav, a long-time street crawler Husky had known for years.

Skidrow Scav had been an algebra teacher at Hollywood High once, but he never really felt like one of the faculty crowd. He preferred to cultivate his image as an ally of the kids. The trouble was, he got a little too far into it and found himself enmeshed in the drug scene on campus and off. That was when he discovered how many ways his students were a great deal more grown-up than he was. Double-crossing a gullible teacher is one of the easier things a smart, street-tough kid can do. The fall of Skidrow Scav's teacher persona was engineered by several of his pupils, and he fell hard.

After a hitch in state prison for trafficking to minors, Scav got back to L.A. and landed on the street he quickly incorporated into his name. He hadn't lost his taste for what he smilingly called controlled substances, however, and cops all over the city had run him in innumerable times.

Scav always got off pretty fast, but then no cop expected a tipper like him to get stuck long. Scav had major inside dope on what he called "real" street people, and he lavished it on any badge that held the hammer on him. He tipped drug operations, kiddie-porn shops, whatever it took. It was a way to stay on the street, but over the years it built him into a weak position. The people who lived out there by the curbs knew you didn't spill your prime beans to Scav, or he'd spill them to some crew-cut next time they tied his wrists together with those cute little plastic cuffs the L.A. heat loved so much.

41

As Husky told Garth about Scav, they got into Garth's car and cruised away from the Sixth Street underpass. Garth pulled a right onto the cross street and climbed the on ramp to head back downtown.

Husky needed to check with Vice. They'd almost certainly have an address where Scav would show his face within twenty-four hours to gas up his veins.

Three

LA BREA AVENUE runs almost the entire length of Los Angeles. It begins as Hawthorne Boulevard in Palos Verdes, near the sea. By the time La Brea exhausts itself, it snakes into the Hollywood Hills as a series of narrow little esses, culminating in a cement-and-barbed-wire gate. The words "Goose-Ass Party Boys," in black and white spray paint, adorn the barrier.

Two-thirds of a mile west of La Brea's conclusion, overlooking a hill-hugging cluster of drab beige apartment houses built in the fifties and sixties, is a small valley. The place is almost always windless, thanks to the rather abrupt inclines on three of four sides.

To the bizarre, unwashed mass of Hollywood Boulevard street people, this place was for years known as Tilly Taco's.

Tilly herself was one of the earliest bag ladies in Hollywood.

Before taking to the street, Tilly claimed she had known Errol Flynn, and swore to anyone who'd listen that this land was once his personal estate.

Years later, Tilly's five-foot-two-inch frame had bloomed to a jovial two-eighty. After eons of waddling past Grauman's and the Egyptian, welching food from sympathetic back doors at restaurants like Musso's or the Tick-Tock, Tilly took to the hills.

Younger street people heard about Tilly's and looked for it. If they played by her rules, which were enforced by the street people who'd known her for years and who now lived with her, they could stay as long as they liked.

There was no protection from the elements, so skins were leathery. Clothes faded fast in sun, wind, and rain, but there was a strange order to the place. It was far better than struggling to exist on Hollywood Boulevard. Proof of this was the fact that newcomers had to forage on that same boulevard for food and bring it back for old-timers. That was rent. It bought relative safety. Only rarely was somebody killed there, and few street people would want to be caught with anything that could be proved stolen from someone living at Tilly Taco's.

Things went smoothly for quite a while, but as Tilly got older her illnesses never seemed to leave completely, and they got progressively nastier. Finally, even the street people decided it was time to carry her out of there and get her to a hospital. While the old lady lay recovering, the place just didn't hold together. In a matter of days, there was fighting.

The fighting drove people so angrily apart, not even Tilly could restore peace and quiet again. Things in Hollywood were meaner and rougher by then, so it was only natural that the hills were becoming worse, too. A lot of the people left Tilly's to take up mass nighttime residence in an old, decaying hotel just east of La Brea on Hollywood Boulevard. These were the worst; the meanest.

In Hell Hotel the rockers, acid boys, and punk people shivered through scathing nights of rough-edged drug rides and even worse nights when they couldn't get drug rides.

The hills kept the hikers, plus the sixties holdovers still worshipping memories of the Grateful Dead and times when Hendrix was king.

That was when there had been marches to join, when they'd felt like they could change the world.

Now they couldn't, so they huddled in the hills. Let the people at Hell Hotel do the confronting, let them piss in old ladies' faces and lurk on the boulevard. For the people at Tilly Taco's, especially during the year or so after her return from the hospital, living was an almost constant exercise in avoidance.

And then, in late 1982, they couldn't avoid anymore.

Edgar Lamp was still down in Texas and probably not ready to even think about butchering any of the twenty-eight young women they would later find. Husky Martin was busy busting a cocaine ring that had accidentally offed a councilman's daughter.

And one night the people who lived in Hell Hotel made their unholy triumphant midnight return to Tilly Taco's.

It was no contest. Many victims didn't even get out of their sleeping rolls.

A few Tilly people ran for it, making it up and over the surrounding peaks. Hell Hotel people didn't chase beyond the peaks, because that would put them up near Mulholland Drive and the real world, where cops could lay you out with hip heat. On Mulholland, Law was law. Down in Tilly Taco's roiling cup of red fiery ground, Hell Hotel people were law.

They weren't the first; they wouldn't be last.

By dawn, Tilly Taco and her loyal friends were buried and their graves covered with brush. The Hell Hotel people, beginning by now to call themselves the Helloids, knew enough to plant weeds into the ground over the bodies.

The police never heard a word of the minor war that night. People came and went from L.A. every day. Keeping track was impossible. Nobody could.

Nobody did. In fact, by the time Edgar Lamp killed the three deputies and ditched the fourth at the car wash, by the time Husky Martin finally sat back in Dr. Beerey's chair to have his root canal while Garth Cheesbro polished off all the back issues of *Newsweek* in Beerey's waiting room, not one of the people from Hell Hotel still lived at Tilly Taco's. A whole new population survived there. Even hungrier, angrier, more ready to strike out for the sheer rush of it.

Into this seething place, Edgar Lamp drove the car he'd finally stolen near the Sixth Street underpass.

He knew these people. He'd spent time here before letting the police run him in so he could see what that was like.

Here they knew him. Here he was King Shit.

Word of King Shit's arrival spread quickly when he was recognized in the car. King Shit was supposed to be convicted. Supposedly due to get similarly reamed back in Dallas. Then it was hard time for King Shit, almost certainly the rest of his life. Maybe the Penalty.

A lot of people breathed easier when they'd heard that. A lot of them didn't have much use for King Shit, but they also didn't know what the hell to do with him when he came around. You had to back down from the guy. You had to know he was completely, permanently screwed on wrong when you got one good, clear look into his eyes.

King Shit was reputed to know the effect he had on

46

people, and he was reputed to like it. Now, getting out of the outrageously middle-class car he came rolling up in, King Shit did the strut right up the middle of the remains of Tilly Taco's haunt. He looked at the lingering human fuzz on the hillsides around him. Most of them looked back when they thought they'd avoided his stare . . . but he caught a lot of them at it and they quickly darted their scared little eyes someplace else. Just waiting for the chance to look back when it was safe again.

Edgar Lamp was taking stock. Trying to see into the minds of whoever had fucked him over while he was gone. Maybe even to see who had fucked him by talking to the cops.

The scary part was that his trial had gone down so quietly in that court, with so much protection for witnesses, that King Shit himself didn't know who had fucked him except of course for the one obvious person who sat there and talked to the judge and jury like a lame-assed straight motherfucker.

That had been Hertzie, the hebe from Philly. Figuring his time at Tilly's was pretty much strung down to zilch, Hertzie played his odds and went cop. He got up with that nervous little grin, constantly looking all over the place, checking to see how his rap was going over with the jury, then the judge, then the lawyers . . . but never right into Edgar Lamp's very eyes. Never into the cauldrons of King Shit.

And now Hertzie was long gone, moved out of town by a happy-to-oblige LAPD and whoever else got involved in such things. Edgar didn't even care about the fucker. He knew Hertzie would live the rest of his life scared beyond comfort that someday he'd accidentally run into King Shit again, when they were alone someplace. Where no cops or anybody could save him.

So now the people on the hill all wondered who else

among them was getting ready to fall before the damning, accusing eyes of King Shit. They all feared. If you were accused, they knew, it didn't matter whether or not you were guilty. He wasn't into fairness as far as anybody there could remember.

Edgar knew perfectly well what they were all thinking, and he knew it did him good to have all these worriers concentrating on him. Because what he wanted right now was everybody staying at a distance. He would never admit it to a soul, he would never even have believed it possible, because it had been years since he'd felt this way, but he was exhausted. Bone fucking tired. He just wanted to lie down and wake up tomorrow.

But first he felt compelled to give everybody a quick scan. Most people he had no fear of, but sometimes you could tell which ones were the cops because like now, when he was walking along and watching the eyes up there on the hillsides, the cops would be the guys who just looked right back at you like they were memorizing you. Like they'd heard your reputation and they wanted to check you against it.

Well, he thought as he kept up his strut, this *is* King Shit, boys. The reputation and the man. He didn't think there were any undercover hambones sitting in the big bowl of Tilly Taco's that early morning.

But he did see one person to worry about. He saw the scowling, mean, close-shaved head of El Chocolate Grande.

El Chocolate Grande was a huge, muscular black dude who looked like he'd been built from boilerplate and then somehow toughened up a little. He'd never liked Edgar Lamp, not for one second. Because El Choc, as most people around here called him, considered *himself* to be King Shit.

El Chocolate Grande just watched as Edgar Lamp went

by, the two of them glaring down and up the hill at each other, not a word being said, nobody else in the place having the guts to intrude on this exchange of hateful looks. It was like a nuclear reactor between the two. You stuck your head in, you got it fucking fried.

And just as Edgar Lamp began to look elsewhere, to go on with his survey and finish it up before going back to his car to sleep, he heard El Chocolate Grande's rasping, annoying voice.

"Hey, Shit."

Lamp turned. The big man was coming down the hill toward him, eyes never wavering. Lamp looked right back at him like he knew something El Choc would never know.

"You convicted, motherfucker." El Choc didn't smile. He probably didn't own a smile.

Lamp didn't reply. He just watched the guy come.

"What you doin' here? You convicted."

"Don't worry, Choc." Now Lamp smiled. He knew Choc *was* worrying. "I'm not gonna stay."

"What the fuck'd I worry for if you was?"

El Chocolate Grande stopped, maybe ten feet away. Everybody in the place was watching, straining to hear.

"Because if I stay, El Choc quits bein' King Shit."

"Ain't the way it goes down now. Since you got cuffed, everybody listens to El Chocolate Grande and nobody dies around here. People like that. People don't want you comin' back, Shit."

"I'm lookin' for pigs, Choc. Then I'm takin' a rest, takin' a piss, and I'm movin'."

"Cops find you, they cut yo' ass. Cops find you *here*, they cut everybody's ass."

"Just a little while, Choc. Don't fuckin' *worry* about it. I didn't come here to fuck with you."

El Chocolate Grande didn't look like he believed anything Edgar Lamp could ever possibly say, but he didn't look like he was in the mood to test himself against his old adversary, either.

"You wanna take yo' rest, do it in yo' damn car. Right where I can see you."

Lamp was checking out the faces of the others here at Tilly Taco's. They didn't want him any more than El Choc did. El Choc saw what he was doing and came closer, until the two men were less than a yard apart, and could speak quietly.

"There's maybe three hundred here, Shit. Maybe three hundred against one. Rest in the car."

"I'm just passing through, Choc. You say rest in the car, I can rest in the car."

Edgar Lamp's smile could've been interpreted as cooperative, but El Chocolate Grande knew better. He knew it was scary. Lamp looked into his eyes for several seconds before moving past him and back toward the car. El Choc stood where he was for the longest time, not moving from where he'd been looking when King Shit was standing there in front of him. Finally, when his heart slowed down enough and the self-control El Choc valued so much had returned, he turned his head, expecting to see Lamp walking back toward the car, moving through the people who had come down off the hill to hear better.

He was surprised to see that Lamp was standing, watching him with an even bigger smile on his face than before, about five feet away. El Chocolate Grande couldn't hide his surprise at this. His eyes gave him away, he knew it.

"Boo," said Edgar Lamp.

And then King Shit turned and walked back to his car, got in, locked the door, and closed his eyes to take a nap.

When Edgar Lamp woke up it was late afternoon and he was hungry. A quick look out the window of the car

50

revealed that El Chocolate Grande had taken a vantage point not far away, and was sitting with his eyes glued to the vehicle. With him were about twenty dudes almost as big and almost as mean as he was. They were watching, too.

Edgar loved it. It proved he was still King Shit. Proved they were scared pissless of him. They must have all kinds of theories about how he got away from the pig boys. Maybe they'd even heard about it on the radio, but they'd never call the Man in here. Not this place. This was the best safe house in L.A. for every killer, thief, and fugitive on the coast. Even to drop King Shit, it would have been too high a price to pay.

Then he noticed how many of the men around El Choc had guns with them. So how come they hadn't riddled this car with bullets and be done with it? He smiled again.

Because they were spooked. Really spooked. They thought he was fucking Superman now, after he'd ditched all those cops. And to tell the truth, Edgar Lamp didn't blame them. He knew he was one scary dude to these people.

But he was also one hungry dude, so he would roll out of the hills and down into town to fill his stomach. Then he'd figure what came next. He'd have to be careful because the cops would by now very likely be looking for the plates on this car, assuming they'd figured out he was the one who'd grabbed it.

Back in Texas when he was just getting started with his killing, when the talent first became apparent and the temptation to use it became more and more impossible to resist, he would never have known enough to think about how the cops would be dealing with *their* problems. But that was the old days. He was much smarter now. He was thinking like his enemies. Like that cop, Martin.

He opened the glove compartment as he turned the engine over, just to see what this guy might've had in there. Maybe a little beef jerky or something. But he couldn't believe his eyes when he did. Couldn't believe his fucking good luck.

Whoever owned this car had kept a *gun* in his glove compartment. A fucking gun. Lamp reclosed the compartment without checking the piece, knowing such a move would scare El Chocolate Grande into taking some stupid action. Lamp wasn't ready for that right now. Not when he'd just awakened and felt this hungry. You had to be in the mood.

So he drove calmly out of Tilly Taco's, cruised down from the hills into Hollywood proper, with El Choc and his boys watching him go.

By the time a few hours had passed he'd eaten, checked out the gun and found it to be a loaded .38, and managed to use it to rob a forty-year-old lady and take *her* car. She had a newer Trans-Am, which he liked much more because it had good power. Then, with what was left of the money he'd taken from the woman's purse, he went to a bar and thought about his situation over a few long-necked Lone Stars.

El Chocolate Grande had pissed him off. The big nigger had been too fucking bold, too fucking brave to tolerate. It was still probably smarter that Edgar leave L.A. within a day or two, but now it seemed a little resolution had to go down first. He thought about sneaking into Tilly Taco's alone in the middle of the night and finding where El Choc slept, but quickly rejected that because Edgar Lamp was King Shit, and King Shit didn't have to sneak into anyplace.

He would do it another way. He grinned to himself. He even bought the guy next to him a beer, he was feeling so damn good. Ideas were coming . . . he wondered if anybody else got them in clusters like he did. This whole problem of El Choc was just reminding him of another thing he had to do . . .

There was no getting around the fact that Martin, the cop, would only quit being a problem for Edgar when Martin quit *living*. But if he was going to take the trouble to risk his ass over killing Martin, which meant he'd have to rub elbows with the police again, then he might as well go all the way.

The other big target Edgar wanted to get to was his grandmother, Alice Lamp Corinth.

There had to be . . . just *had* to be a way to do them both, possibly even at the same time. It was the kind of idea worthy of King Shit. He would have to consider the possibilities. Martin would follow him anyplace to catch him. His grandmother had hated him for as long as he could remember, and he more than returned the sentiment.

Maybe there was some signal he could send Martin, even while he continued to make the guy look bad.

Maybe it was time for the secret Edgar believed he carried in his soul to come rising, finally, to the top.

■ ■ ■ ■ ■

Nobody else had called attention to it. Not one of the other cops on the Lamp investigative task force, all of whom got copies of the report on the murders of the three sheriff's deputies.

But to Husky Martin, the inconsistency kept jumping out at him while he waited in his office for Vice to tell him where he'd most likely run across Skidrow Scav.

The deputy who'd been sitting on Lamp's right and who was the first victim had not only suffered the gunshot wound and the subsequent internal injuries from the bul-

let that stopped in his lung. He'd also, for reasons that no one had discerned and the medical examiner had relegated to "high-stress physical breakdown" at the moment of mortal attack, suffered what seemed to be quite literally an exploded heart.

There was nothing unusual about the second deputy, who had been shot in the temple.

But the third victim, though shot only in the chest and directly through the heart, had a ruptured *stomach and liver.*

The medical examiner stated that he could not determine what caused these developments at all, apparently abandoning his "high stress" theory when it happened more than once in a single incident.

When Husky called the ME's office, everybody was either at lunch, taking somebody apart, or "unavailable." He left word for Dr. Sillitoe to call back. Sillitoe was head man down there, and also the guy who'd written these reports.

■ ■ ■ ■ ■

Husky and Garth waited in the car outside the small house in the eastern reaches of Hollywood. The windows were rolled up tight and the doors were locked. Pushers didn't seem to live in very good areas, Garth had observed.

A few minutes before, Skidrow Scav had walked, big as life, up to that front door and knocked, *in code.* Husky had held his laugh inside.

"Why don't we take him?" Garth had asked.

"Wait'll he makes his deal. Then we catch him with goods, he's got no choice but to cooperate. Catch him before, he can say we're harassing an innocent citizen."

A little time passed. Husky couldn't stop thinking about

that ME report. He hadn't mentioned it to Garth because he didn't want to hear the weird theories he knew it would provoke.

"If he doesn't come out that door pretty quick, we quit sitting here and do some Scav grabbing."

"You mean go into the house?"

"I mean we better figure he's made us . . . or somebody in there has," Husky said quietly. He was looking up and down the block, gauging distances.

"You're not even sure he knows about Lamp."

"Scooter's reliable. Scav must've said something."

"But he might only know the guy's halfway to Canada."

"That's a hundred percent more than we know." Husky still hadn't taken his eyes off the house.

"So where is he?" Garth finally said.

And Husky was opening the door.

"He might be running. We're gonna find out. I'll go over there," he said, pointing to the left. "You drive the other way. Turn the corner up there and come up the next street, meet me coming the other way. I think he jumped on us."

And Husky was gone. Garth sat unmoving behind the wheel for a moment, feeling desperately in need of a good urinal to fill. He rolled down his window.

"Are you sure?" he leaned out and yelled.

Husky looked back and waved for him to just go on, already. Garth rolled the window back up and started the car in the direction Husky had pointed. He was excited, scared, and wondering if he would do this correctly. He told himself Scav wasn't very big according to the description he'd read. He rationalized: he could probably take the guy, especially if he was smashed on heroin, which would leave Scav slowed down and an easy mark.

And just then he saw Skidrow Scav dart across the

street he'd turned down according to Husky's instructions.

Garth gasped, fighting down his panic. He swerved to keep the Scav in his headlights and simultaneously leaned on the horn. Scav was moving surprisingly fast—much faster than Garth's rationalizing had given him credit for. Garth stepped on the gas now, trying to cut the guy off before he could cross.

At the other end of the block, Husky heard the horn, cussed under his breath, and started running at a full-ass sprint right down the street, right past the dope house and on after Garth.

When Garth floored it, Scav tried to slow down but only managed to run into the side of Garth's car just as Garth was again braking and attempting to form a one-car barricade in the middle of the street.

Scav was seriously stoned, so he hit the car pretty hard and took a couple seconds to collect himself. The pain was in there, but it was muffled by the high.

"Oh fuck," came the groan as Scav grabbed his knee, which he was pretty sure represented the source of the pain now moving up his leg toward his dick.

Scav reeled away finally and looked back when he heard the door opening. He had no idea who this guy was, except he obviously *wasn't* a friend. Scav tried to start running again while looking back and telling the guy to keep the fuck back, he had a butcher knife—which he didn't—but as he said this his feet got messed up and he proned out on the asphalt. Now the sting was all over his body, and he sank into it. He swam in the uncoordinated ooze of his high and his pain, feeling for his elbows and feeling wet when he found them.

"Shit." Getting to his knees, he realized he was bleeding.

He turned just as a very scared Garth was getting to

him, fearful beyond reason. The fear was probably why Garth took a running jump and threw himself through the air. He tackled Skidrow Scav, who was just then up to his knees and thinking how much he hated to bleed. He hated like the fuck to bleed.

Garth's Lyle Alzado imitation was pretty fair for a radio columnist/author. Skidrow Scav flattened faster than a soufflé in a terrorist attack and stayed down, knocked cold when his chin hit the tar.

Garth, not sure what he'd done or hadn't done, grabbed for the unconscious man's wrists and pulled them behind him. He was wondering if he should be saying something about this guy's having the right to remain silent when he heard footsteps. He looked up in fear, letting go of the wrists, which stayed right where they were.

Husky came running up to find his friend all set to be attacked by imagined hordes of East Hollywood street carnivores.

"Husky?" Came the question.

Husky stopped. He couldn't believe what he saw. Garth had coldcocked the guy and had him pinned while the car . . . was *rolling* away!

Without answering, Husky bolted after Garth's vehicle. Garth turned in confusion to watch, and his heart nearly exploded as he saw his property in desperately close range of a streetlamp. Now *that* would bring out the locals. And fuck everything up.

But Husky surprised his friend by getting to the open driver's door—left open by Garth when he'd leaped out— and hopping in, to hit the brakes.

Then he put it in reverse, and backed up to within three feet of Garth and the slumbering Skidrow Scav.

"Garth," said Husky with winded bemusement, "what the fuck did you do to this man?"

When he came to, the first thing Scav smelled was food. A hamburger and fries, to be exact. As the eyes started operating again, he realized he was in the back seat of a car . . . now he remembered the car. The food was somewhere in the front seat.

He tried sitting up and saw Husky Martin. Scav stared in shock, then groaned and sank back down on the seat. With Husky in front was . . . whoever that prick who practically killed him was. They were doing the eating.

"Want something?" Husky asked as the two captors looked over the backs of their seats at him.

Food was the very last thing Scav would ever want. For some reason he seemed to be in deep shit here. After these guys ate, if he knew Martin, they would probably beat the macaroni out of his guts. Cops.

"You were gonna tell us about Edgar Lamp," Husky offered.

"I *was?*"

Scav looked out the window. This was the parking lot of . . . what . . . an Arby's. Jesus, Arby's? He stayed down on the seat and thought about it as he stared out the back window at dark sky and one rather bright blue gas lamp in the parking lot.

"Yeah. You didn't know it yet, but you were. Woulda been much easier if you hadn't run when you knew we were there," Husky said.

"Well, how did I know who it *was?*" whined Scav.

"This is all below you, Scav," Husky answered. "I mean, you and me, we go back, huh? We've been straight with each other on ten, maybe fifteen occasions. Have I ever burned you? Have I ever fucked you over?"

"I saw *him*"—pointing at Garth—"not you."

"You didn't give him a chance."

"To say what? Hi there, buddy, Husky sent me?"

Husky looked at Garth. "Would you've said that?"

"Is that burger or roast beef?" Scav ventured.

"One of each," Husky said. "You want some, you talk first."

"Purely informational curiosity," Scav told him, realizing that he was coming down off the horse now. At least into the verbal zone.

"Quit fucking with us." Husky reached over and grabbed Scav's scummy shirt. He pulled him up so they were face to face. "Quit fucking with the world, okay? Scooter tells me you know something about Edgar Lamp and he did it in a way that kept you covered with your other buddies. But if you don't play gossip column with me right now, I swear to God you're goin' downtown." Husky let him go. Scav didn't sink back down. "Or maybe I'll just dump you on somebody else I know wants to see you and maybe I forget I did it."

"Cops can't bluff for shit." Scav straight-faced him.

"Jackie Preen," Husky said right back.

Jackie Preen was a bad name to say to Scav. Jackie was a two-time loser Scav had set up for Husky to nail on his last drug rap. There had been a killing involved, that of an old man. Jackie had managed to dodge it, but the killing brought Husky, a homicide officer, into the case. Both Scav and Husky knew Jackie had done the hit and ducked the charge on a tech.

They both also knew Jackie Preen would gladly kill Skidrow Scav and take his third trip to the land of high walls with a smile on his face. As long as he'd had his revenge.

"You're a cold fuck," Scav said. He sat up in the back seat. Now he got a good look at Garth, who just stared as

59

he munched a fry. Scav wondered how he'd ever been stoned enough to let a pig like that grind his face in the street.

"I saw Lamp under the freeway at Sixth."

"Yeah . . ."

"And then . . . and I really couldn't *believe* this . . . I saw the guy *again.*"

"You followed him?"

Scav shook his head. "I was at Tilly's."

"Tilly's is deserted. We cleaned it out."

"The fuck you did. Cops always believe what they do is final."

"So you were at Tilly's and Lamp was there?"

"I watched him come in driving this brown Ford."

"You get the plates?"

"I was fucked up, Husky." Scav smiled.

"Then how do you know it was him."

"I've never been *that* fucked up. It was him. He had this cozy little moment with El Chocolate Grande, right there in front of God and everybody."

Garth looked lost. Husky just held up a hand. He'd explain later.

"So what did he do?"

"He went back to his car and took a nap. Then this morning he took off. That was it. Over and out."

Husky thought about that for a moment. Then he slowly put the remains of his burger back in the bag it came in. Garth watched expectantly.

"Scav," Husky said with a sigh, "I always thought you were a smart man."

"I am smart. I used to teach algebra."

"Yeah. I really always did think you were smart. Seriously. And that's why I'm gonna ask you to do us a favor here."

60

Now Scav was looking worried. He hadn't expected a twist.

"I'm gonna ask you to go back there to Tilly's and be my eyeballs."

"You're nuts."

"No," said Husky, "I'm callin' the shots, that's all. Remember?"

Yeah, Scav remembered, all right. He remembered Jackie Preen. He remembered the city lockup and courts and the eventual road to state prison. Finally, he nodded and sank a little farther into the back seat. He wished he was still unconscious. Maybe, it occurred to him, he actually was and this whole thing would be over soon, just another bad dope dream.

Then the pig behind the wheel took another bite of his sandwich, releasing the cooked stringy beef smell all over again, and Skidrow Scav knew his bad luck was real. You never smelled stuff in dope dreams. You just smelled bad afterwards.

Four

EDGAR LAMP loved nothing more than strutting right into the mouth of the tiger. He had done it when he went back to Tilly Taco's. But what he was doing now made that look like wimp shit.

He was entering the visitors' waiting lobby at Los Angeles County Central Jail. Here lingered families, friends, lovers, whoever wanted to come see the hard-asses jammed inside this place. They all congregated, waiting until the right name was called.

Edgar felt like King Shit all over again here. Baddism incorporated. Badder than the short, cocky Mexican dudes in their gray janitor pants and white T-shirts. Badder than the blacks with their little berets and spectacular assortment of hairdos over bright-colored jumpsuits, running suits, pimp suits . . . whatever suits.

And yet not one man in the place could carry El Chocolate Grande's jock in a one-on-one.

But Edgar Lamp, his King Shit persona surging to the driver's seat of his cerebral cortex, had no interest whatever in anything remotely like one-on-one with any living soul just now. He was talking build the Army. Build the Force. Build the sweeping dark tide of death to come down the backside of the hill at Tilly Taco's.

He was looking for bad meat to mold, and he knew he could mold it because *he had a secret. A bad* secret.

He took the little white visitor's request form from the deputy at the door, just like the steady stream of other visitors, but he didn't fill anything out. He had no desire to see anybody incarcerated here. Incarceration was a downer to Edgar.

It was the *out*carcerated faces he scanned; hard faces on hard cases sitting on wooden hard-backed benches while the PA boomed.

"Visitor passes for Rodríguez . . . Gee-yair-mo Rodríguez. Sammy Johnson. Pass for Gazziz, Ahmet Gazziz . . . third and last call for Pasqual . . . Chuckie Pasqual . . ."

And on, and on.

There were too many young fools here tonight. High school crowds; doinks with nothing better to do than come down to this pisshole and wave through the glass partition at the biggest jerk in the whole gang. The one who managed to get himself caught while he was ripping off a tire. Or swiping some old fucking woman's handbag. Or slitting some drunk.

"Hey, you gonna get out, man, it's gonna be party fuckin' time. All right, dude?"

And the dude would grin like he'd suddenly been hit by mental retardation behind the little window. And he'd be thinking how much he fucking wished it was the other guy in here, the foolish greased-back masturbator who was waving to him from outside. *In here* so they could fuck *you* in the ass, cute boy.

Edgar remembered how it felt being on the inside when a couple of his old buddies had rambled in one time. They thought they were hot shit telling him what they were driving, who they were fucking, and what a goddamn drag it was to wait in these lines just to get fifteen or twenty minutes with him.

That was the only time anybody visited Edgar Lamp while he was in County waiting for trial.

It was easy to remember because it had happened less than an hour after one of the "old men" in the jail, a true old Mafioso, had tried to kill Edgar because he was supposedly "crazy."

The Mafia boys didn't respect the way he'd done his killing.

As Edgar and the Mafioso struggled over the knife, deadlocked, the old man had suddenly suffered a massive heart attack. Edgar split from the hall where it happened, and no one knew he'd been involved. Furthermore, no one knew—except Edgar—that the heart attack had come when he'd been staring . . . *staring* intently at the old man's chest.

At his heart.

Ever since, Edgar had believed it was no accident.

He'd become certain he could make things happen almost as if he'd willed them.

That was his secret.

He'd spoken to no one about it, but the thought had been with him now and again since. Soon, he would need to test his theory further. He would need to prove it.

He checked out the women in the visiting area. A mess of Chicanas with makeup way too thick; a lot of purple and rouge and whatever that shit was on their cheeks. Way up the sides. Black velvet paintings sprung to real life.

64

Real eyebrows plucked carefully; phony ones drawn in, looking almost Japanese. Edgar couldn't remember what you called that kind of makeup, but it looked Nip.

He wandered to the other end of the lobby. Slim pickings tonight; nobody he knew. Running into a buddy here was pretty good odds, too. The same people were always either inside looking out or vice versa. Time after time. So they hung out together on both sides. And through the glass, talking on the dirty, grease-coated little phones to each other.

And then, as he scanned the front entrance again, just about ready to admit he was bored and empty-handed enough to split and forget the fun of strutting around right under the Man's ignorant nostrils, he saw Frito.

Frito was short for Fred Zito, a guy Edgar had known before he was ever caught. A guy who had more than once tried to get on Edgar's good side because he thought it would be cool to get together and bust some heads.

Frito was a man who prayed to God every day that he could be cut from the same cloth as King Shit. Only he wasn't as smart, cunning, or ultimately as brutal.

Edgar knew all this about Frito. The guy was a definite killer, but he killed like a tractor instead of a good hunter. The good hunter would have to drive the tractor, then jump off for a good view while it mashed squirrels.

As Edgar moved toward him, Frito scowled at the piece of paper the deputy had handed him. Frito would be having trouble with words like "it" or "the."

"Hey, Frito . . ."

Edgar didn't smile when Frito looked up. He was establishing that it was serious time. So he just looked, like he was real cold inside, at Frito. Frito's quick, easy dumbshit grin dropped off his face when he saw King Shit wasn't showing teeth.

"This a big visit?" Edgar pushed it.

65

Frito shook his head.

"My cousin. You wanna talk? Fuck him."

Edgar nodded, indicated for Frito to follow. They wound up in the men's room, where graffiti literally covered every square inch. On the chrome pipes, the handle of the urinal, the metal shitter partition. Even the light bulbs in the ceiling and every inch of wall.

They waited for an old black man in baggy brown slacks and a tired Eisenhower jacket to straighten his formal hat and get the fuck out.

"I thought they bagged you," Frito said.

"Everybody thought that. But I'm unbagged now, right?"

It looked right to Frito.

"So the deal I'm lookin' for is a little help, all right? I mean like a little move-in-and-crush-it-type help."

"You need that?"

Edgar never wavered, never broke a smile on this dumbshit. He knew guys like Frito loved to hitch on to something they thought was bad-ass and then break out and go their own way at a crucial moment. Edgar wanted to be sure this never entered Frito's head.

"I got the whole thing wired to the last inch, man. All's I need is arms and legs to help me out. Now you got limbs for rent or you don't. What is it?"

Frito, dazzled by the idea that the man had an actual plan, nodded and held out his hands like he was ready for anything. Which he was. He was deciding he really liked King Shit. He liked anybody who could really think, liked to be around them and listen when they talked. Frito knew he wasn't real big in this department, and he knew he needed to hook up with guys who were. Together with them, he would get the feeling that nothing could stop him. And besides, he'd wanted to do some skull smashing with King Shit for the *longest* time.

66

"So what's the idea you got?" Frito wasn't smiling anymore now, either. He'd caught on that smiling was playing too loose. This guy didn't want to be pals.

Edgar leaned in a little.

"I need you and about five, maybe six other guys. I think you might know some, huh? Then we all get together and go up to Mulholland . . ."

Frito frowned. He wasn't into cars or anything, and Mulholland was where guys went to race.

"If this is cars and shit . . ."

"Not cars," Edgar hissed. And all of a sudden he got a little antsy in this place. The bathroom of the fucking visitors' lounge at the fucking county lockup, for shit's sake! Was he out of his mind?

And without pausing a moment he started walking out of the bathroom. Frito just watched him as he took the first couple steps.

"Come on," Edgar said back over his shoulder. "I don't wanna talk in here anymore. I'm sick of smelling shit."

Edgar started talking again when they got to the parking structure adjacent to the county jail. In some ways it was scarier than the waiting room. Deep shadows and remote corners invited damn near anybody to do anything to anybody else. The deputies wouldn't know for hours 'cause they lacked the balls or interest to go check it out. This was outside the realm of their armed cordon. Outside the checkpoint at the front door and into the hostile real world where people like King Shit and Frito could blend into dark places.

"So if it's not cars on Mulholland, then what the fuck're we talking about here?" Frito was hooked. Edgar still didn't allow himself a smile.

"Mulholland is just to get up there to the top of the hill,

man. To get behind some people down on the Hollywood side."

Now Frito was shutting up. Just listening. The mention of getting behind some people was more his speed. It didn't matter who or why to him. It was the idea of doing some people. For a moment Edgar remembered about Frito, and he knew he'd chosen right. Frito had no idea of fair or right and wrong. Frito could make snakes puke, he was such an asshole.

Just what Edgar needed. King Shit and the Assholes, he thought. And liked it.

"You ever been to a place called Tilly Taco's?"

Frito nodded. He sure had.

"There's a guy there . . . black dude everybody calls El Chocolate Grande? Since they busted me, he's goin' around like *he* was King Shit. Like it was all his up there and just 'cause I'm out I got no right to take it back."

Now King Shit smiled.

"Well, he's about due. And I'm about ready to *prove* something."

Frito had no idea of the kind of proof Edgar had in mind, but loved it. His blood was racing. His skin was tingling. He brushed the hair out of his eyes. Just now a huge black man, at least four hundred pounds of sheer mass, turned on one of those shoulder-pack blower machines and started blasting the litter out of a nearby corner of the parking structure.

Against the thunder of the sound the cleanup man made, Frito moved a little closer to Edgar Lamp. He took a quick look at the huge cleanup man, who was moving away.

"I can get you five more boys. You know, when I wanted to get together with you before? Back when you weren't busted yet? *These* were the guys I was trying to tell you about, man. The Demon Viejo Dukes. These guys are *per*fect. All right, man?"

"I wanna meet them right away. Can we do that?" Now Edgar was excited, too. It was falling into line. The Demon Viejo Dukes would be his little squad. The idea of sweeping down that hillside to kick the shit out of El Choc and his boys was sounding better and better.

Then, when he did leave L.A., there would be no doubt at all in *anyone's* mind about who was King Shit and who was not. He could even leave L.A. to somebody like Frito, who would never try to say he was another King Shit.

Because Frito, like the other boys he was going to meet for this little war, was going to see Edgar *prove* what he had in mind. That was it. A full-on *Proving.* Just like Grandpa Harper Lamp had chattered about all the time: "The Lord will come a-proving Himself to you, boy. The Lord will lay down the facts and there will be a Proving and you will believe what you see because it will be a miracle. And you won't know it's comin' till it gets here, but when it does you can't miss it. 'Cause the whole world wants a miracle. And the miracle is in the Proving."

Grandpa Harper Lamp had been just a little bit wrong. Edgar could feel it coming. He could almost taste it, almost name it and describe it. And it would definitely be a Proving.

Edgar could think of his grandfather and smile the sweet smile of knowing where the last laugh had fallen, and to whom. Grandpa Harper hadn't proved a damn thing in his life except what a jackass he was.

His God and all the miracles and Provings and the other bullshit he'd laid down were washed away and forgotten. Just as dead as he was himself, and just as easy to kill. Edgar had only raised the ax, he'd never had to bring it down.

Harper's death had shown Edgar how weak his grandfa-

69

ther had been . . . and how strong he himself was. Strong enough to bring about what skinny, quaking, monkey-eyed Harper Lamp with his sweaty-handed, arm-grabbing urgency had never even been able to approach.

Real Provings. And what they proved, Harper would never have believed. It was the kind of stuff that scared the shit out of skinny old men and big strong young ones. Every single man and woman Edgar Lamp had killed had been a Proving. A miracle. His miracle.

The whole world wants a miracle, Edgar thought, smiling to himself, but the whole world better be careful what it wishes for.

As Edgar and Frito drove in Frito's car toward the lair of the Demon Viejo Dukes, Edgar rolled down the window and closed his eyes. He let the air play over his face, mess up his hair. He felt like the smartest man on earth, like he was unlocking the secret and he could bring it down like a hammer on anyone who got in his way. Like the knowledge of what he could do was coming closer and closer to the surface . . .

Maybe he wouldn't leave L.A. that soon after all. If King Shit found the right Assholes, maybe he could stay as long as he liked.

This pleased Edgar. His plans soared, his confidence bloated. Martin and his cunt grandmother would shit to hear his thoughts.

When Martin got Edgar's message, his grandmother would feel it, too. It would be sent to her as much as him, and she would know to get ready.

The car slid through the night haze into East L.A. Into Frito's World and Frito's Territory.

"You wouldn't fuck with me, right?" Edgar said to Frito. " 'Cause, man, you won't believe what I've got working against that nigger."

No, no way. Frito's smile said it all. Not he or the flying spider monkeys he had waiting in some warehouse around here, working on their motors and shining up their hardware. These were guys who couldn't wait to see what King Shit called a Proving.

"So what does it prove, man?" Frito looked eager to learn.

"Proves the world is flat, Jack. If I say it is . . ."

Edgar Lamp wasn't smiling. He was much too busy believing himself.

■ ■ ■ ■ ■

Of Fright

After Harper Lamp fled from the town of Gullickson, Alice Lamp thought Edgar might've been happier for a little while. But even that was conjecture, since Edgar didn't register things like happiness or sadness too clearly, even at that young age.

A little later it would become much easier to recognize when he was upset.

Alice kept hoping to hear some message of reassurance from her husband, or from the authorities regarding his whereabouts. In time, she even hoped to hear that he had been found dead somewhere, so she could stop living in doubt and constant tentative fear.

The presence of Edgar in the house, though the boy kept to himself a great deal of the time—to avoid her, she knew—was a persistent aggravation of her existence in limbo.

Finally, a break came. Edgar, barely fifteen, also left the Lamp house. He packed the same single suitcase he had arrived with, and simply walked out in the middle of the night without so much as a goodbye.

Edgar virtually disappeared from the face of the earth for the

71

next few years. No hard facts are available, but it must be assumed that he hitchhiked throughout Texas and possibly the rest of the Southwest during that time. To conclude that he had gone in search of his grandfather was, in the eyes of the police, stretching the matter past any point the evidence of the old man's eventual death could support.

True, fourteen months after Edgar left Gullickson, Harper Lamp's body, long and thin and bony-faced as ever, was found on a deserted hillside overlooking a small company oil town. Also true, despite the fact that it appeared to have been roughly two weeks since the death, the expression on the dead man's face was one of sheer terror.

Of course, the elements and various animals had taken their toll on the remains, but the gaping mouth and general posture of the body, even in rigor mortis, were hard to misinterpret.

The only cogent attack anyone could muster against Edgar was the fact that Edgar had sworn, in one of his few expressions of any emotion at all as a youth, that he would love to kill his grandfather . . . to do it personally and by himself. Without a gun or any other weapon. Just by himself.

Even this recollection by Alice Lamp Corinth of her grandson's homicidal fantasy, however, was hearsay. Furthermore, Edgar's exact whereabouts during the time of Harper Lamp's death could not be determined at all. Months later, he was seen near the northernmost tip of Arkansas, far from his grandfather's death site. Edgar's account of where he'd wandered was vague, but the few particulars he could provide were verified.

The final factor that caused Arkansas State Police to simply release Edgar Lamp was the condition of Harper's body. There were no apparently mortal wounds of any kind, anywhere on the body. Nothing resembling a deathblow, strangulation, gunshot or knife wounds. Perhaps animals had chewed away such telltale evidence, but police could not tell.

The man seemed to have died of fright.

72

Five

SKIDROW SCAV was on maximum hunker, his defenses high, his danger antenna doing three-sixty sweeps.

He'd never liked Tilly Taco's, even as a last-ditch overnight stopgap. Now, with an air of uneasiness permeating the place, he'd gladly doze in the dankest urine-soaked rut in the worst deserted building in the city before being here.

The consensus among the other nighttime denizens of the Taco was King Shit would resurface, wanting ugly revenge for the snub he'd gotten here earlier.

El Choc, strutting amid his cadre of watchful, nervous sympathizers, made it loudly known that King Shit had realized his time at Tilly Taco's was over. He no longer had power here, no longer had friends here, no longer had a welcome here.

There wasn't one fucking soul in the place who put any value in what El Choc said. Well, maybe fat nineteen-year-old Jill, who was into buffing stop signs when she wandered the streets. She muttered about the importance of keeping the letters on them clear, since you never knew when a driver might miss seeing one.

Skidrow Scav watched her sit alone, knees gathered up close so her skirt rode high, her filthy underwear blaring tattered green ass cheeks at the world as she watched El Choc with admiration. Caught in his thrall. He looked more dramatic than King Shit from a distance, and Jill never got closer to reality than a distance.

Scav thought about thrall. People here either got caught up in it or dished it out. Scav personally didn't buy thrall. He set himself apart from the others—givers or takers—because of his education. He saw it all as hype and gullibility, so he sat back, did his occasional fix, and kept clear of thrall.

But a lot of thrall was going down around him. Right now who commanded it was up for grabs, and even *that* carried its own thrall factor. Scav felt like a reporter on the scene, clutching the mike on behalf of some impersonal electronic grid feeding into millions of homes, disseminating slightly altered truth. But Scav wasn't really broadcasting anything to anybody except two cops, named Skakel and Purdue. They were in plainclothes; feeling pretty jacked about shedding blue suits for this assignment. They sat in their obvious green unmarked metro car a few blocks from Tilly Taco's and waited for an electronic beep signaling trouble. It would mean the arrival of Edgar Lamp, and at the very least the impending commencement of serious violence.

Scav knew the cops waiting out there would have healthy respect for King Shit, so King Shit held even *them* in his thrall.

Scav was eyeballing escape routes, thinking how nice San Diego would be this time of year. He felt in his jacket pocket and touched the small electronic device Husky Martin had given him. It was the signal unit, a beeper of the simplest order. Just click the little switch part over to where it showed green instead of red, and you were emitting a pulse signal that caused a receiver in the unmarked car to beep repeatedly.

Scav was a beacon, a fruitfly trap, a veritable King Shit narc. He'd always wondered how narcing felt, and now he squirmed inwardly with the fear that somehow, some *way*, everybody here would divine the fact that his were dirty little cop eyes dropped into the body of an otherwise perfectly respectable derelict.

He wondered where Husky Martin might be; biting his nails and wondering if he'd made the right decision by even halfway trusting such a being as Scav. He'd sure made a lot of noise about Scav's algebraic past. About how once Scav had shown he was *meant* to be a real contributing member of society. About how there must be some shred of that decency he'd once worn proudly left in there. And how everything that had gone wrong was only a terrible mistake and shouldn't really have happened like it did.

So Scav hated Husky Martin. Because Husky had tapped into Scav's own most secretly cherished idea about himself. Tapped in like a mosquito settling on a good, greasy skin spot to plunge that poker right in.

Sure, Scav knew King Shit was the worst news ever dropped on any city, and he didn't want the guy roaming out there any more than that respectable, homeowning, TV-watching diarrheic pile of a society out there did. Scav was just as scared of him as they were. More. After all, he was right out here in the guy's stomping grounds.

With a beeper, for shit's sake.

Scav pawed at some dirt, tossed a pebble and watched it bounce downhill a little. Yeah, Husky Martin had fucked him over perfectly; caught him in his own guilt and delivered him to his own conscience.

■ ■ ■ ■ ■

The three cars parked on the soft shoulder along Mulholland and the lights went off. The figures inside waited. Edgar Lamp wanted it to get later, so the population of Tilly Taco's, just over the ridge and down the hill below them, would be largely asleep.

Edgar sat in the passenger seat of the first car, next to a very wired, fidgety Frito. Edgar knew how cranked Frito was and didn't like it. The others had more control over their cool.

Not that he liked them, either. The scene back at the warehouse in Pico Rivera had been tense. None of those guys wanted to trust Edgar. They watched him when they thought he wasn't watching them.

They'd probably argued behind his back about wasting him when they went into the next room to decide. Argued about giving him to the Man and sucking up to the approval of the whole fucking city.

But they hadn't because Edgar had come in, King Shit eyes all cold and primed and full of that *calm* he could give them. They knew it was better to go with him.

Edgar had told them, his eyes full of an excitement that almost betrayed him, that he would put on a Proving. He said it in a way that sounded so much like his fucking dead grandfather Harper Lamp that it'd even freaked him a little.

He said tonight we *do* some people. He asked them if the Demon Viejo Dukes had the balls, and even though Frito laughed his hollow, wimp-ass laugh, the other five just looked at him. Checked him out.

He scanned them back, commanding and challenging with his midnight-black eyes for any of them to step up and say fuck you, Jack, you couldn't *prove* dick.

But the Dukes just watched, thinking he was fucking crazy, just like he wanted them to.

Then he started talking battle, and they saw he wasn't crazy at all. He would lead them down to cut faces at Tilly Taco's. It would rain broken glass and nails in that natural bowl and they would *be* that rain. They would love that, he knew. They wanted the same tribal rush Frito wanted, but they would draw that rush into darker souls than Frito could ever hope to have.

They were war boys; quiet, dangerous, and so, so proud.

Edgar could see how Frito, stupid and scared, was low man. He licked their cracks. They had used him exactly as Edgar had used him, to connect. He'd set them up with King Shit and now he didn't matter.

Edgar controlled the game. The Dukes waited for his Proving. If they liked it, then for a while they'd do any fucking thing he wanted.

■ ■ ■ ■ ■

They got out of the cars and stood in a line in the moonlight, looking down the dark hill at the cluster of sad humanity below. Tilly Taco's was just as easy and open to attack now as it had been when the people from Hell Hotel had murdered and triumphed.

The Duke called Little Cholo felt his lean body heat up with excitement, fending off the cold night air as if it wasn't there. On another night he might have shivered, but not just now. He was a Demon Viejo Duke. He was ready to *fly*. One of the others standing with Edgar and Frito was Little Cholo's brother. Their mother had named him Wilson, so he wouldn't sound like a Mexican when he introduced himself. He hated the name and had invented a new one, Mr. Yogie. The other Dukes liked it because Mr. Yogie sounded like a thinker. And that he was.

It had been Mr. Yogie who had convinced the other three—quiet boys of twenty or twenty-one named Zero, Quiet Carlos, and Spider Lobo—to shut up and let King Shit make his play. Nothing would happen to them. Their fast gray-primered engines would wait on the Mulholland pavement not far away. If the pigs showed, they could vanish back into the dark hillside like ghosts and leave King Shit to stand around and wonder what had happened. The pigs would not outflank them, because behind them would be only the hillside and the winding Mulholland darkness. They knew all of this because of the many times they had come up here before to drive. On those drives they had seen the big houses and they had decided to rob some. They had even killed up here twice, vanishing down into the valley to take the freeways east and back to the safety of the city.

Their own small, safe streets. And the warehouse.

So while Little Cholo nodded, Mr. Yogie had reminded Zero, Quiet Carlos, and Spider Lobo that they had the hardware and they knew the roads. While Frito and King Shit stood waiting in the next room, staring at their feet and scratching their dicks, the five Demon Viejo Dukes tried to imagine what King Shit meant by a Proving. They remembered what Frito had told them before about King Shit, telling them how it was the perfect combination. Frito had sworn this one was special like they were, a thinker, a real one, and sooner or later they would want to get together and start doing some people with him because it would be like fate or something. Frito had been very excited. More excited than any of them had *ever* seen him, and they all knew that was *something* because Frito got excited easily. So they were curious.

And now, above Tilly Taco's, they were feeling that heat come up from their crotches to warm chests and shoulders. It burned away worries about pigs. By the time they started down the hill together all the bad shit was gone for all of them. Little Cholo thought for a second about how much he liked his name, which meant fox. He moved through the weeds and brush, taking the declining hillside as if he was born for it.

Edgar Lamp watched all of them as they moved downhill. He knew Frito wanted to yell out, crush the first head he came to. He would want to fuck the women and kill everybody. Edgar motioned for him to be silent, repeating a warning he'd given in the car. "You gotta stay quiet. Wait to get to the bottom, you know? Wait till we all start." Frito had looked like a little kid getting punished by his teacher, but he'd finally nodded, driving along.

The others, Edgar could see, were going to be no problem at all. At his hand signal, they stopped about halfway down. Edgar pointed to a fire in the center of the three blazes. That would be where El Choc sat. Edgar thought he could see his back, heavy with muscles, among several other men.

Edgar was already seeing what would happen to El Choc in his mind's eye.

Everybody coming down the hill brought out their guns. Light, easy-to-carry little pieces. Plenty of shells in every pocket they had. They kept moving, silent.

Edgar felt more alive than he had in weeks. His head was clear. Everything seemed brighter and louder than even a few minutes before. He believed now more strongly than ever that he could kill El Choc the way he had killed the old Mafioso in the county jail.

They attacked the people highest on the hill in utter

silence, using the guns as heavy fists. Quick blows to backs of heads. In teams, they caught sleeping street people unaware. A hand would clamp over a mouth to muffle sound, and as the head turned to get a look the second member of the team brought the small but terribly hard butt of the pistol down on the temple, the forehead, the cheekbone. Crushing or simply impact killing, if the blow was right.

Skidrow Scav was not one of the first ones they reached. He was lying wide awake. He heard rustling above him on the hill. He didn't move, not even when the sounds became louder and closer. He misjudged how quickly it would come upon him because he never imagined seven of them working in quick little teams of two, with Edgar Lamp cruising, watching, picking up and taking out the odd, surprising sleeper they hadn't expected.

Scav had his hand in his pocket and his fingers wrapped, ready, around the beeper when Quiet Carlos covered his mouth and jerked his face around for Spider Lobo to smash. Spider Lobo looked a thousand feet tall to Scav in the split second before the pain in his cheekbone blinded him. His scream was cut off by a second punch to the abdomen, blasting air and loose mucus out his nose. Finally there was another rather sloppy blow to the face. Scav seemed out cold, but he wasn't close to being dead. They went on, misjudging the damage. They had no idea about the beeper, which had come out of Scav's pocket and lay on the ground nearby.

But Scav, in the pain that rocked his senses and blew his mind, had never clicked the switch from red to green. He lay almost unconscious as they continued down the hill quietly, nearing El Choc.

■　■　■　■　■

The men around the center campfire realized that they had visitors far too late. They sprang up, reaching for guns kept in their belts or by their sides, but Cholo's mean little voice rasped out at them.

"Don' do it, man."

Another voice penetrated the campfire. As it did, the men around it looked to El Chocolate Grande, who stared coolly into the darkness.

The other voice was more recognizable.

"Nobody do *any*thing. Just lemme hear fuckin' guns hit fuckin' dirt."

The voice was Edgar Lamp's. El Choc told himself this was it. Part of him, down deep, was glad. Let it be decided. He knew the adrenal rush he was getting meant he would in moments be ready to do anything he had to. His hard body was animal-coiled while his mind remained calm.

A couple of the men who stood near El Choc made a move. They were surprised to discover that there were adversaries on all sides. Edgar had cautioned the five friends of Frito not to shoot El Choc under any circumstances. They remembered, and only the two men who moved, plus three others who moved a moment later, were chopped down in a short burst from the darkness around them.

There were a few moments of silence while the results sank in for El Choc and his people. Then their guns did indeed begin to hit the dirt.

El Choc had not flinched. He had found the figure of Edgar Lamp in the darkness and he had fixed on it. He knew King Shit was just as fixed on him.

The seven invaders closed the circle quickly now. Quiet Carlos and Spider Lobo picked up the dropped guns and separated them from their owners. Frito was hyperventilating like he was in heat, keeping fingers tight on his gun.

Edgar saw this. He stepped in front of Frito, facing El Choc as he entered the light.

"I'm back." He smiled.

Choc didn't move a muscle.

"Told you I could take what was mine. Now I'm standing here with all these bad people you were telling me would hand me my ass. And they ain't moving a thing but their bowels." He paused, stepped closer, inches away. "How come you think that's happening?"

Edgar brought the gun up very fast, whipping its barrel across El Choc's jawbone in a wicked slap. The big man stepped back a little, but the blow hadn't done much to him. His eyes flared down at Edgar, who loved it and peered up into them. His was a deadly child's fascination as he prepared to rip the wings off a moth. And then Edgar Lamp turned to Cholo, who stood just a couple feet away, transfixed with the face-off like all the rest in this darkened hill break, and handed him the gun.

"I'm gonna show you something, Chockie. I'm gonna show you and everybody here something I can do."

And Edgar Lamp, his King Shit confidence surging and buzzing through every artery and vein, moved back a step. He said, "The whole world wants a miracle, Chockie."

El Chocolate Grande looked at him with a mixture of fear and confusion. He thought Edgar Lamp was flat out of his mind.

But Edgar had been feeling more and more certain about himself. When he'd taken control at the campfire he'd realized this would be bigger—*better* than with the old man in the county jail. Now he felt a clear, definite hunger to do his own special Proving.

"This is the miracle," Edgar said. His expression momentarily took on a quizzical, straining quality that quickly changed to absolute concentration. He did not seem to see El Choc before him, but some small animal;

something to kill. El Choc felt something lurch in his solar plexus. His hands moved to his middle as if on reflex.

Edgar was buoyed, lost in the knowledge of what his mind could do to another person. He also realized that he was the most vulnerable man in Tilly Taco's at this moment of his Proving on El Choc. Vulnerable to anyone else except El Choc.

But no one would ever imagine this. They would be far too surprised at what they were seeing. They would concentrate on it almost as hard as Edgar himself.

And they were. Nobody moved. Not Edgar's friends or foes. Edgar lost track of conscious thoughts. The big man felt himself being moved backward, *physically* backward, though nothing was touching his body. There was only the scowl on King Shit's face.

It was a face beyond meanness or hate, unlike anything El Choc had ever seen. For a moment, despite the pain in his middle that suddenly rose as if he'd been speared, despite his airless gasp and backward stumbling, all he could see was that face.

El Chocolate Grande struggled desperately to regain control of his own thoughts, his own destiny. He told himself nothing was pushing him backward. Nothing was ripping at his insides. He determined to plant his feet in something like a football lineman's stance and push forward against whatever this was. He managed to get his right heel dug in, skidded a little, but had time to do the same with his left. Now he was plainly straining against some force no one could see, looking for all the world like a man walking through a powerful river current.

Now El Choc brought his eyes up, the struggle forcing him to use every ounce of power in his huge, pile-driver body. The utter relaxation and calm of the features of King Shit's face was instantly demoralizing, but El Choc didn't let down his effort. The eyes told it all.

83

King Shit's eyes were boring holes in El Choc, or so it felt.

Edgar realized that this was not as easy as he had expected. Something in him felt a moment of anger, irritation that El Choc could throw up a blockage of sheer will. He experienced the panicky flare of an idea: maybe El Choc would be able to *keep* him from doing it?

Edgar acted quickly. Never letting up on his concentration, never stopping the mental chant: "The whole world wants a miracle," Edgar took two quick steps forward. His eyes never left El Choc's face as he thrust his hands forward with a single animal shout he was not even aware of.

El Choc could not believe what he was feeling. He looked down, moaning in pain. Edgar Lamp, staring down there, was also pulling now at El Choc's solar plexus with his bare hands, helping the sensation of separation, the driving pressure that was inside, trying to get out.

El Choc tried to put his hands around Edgar's throat, tried to make his comeback, but his hands proved harmlessly weak. They were unable to remain at neck level, much less cut off the air. They fell back to El Choc's sides.

His knees gave, his strength suddenly abdicated. There was a final little gasp as he fell back before King Shit, who stayed with him as if clamped to his belly, forcing him down. And then suddenly there was a sickening plosive sound, a breaking of bone, skin, and muscle as the strong, hard body of El Chocolate Grande gave a violent, unnatural jerk.

The torso opened up from navel to sternum in one sudden action, one warm gust of air. Ribs snapped as one, and bent up to face the stars. Internal organs rushed past the ribs and the outer perimeter of El Choc's body, flying past and around the invading form of Edgar Lamp as though he and they were the like poles of two different magnets.

84

Only the blood spattered his face and chest and arms. His hands were bathed in it.

No one around him, no one in all of Tilly Taco's, uttered a sound. Edgar was unaware of them anyway. He could think only of his Proving. Right here. Tangible. In his own grasp. And suddenly, with a bellow of conquest, he thrust his hands into the warm, emptied, oozing husk of what was once El Chocolate Grande's chest. He violated that sanctity again in one final plunging of fists and forearms, clear to the elbows. For all of them to see. And he let a sigh pass his lips, his satisfaction immense, sensual, undeniable.

From the hillside above, like all the others, Skidrow Scav had witnessed the Proving Edgar Lamp had brought to occur. Scav half sat up, half rested on an elbow that would not stop aching. He had to get away from this place, away from these people who might find him crawling and finish their job.

But he *couldn't* take his eyes off the figure of King Shit, now standing in a feral crouch over the oddly turned, twisted corpse of El Chocolate Grande, staring down at it as the others stared at him.

Scav's head was killing him. His major activity for the last five minutes, besides watching the spectacle below, was wiping recurrent blood from his eyes. He never wanted to see his own reflection again, certain it would be a scarred rubble of what it once was.

He tore himself away from the quiet gathering below to crawl unnoticed up the hill. Then he remembered. The attack, the blow to the head, finally the awakening to the strange, haunting encounter thirty yards below him on the hillside—all had kept him from remembering.

Now he stopped and reached hastily, desperately into his pocket for the remote signal device.

Jesus, it wasn't there. He tried his other pockets. Maybe

he'd forgotten where he kept it after getting hit. No dice. Angry frustration rose. He would have to crawl back to where he'd been and *find* the damn thing!

He attempted to be as quiet as humanly possible as he looked for it. Certain he'd be detected and shot at any moment, he stayed on hands and knees. In darkness at ground level he knew he might as well be stone blind.

Stevie Wonder attempts to find his garage-door opener.

Scav didn't laugh aloud, but resolved to share that one with somebody if he survived this. And suddenly there it was, right under his shin. He'd passed it right by and nearly crushed it with his knee.

But he had to hurry because the attackers were following Edgar Lamp up the hill and out of Tilly Taco's. This wasn't takeover, just murder. Scav clicked the switch from red to green and the little red light on the side of the unit flickered. It was still working.

As he looked around, Scav realized he could begin to relax now. In moments he would be almost the only living person in Tilly Taco's. Lamp and his group were well up the hillside toward Mulholland. Others who could still walk fled from the body of El Chocolate Grande and the three campfires.

Scav wondered what might have happened to Jill, the girl who cleaned the stop signs and admired El Choc from afar. There'd be no way to know if she'd survived this. Or if she had stared in fixated wonder, caught just like Scav himself in the full grip of King Shit's bona fide unadulterated thrall.

He didn't think about her long. His attention was caught by the beacon of Skakel and Purdue's approaching metro car. There were rapidly following flashers from the squad cars they'd called for backup, too.

So blues and yellows mingled with the reds, throwing Tilly Taco's into a bizarre Christmastime color bath. The light played over the motionless forms at the hill's bottom, each color casting a shadow of slightly different darkness.

■ ■ ■ ■ ■

Edgar controlled his exultant feeling as he rode with Cholo, who was newly wary and unable to understand what had just happened.

"I told you I'd do a Proving tonight," Edgar said, staring over at him. He wondered how he could be sounding so calm.

Cholo kept his eyes on the road. They were nearly into the valley, taking their winding back-roads route through the quiet affluent neighborhood in the hills above Studio City.

"Didn't know what you meant," Cholo finally answered quietly.

"You know now?" A little smile.

Cholo didn't answer that one.

"Nobody's ever seen me do that," Edgar finally went on, putting more fatigue in his voice than he really felt. He wanted Cholo to think it was harder than it actually was.

"Make you tired?"

"Little bit."

"That what you did to all those people? . . . You know . . ."

Edgar felt his commanding past enter the conversation.

"The ones I offed, you mean? The ones in Texas and out here?" He just looked at Cholo for a moment. Then, when Cholo finally threw a questioning look back at him: "Yeah, that's how it went down," he lied.

Cholo had thought as much as soon as he'd seen what was happening to El Choc. It had not been easy out there

87

for King Shit tonight, that was for sure. El Choc was a huge, strong man. He had not wanted to die and he had fought harder than most men do. Cholo had quietly hoped El Choc could surprise King Shit, but he had never really believed it possible once that hex or whatever it was had really taken effect. Now Cholo was rethinking his own opinion of King Shit. There could be no easy way to end a friendship with this one. There could only be the death of King Shit, or the deaths of Cholo and the Demon Viejo Dukes. Cholo was quite sure King Shit had already figured it all out, and he felt nervous about coming to this conclusion so late himself. Maybe King Shit had already decided how and where he would try to rip the bodies of Cholo and his friends open. And maybe there would be nothing Cholo could do to stop it.

Cholo kept driving, coming to the freeway and taking it, seeing the other cars behind in the rearview. Now they would be safe for tonight. Freeways were the great black safe zones they caught and slid away on; the finely surfaced asphalt jet-stream escape from reality. Sometime later, they would reemerge into a different, disconnected reality; San Fernando Valley replaced twenty-five minutes later by East Los Angeles. The safety of Pico Rivera. Familiar streets and reliable hiding places. The warehouse. Where Cholo and the others could decide how to deal with King Shit. And when.

Edgar was still stunned at what he could do, still almost giddy when he relived it as they rode back to the warehouse. He had done his Proving. El Choc, though surprisingly strong and no easy victim, had gone down. Edgar could smell the man's blood drying on him. He was surprised he hadn't noticed it before. Maybe it had been the fact that immediately after the Proving, he was suddenly so alert to everything else. He'd known the pigs would be coming, though he wasn't sure how they knew. He'd known to get out of there right then; no burials, no victory celebration, nothing. And he'd been right. By the time they'd reached the top, the place had been swarming with blue suits and badges. But they hadn't known to look up the hill. At least not until he was gone.

Now he thought about what to do next. There was always the idea of getting out of town completely, but things were turning him away from that. He couldn't trust Cholo or the other Dukes beyond his line of sight, but he sensed they were fascinated with him. They wanted to see how his mind worked, what he would do next, what was in it for them. It flattered him, and flattery was something Edgar had rarely ever received from anyone except himself. So he thought about staying and carrying things the next step.

Looking out the window at the freeway lights, Edgar thought about that cop. Martin. He would know what Edgar had done tonight.

He'd probably even been one of the cops rushing in so quickly after the death of El Choc. Edgar liked that idea.

A near-miss. A game of inches.

But this was not enough. This was not the Big Message to his friend Mr. Martin, though Martin would be coming after him with everything, and Edgar would now be item number one in Pigland.

That would require some fitting reply. Some new kind of miracle for the whole world to see. Some new kind of Proving. And *that* would contain Edgar's message; his promise.

There was no idea Edgar could've liked more.

Six

SCAV HADN'T LIKED the emergency room, and he liked this fucking interrogation chamber even less. He hadn't been hit with a case of nerves like this since he'd tried going cold turkey about six months earlier. He couldn't stop chattering, talking as if the editor that usually rode around in his brain cavity was on a major vacation.

At the same time, he hurt in places he'd never thought about, bending forward in his chair, clutching his ribs—which only hurt his ribs *and* his arms even more—while sucking on a cigarette and wincing. Shit, even the pressure of sucking on the smoke created new shooting pains inside his mouth. The tender flesh there had been torn by his own teeth, courtesy of the blows to his face.

That face was twisted into a deep frown as he listened to himself talking at Husky Martin, who was in no mood to play Florence Anybody.

"The guy . . . the guy is fucking just *bad* news, man. I

mean, he took him right out . . . just took him like that
. . . I don't know, I don't know . . . it was dark. Fuckin'
dark. Maybe I didn't see right."

Husky moved quicker than Scav thought he could, grabbing a fistful of shirt.

"Throw some fucking *light* on it."

"I can't, man . . . you know . . . I'm hurt, right?
Can't you see this?"

Husky let go of Scav's shirt, calmed himself. "I've seen
guys hurt twice as bad as you pull eight-hour shifts with a
smile."

Scav didn't look up, didn't want to deal with Martin's
eyes, but he nodded at the floor.

"Look . . . all right . . . look, I mean I don't know
what the fuck happens when this guy goes one-on-one,
okay? Only you bought a mess, here. First they come
down the hill behind where I'm laying, right? I mean like
seven guys including Lamp, and I only hear sounds at
almost the very last second, and then they're on me and
everybody else. I never saw so many dead people or
bloody people or whatever they were . . ."

"We know. We found 'em." Husky was tapping an impatient finger on the desk top. Garth just watched Scav. Scav
finally noticed and stared back at him for as long as he
could stare at anybody just now. Finally, looking down
again: "Who *is* this guy? He Vice or something?"

"Friend of mine," Husky told him. "Don't worry, he's
here helping us."

More rapid nodding of Scav's head. He couldn't get the
picture of what had happened out of his mind. Maybe it
would help if he told them about it.

"When did you come around?" Husky tried to lead him.

"Oh shit . . . couple minutes maybe? Later, anyway,
but not before the whole thing went . . . five minutes, I'd
say." He shook his head to clear it. Rubbed his hands

across his face, lit another ciggie. "They were already down by the fires where El Choc was . . . sort of all around 'em. Couple guys were already lying in the dirt down there. I guess they were shot by then, huh?"

Husky nodded, waiting to get to the meat of it. Scav understood; did some more rapid-fire head bobbing.

"This guy Lamp . . . I don't know how but he didn't use a gun on Choc, okay? He didn't use *anything*, man. He just *looked* at him real hard. I fuckin' expected the guy to just suddenly go '*Hee-aah!*' You know, like some fuckin' TV preacher, right? I didn't know *what* was goin' on, but it looks like he wrinkles his forehead and you get your fuckin' ticket punched."

"What?" Garth said.

Husky just kept his eyes on Scav for a long moment. Scav didn't look away. He wanted to be believed.

"He used *nothin'.*"

"No knife? I mean, there were guts all over that ravine. The guy was empty. His ribs were bent."

"No knife. No crowbar, no lead pipe. Nothing." Scav just kept staring at Husky for a moment, then seemed to get hit by a new wave of his personal aftershock to the whole experience, and began to shiver and rock and bob again.

"Try and give it to me one step at a time," Husky told him.

"He went in"—Scav was nodding as he spoke—"he disarmed the other guys and said he was gonna . . . *prove* something. Like he was gonna have this proving? That make any sense?"

"What was he gonna prove?" Husky asked.

"You nuts? He proved you're crazy if you fuck with him. He proved guys like me shouldn't tell guys like you a thing."

92

Husky nodded. "I may weep. Keep tellin', and no bull-shit."

Scav almost laughed. As if he could possibly make himself *stop* talking at this moment.

"All right . . . all right . . . it sounds like I'm in fucking withdrawals, but what he did was he made the guy *explode*. It looked like a charge went off in his solar plexus."

They just stared at him, waiting.

"I wouldn't shit you, the guy's *insides* came blowing out. Like they'd been launched." Scav looked from Husky to Garth and back again. "I'm telling you the fucking *truth!*" Scav's sudden shout made Garth jump, but Husky was unmoved. He was thinking very hard about several of the things he'd seen recently.

"Well . . . how did he do something like that?" Husky's words were at an ultra-calm level, sharply contrasting Scav's.

Scav did laugh now, as he waved his arms.

"Hey, I just saw it. I didn't go down asking for a guidebook, did I? I mean, he leaned in, right? He puts out his hands, all right? He makes this big strong black dude could rip your goddamn head off just flat *die* 'cause he couldn't lift his *hands* . . . he couldn't *fight* the man . . . he couldn't protect himself!" Scav was half standing up out of the chair. The two faces watched, looking up at him. "It was a goddamn Klansman's dream! Put his hands up around Lamp's neck and couldn't choke him. El Choc's just twitchin' and jerkin' all over the place and then . . . and then . . . he goes down on his knees and looks right up into Lamp's face, and flops down on his back 'cause he's lost it and then he . . . *just* . . . *came* . . . *apart.*" Scav looked at them hard, then sat back down. "And if you think I'm lying to you guys here, then do me a favor, you fuck off and die."

Scav was shaking. He and Husky stared at one another for a few moments.

"Can I ask a question?" Garth ventured.

Husky glowered for a moment, then made a gesture for his friend to go ahead. He'd hear anything, any question right now.

"What about the other people? The people around there?"

Scav looked at the ceiling, hearing himself chatter into what must surely be deeper trouble.

"What would *you* have done, man? This guy comes down the hill with his little barrio *strike* force and catches you by surprise in the middle of the night? He kills off God knows how many on the way down the hill and stands around with his guns aimed at your balls? You gonna fight him?"

Garth had no answer. Husky thought about the cleaned-out torso of the man he'd seen in the cold little valley when he'd arrived for a personal look. El Chocolate Grande had seemed frail, his shattered body gone gray after its ordeal. Husky thought about hearts that had seemed to explode, stomachs and livers ruptured even though no bullet or other instrument of death had come near them.

Scav watched him. He could see Husky was believing him, but unwilling to say so. Here was the cop, trying to make a cop's sense of this.

"I'll tell ya, man, the guy had us all in his fucking thrall. Everybody there. Roman Colosseum time, and El Choc was the big Christian." He reached for another smoke. "But it didn't have to be that way."

"No?" Garth asked.

"No. We were afraid of what we didn't understand."

"You read too much science fiction." Husky fought what he now knew was inevitable.

94

"This was science *fact.*" The challenge in Scav's eyes was direct. "I don't believe in the devil and I don't think the dude's from Mars. But he *did* what I *saw.* Everybody there saw it. He gets up and says okay, gang, I'm gonna stand here and show it to you, whip it out right onstage and everything and show you it's bigger than yours, and the ol' crowd just stops and stands there to watch. And they're *not* gonna think about stopping the guy or shooting the guy, for God's sake, because people wanna see if it really *is* bigger than theirs. Because they've gotta *know,* right? They just do. So he went ahead and did his number on El Choc, just like that, made his point."

"With everybody in his thrall . . ." Husky said softly.

Scav laughed again, and found it a little hard to stop. When he finally did, he pointed at Husky.

"You're comin' around, aren't you?"

Husky just looked at him. Just looked straight through him.

"You said it didn't have to be that way."

Scav took a drag, snuffed the butt.

"It didn't. 'Cause of how hard the bastard was having to *concentrate!* I thought his eyebrows were gonna fall out. He was giving it everything he *had.*"

"So you think if somebody's behind him . . ."

Scav nodded, right into Husky's eyes.

Husky thought about this. About everything. He could see Garth considered Skidrow Scav to have been so traumatized by his beating at the hands of Lamp's buddies that he'd become completely unreliable.

Husky couldn't bring himself to feel the same way.

In fact, considering evidence at hand on all sides, Husky felt quite the opposite. He was evolving a theory about Edgar Lamp. It excited and terrified him. It was also, to Husky, plain as day.

If Scav was telling the truth, and Husky thought he

was, then Edgar Lamp was a killer like no other *known* killer before him.

He was also a complete sociopath, although that was no news to anybody.

He would have a lower palm temperature than most people, just as is common among sociopaths. He would be incapable of remorse or guilt. He would come into situations like the one in which he'd killed El Chocolate Grande, and he would be *partying*. It was the time at which he doubtless felt more completely alive and powerful than at any other. If the opportunity was there to kill someone, to experience the rush of control which that contained, there was no way Edgar Lamp could resist it. It was his drug.

And now it seemed that he could do it with his *mind!* Jesus, the amazement the man must be feeling at that, thought Husky. How could he possibly stop when the intoxicant was so close to him? So easy to come by?

How could nature create a human shark more perfect than a *telekinetic sociopath?*

Husky couldn't stop the wave of depression. He knew he was dead-on about Edgar, but to come out with his theory would sound like pure idiocy. Retirement time. He looked off, wondering how to get it across without giving Edgar Lamp the biggest victory of all in the process.

Both Scav and Garth had been watching him, waiting for some reaction.

"You wanna go into a detox, Scav?"

Scav looked frightened. "I'm not lyin' to you, Husky. How could I make this much shit up? C'mon . . ."

Husky was shaking his head. Put a hand on Scav's shoulder. "Not 'cause you're lying. 'Cause I owe you. I'm offering to put you in . . . under an assumed name so nobody knows . . . waive whatever charges are pending against you."

96

Scav looked into Husky's eyes, hardly able to believe it. Neither was Garth, at whom Husky just smiled.

"Relax, Garthie. We just found out Lamp's got a weak side. He's gotta concentrate, right?"

Part Two

Part Two

Seven

THE WAREHOUSE got clammy when it rained. The pummeling of the aged corrugated-metal roof made Edgar want to do the skin hop.

He heard the others sleeping, but knew Cholo was awake. They had decided to go to the mattresses with him here tonight on the chance in a million somebody had known them, seen them, and survived. This way, if fingers were pointed at the homes of their mothers and fathers, guilty sons wouldn't be around.

Edgar had grinned when they'd made that decision, parading his contempt for boys who wanted to be men. His eyes cut them: *still living at home?*

They'd looked back with hate. Cholo hadn't spoken again all evening, his eyes relentlessly on Edgar.

Frito, on the other hand, kept going over the events at Tilly Taco's to the point of stupidity. Edgar realized he wanted Frito to be their first casualty, but he needed to do it right.

Edgar waited a while before revealing the full panorama of what he planned next. He'd been thinking all the way back from Tilly's about what he had done. Strangely, he no longer felt surprised about it. The whole thing made sense to him. And the clear image of how he could send notice to both Husky Martin and Alice Lamp Corinth had flooded into his consciousness even before the thrill of conquering El Choc had faded.

It was as if the shadowy confrontation at Tilly Taco's had been necessary to understand what came next.

It would be a new kind of Proving.

The first part of it required that the Demon Viejo Dukes prove something to *him*. When he announced this, they all paid attention. Even Cholo, though he still wasn't talking.

Edgar had never had an idea so personally exciting for him.

He'd been thrilled tonight. The first realization that it was *really happening* had excited him so much he'd almost lost concentration on El Choc. He'd been lifted high by the power it gave him, the knowledge that he could do it again and again, at will.

But the idea he now called Multiple Grandmas was the all-time mind blower.

Martin would think he was the devil come to personally rub his nose in shit.

Multiple Grandmas, he told the five listening faces, was going to go down all at once, all over the city. It would look as if Edgar Lamp had done them all at exactly the same moment. *Miles* apart.

"What the fuck does that do?" Frito wasn't with him right away. As usual.

"It makes the cops think I'm in six places at once, shithead." Then he started to grin. "How'd you like to try

catching some dude could be in *six* places at *one* time?"
Edgar started to laugh his dry, reedy little laugh.

Though a couple of the Dukes laughed with him, Cholo
didn't. He just watched Edgar, who now looked right back
at him.

"Got a grandma, Cholo?" Edgar asked him with a smile,
almost able to repress the laugh. The others kept laughing
right with him, starkly contrasting the stoniness of
Cholo's face.

That had been hours before.

Now, under the broad rattle of the rain, Edgar peered
through the dark as Cholo got up from where he'd been
sleeping. Cholo stood, silently staring at Edgar for long
moments, unaware Edgar was awake.

So when Cholo turned to go to the next room and be
alone—to load his zip gun?—Edgar rose in cat silence and
followed.

Cholo was stunned to turn and see Edgar silently
watching him from the doorway.

Edgar was glad Cholo had only moved into this room
for a smoke, for a few private thoughts. There was no
weapon.

But his loathing look hadn't abated.

"You didn't like my idea," Edgar said quietly.

"Your idea's okay . . ."

"You didn't like it that I was fuckin' with your head,
then. About living at home. And your grandmother."

The look that came back confirmed it. Edgar nodded.
But he'd taken a permanent and unshakable advantage
over Cholo, who would either work ceaselessly to prove
himself as much a man as Edgar or simply try to kill for
revenge. Because Edgar knew this, he could be the puppe-
teer.

"You wanna show me I'm wrong, Cholo?" Edgar moved

103

close, working the mental strings. "Then you take somebody's grandma you know. Somebody on your street."

"You crazy, King Shit."

Edgar smiled as if he was, indeed, a little crazy. He could see Cholo's mind working hard, wrestling with what he'd said.

"I mean it. I need you to prove this to me. You do, and I don't never worry about Cholo again, you know? I never think well, maybe Cholo shouldn't be the number one right-hand man to King Shit. There wouldn't be any doubt about it."

Cholo took it all in.

He couldn't believe his own thoughts. They didn't run to revenge against this pale-skinned motherfucker lunatic, and they didn't run to getting as far from him as possible, either.

They ran back to his own street, to one specific old woman who was unhappy with her life and disgusted with her great, fat body and her stinking wreck of a family. She had screamed obscenities at him. He'd been a child playing baseball. The ball flew into her backyard, and she'd gone apeshit on Cholo, who had been the one to sneak over the wall and come face to face with her. She was holding the ball high over her head, far out of his reach, shrieking like he was a dog who'd pissed on her carpet.

Cholo remembered his embarrassment at her disgusting anger, her power over him to keep the ball, and the hysterical amusement it had given his friends. From that day on, the essence of an old woman worth hating had been that woman, Grandmother Carlotta Rodríguez.

If there was any grandmother he would kill on his own street to prove himself to King Shit, she was the one.

There was only one problem.

Grandmother Carlotta Rodríguez was *Frito's* grandmother. On his mother's side of the family. To do her would be danger of a different nature for Cholo. But he told King Shit anyway.

Edgar looked down at Cholo. This was better than he could've hoped.

"Frito scare you?"

Cholo's brown eyes did a laughing jump, after which he couldn't keep the grin from appearing on his face.

"Didn't think so," said Edgar.

Then he told Cholo, before he told any of the others, how they would need to get parts to make five very small bombs. Edgar had read all about how to do it while in jail waiting for his L.A. trial.

The plan was to take the bombs, each attached to the end of a wire, and forcibly stuff them down the throats of their old-lady victims.

Each old-lady victim had to be miles and *miles* from the nearest one.

It didn't matter if the strangulation killed them. It only mattered that once the mini-bombs were shoved down their throats, they were set off, blowing the guts out of the old women.

"And you?" Cholo asked.

"Doin' it for real, right at the same time."

Cholo looked down at the ground, thinking, then looked back at Edgar Lamp, meeting his stare unafraid.

"Is a good plan."

Yeah, Edgar knew that.

Eight

"ARE YOU SORRY you're writing this book?" Husky asked Garth.

He plunked a just barbecued steak onto Garth's plate, leaving his own on the grill a minute or two longer. They were in Husky's backyard. It was nearly sundown and the two old friends had given themselves a few hours to clear their heads. Away from Parker Center, Edgar Lamp's toxic influence, and everything except a couple nice, thick T-bones.

Fred never left Husky's side while he cooked. Garth couldn't decide whether it was because the dog missed his master or the chances of getting a stray morsel were pretty good just now.

Garth sighed as he thought about the book.

"I've done what, twenty years of radio columns? More?" Shit, he didn't even know anymore. "I wish maybe the . . . subject matter of this was a little easier to stomach."

Husky nodded. "So do I."

"But if I wasn't writing it . . . somebody else probably would be. Most likely after the fact, which means they'd miss a lot."

Husky looked over at him, just about to spear his own steak and plate-plunk it.

"You think there's anything to my theory? Telekinetic sociopath?"

Garth picked up his knife and fork. Looked at his steak and salad, then put the utensils back down.

"I've spent about as much time with the guy as anybody has who's lived. I've never seen one thing that supports what you're thinking about him . . . but then I've never seen him do anything at *all* except wise off at the mouth. For all I could prove, he could kill people any of a hundred ways."

"You're not answering my question."

"I'm getting to it," Garth said as Husky sat down and dug in. "The medical examiner's report on the deputies who died in that sheriff's car does tend to corroborate what Scav said and what you're thinking."

"There's more," Husky said.

"What?" Garth looked up, a little surprised he'd missed a point.

"When I talked with Patton right before we left headquarters to come here, he told me he'd run a check I asked him to. In all the victims Edgar Lamp has left behind, about forty percent of the autopsies showed unexplainable internal organ damage similar to the deputies'."

"Back to the beginning?" Garth was amazed.

"Almost. At the very outset, there don't seem to be any splattered kidneys. But as time went on they started showing up, and in the most recent killings it's up to about eighty percent of the victims."

Garth sat silently, feeling a bona fide chill go down his

107

spine. Fred sort of snooped around their laps, getting the message that leftovers weren't ready for him yet, so he curled up near Husky, snuggling his foot.

"Okay"—Garth tried to keep his balance in the conversation—"so where does that leave you?"

"He's still a murderer. He's still sociopathic," Husky said. "It's like you've been writing in your book. This man lives as if taking other people's lives was his function, reason . . . whatever you wanna call it."

"And you think he's vulnerable."

"We caught him once, we can probably catch him again."

"You don't think Scav was exaggerating?"

Husky looked at his friend.

"Garthie, is it just that you truly don't believe it, or that you don't *want* to? Scav wasn't telling us a fairy tale, he'd been living with that shit. I've seen all kinds of guys tell stories and tell lies and I'm telling you what he gave us was neither. He can't get it out of his mind. That's why it was so hard for him to confront. He was showing us what bothered him the very most right now."

There was another facet of the whole thing that Husky couldn't put out of his mind as he worked on his T-bone. He'd met El Chocolate Grande himself many times during investigations, and he'd certainly met Edgar Lamp far more times than any human should have to.

There was no possible physical way Edgar Lamp could've killed El Choc with anything less than a large gun at point-blank range—unless Skidrow Scav was right.

Not wanting to go back to the fray just yet, Husky and Garth went into the living room to have cigars and bullshit some more. They didn't want to admit it, but both of them needed this temporary hiding ploy a great deal.

Husky sighed when the phone rang at him. He knew it would be Chief Nash before he got the receiver to his ear.

108

"Did you just figure to check into a health spa or something, Martin?"

"My friends know I lack sufficient nerve, Chief."

Nash didn't get the joke, much too intent on his own reason for the discussion. Husky noticed Garth's ears were on full zap.

"I just want you to know I personally suspect whoever checked El Chocolate Grande's hat and coat is almost certainly Edgar Lamp."

Husky knew the drill. Nash had read every word of every report on it, had heard from his spies in Homicide that Husky had reason to know for certain it was Lamp, and was now "officially" covering his ass and sounding like the Great Commander that he usually wasn't.

"We've got a positive eyewitness ID on him, sir, but none on the accomplices. There's an all-points. We're doing a major song and dance at every squad-room meeting from right now till we take him down. Anybody on the street who's ever given us so much as a head cold is getting a free trip to Acapulco dangled in front of them if they deliver."

"I don't care much for the levity, Martin."

"Well, I don't care much for Edgar Lamp, Chief. Give me the room to keep myself giggling, huh?"

The two had never liked each other, never approached their work in similar ways.

"Don't drop him, Husky. No matter how good your smiling fat-guy image is, you'd never get your toes out of the way."

The chief had hung up before Husky could tell him he was on top of it, or to fuck off, or whatever would've come out first. He put the phone back down and looked at it. "Fuck you," he told it.

"Close relationship you've got with the chief."

109

"Don't you have a disc jockey you could be raping?" Husky stared out the window.

"I meant to tell you . . . I've decided to chuck the AM/FM persona as soon as I'm done with Edgar's last chapters."

Husky smiled. "You wouldn't be pressuring me to catch him, too, would you?"

Garth grinned back. "Catch him or lose him, I've already mapped out the last phase of the book in either eventuality. All I do now is wait for the collar . . . or not."

"When do you decide it's *not?*"

Garth shrugged. "The gut'll tell me, I guess. And the publisher, tapping me on the shoulder with his deadline finger."

For a moment envy resonated in Husky's consciousness. Garth was talking about publishers, deadlines already engaged and out there waiting for his book.

Garth was *doing* it. Of course, Husky had allowed him to observe the case quite literally from over the shoulder of the investigating officer. And the investigating officer was very likely to be the book's hero. Hence, without Husky, Garth *couldn't* be doing it.

"Well, Garthie"—Husky finally sat back down—"I've gotta tell ya, I'm glad one of us is getting into the world of legit letters, anyway." He smiled, puffing his cigar. "And I don't exactly mind getting all that page space you're giving me."

Garth laughed along at this, nodding his precise understanding of Husky's meaning. Both cigars lofted blue clouds to accompany the ironic amusement.

"Couple old fucks gettin' some glory," Husky finally said. "Bread-and-butter cops don't get hooked into surefire best-sellers on a weekly basis."

110

"Best-*seller?*" Garth looked at Husky; shook his head. "I'll be happy getting into print."

"Lamp makes it the best-seller, Garthie. Whole damn country reads about Lamp in the papers, hears about him on TV. Book comes out, they like to drag their asses through it again, only in much more detail. So a cop like me does get in a best-seller."

"You gonna tell Chief Nash to stick it up his ass when this is over?"

Husky had to smile. Garth smiled back.

"Before I got complacent at the paper, I had ulcers every time an opening would come up in the film critic's slot. Finally quit worrying 'cause it got too close to pension time. And then no sooner did I calm down to enjoy life a little bit, you come along and tell me I oughta write this Lamp book. And then there's agents falling all over me when I tell 'em about it and what my contact is to the case." He shook his head.

Husky'd been eyeing his own pension, so he knew Garth's feeling of what-the-hellism, however fleeting it may have been. But Husky had also always been hungrier for any kind of pulse quickener than Garth. That was one reason he'd become a cop.

"I wasn't sure you'd wanna do the book at first," Husky admitted. "I figured I was the one who still had the ol' disease for stickin' my neck out, not you."

"Worth it?" Garth asked.

Husky gave a one-shoulder shrug. "Spent a lotta years stepping on my own dick 'cause the right people at the right parties made me puke. Very self-destructive."

"You were never exactly a team man."

"Long-distance runner with a perpetual hard-on to be the romantic hero," Husky agreed. "So I punish myself with this bug up my ass about leaving some kind of *mark*. You'd think I'd know better, but every cop wants a plaque

111

in the lobby at headquarters commemorating his bravery. How he cracked some impossible Chinese box. We all want a TV movie about ourselves."

Garth didn't like this. Most of the guys on plaques out in those lobbies were ex-chiefs. Or dead in the line of duty. Husky knew that.

"You think I'm nuts, right?" Husky peered at his friend.

"I never said that."

Fred shifted on the floor.

"Oughta see your mug."

Garth decided to be blunt.

"Why *didn't* you ever play the politics?"

"I figured it didn't really matter. I know guys hovering right around Badge One you never heard of. They plugged it from sunup till long after their wives went to sleep for twenty years. All they got was prostate cancer from too much takeout pastrami. I figured if I was gonna have to be one more fleshy gray face, I'd at least let 'em *know* when I thought the department was bullshit."

Garth looked down. "People never change."

"You learn that around here."

"What I meant was you used to piss the profs off back at school, too."

"And now the prof is Nash?"

"Whoever. I used to tell myself the Great Crusader would learn. But you still want the plaque, even *after* you've spent years taking leaks on people's desks."

"If I didn't have the Big Movie, I'd go to sleep on myself." Husky dug his nails into the fabric of the arm of his chair. "But I will tell you one thing. One secret, Garthie. Lots of times I don't know if, when the Movie's over, I was the guy in the white hat."

"You're Homicide. How could you not be the white hat?"

"Gimme a fuckin' break. Look at this case. In this particular case I'm no more moral than the criminal."

"Bullshit." Garth didn't hide his disgust. "You're fishing for fucking sympathy."

Husky shook his head. "Absolutely no way. But I'm just as bad. Look, I'm sitting here, hoping I get the glory for draining him, right? Guy who's now apparently figured out how to yank people's guts out while having a hell of a good time. So as long as I'm sittin' back in my easy chair playing chess with the motherfucker, hoping I get on the six o'clock news, then I'm *living* off him." Husky leaned forward and pointed a finger at Garth for emphasis. "You gonna tell me that's better than he is?"

"Sure I am. You didn't start it. You didn't go around killing people."

"That's a bullshit answer, because I *do* go around killing people when I have to. It's just that I've got society's sanction to *do* it. See, I don't *mind* necessarily that I'm as bad as Lamp. I'm just saying I *know* it. I can't tell you how many guys on the force *don't*. I can't tell you how many cops I've watched go digging like prospectors, for Christ's sake, after some misfit with congenital brain rot. I can't tell you all the victims I've seen . . . families, kids who got left behind by the dead . . . little blue-haired ladies whose 'babies' turn up dismembered or something in a trash bag behind a dime store. I can't tell you how many I've seen 'cause I can't *bring* myself to count that high. But I *can* tell you all those people made me understand it's *all right* if I'm just as bad as the criminal. As long as I *catch* him."

"That makes no fucking sense." Garth looked totally disgusted. He took a drag on his cigar.

"Makes perfect sense. 'Cause somebody, somewhere in this whole, unintelligible mess oughta get some payoff. Somebody besides the killer, who already got his power rush when he murdered somebody."

113

Garth stared at him for an uncomfortably long time.

"What is it?" Husky asked. "Have I got a booger?"

"I guess it never occurred to me in all this time how you had to be this cynical to survive."

Husky laughed. "Cynical? I'm a fucking pussycat bleeding-heart liberal! Always wanted to write, always wanted to dump the *chorizo* of my soul but never had the talent of a Joe Wambaugh. So instead I become this bitching machine who tromps along, slightly out of kilter, making every other cop uneasy."

"Am I supposed to be getting this down?" Garth's smile was starting to come back. But he knew what he was seeing.

This was what Husky Martin, on some darkly honest level, really thought of himself and the life he'd been carrying on.

Husky sighed and patted Fred on his broad back.

"You never really know somebody till you travel with 'em, right Garthie?"

■ ■ ■ ■ ■

Bad Penny

Four years after Edgar had left the Lamp farm in Gullickson, Texas, in the middle of the night, he abruptly and briefly returned.

Alice was by then remarried to a farmer named Johnny Corinth, who had been a childhood friend and had become a widower since Harper's departure. Alice was well on her way to forgetting the unquiet life she'd led with Harper and his family, so her shock and anxiety at Edgar's arrival were understandable. They were even more so because, in the years that had passed, Edgar had grown to look alarmingly like Harper Lamp himself. The same tall, thin, bony, wild-eyed features. The same voice . . . that voice that sometimes came to her in dreams and caught her by surprise.

Edgar came up to the house late one night and pounded on the door. Johnny went to answer, so Alice got up and went right behind him. The two padded barefoot across the cold living-room floor of the same small two-story farmhouse in which Harper had lived for so long. As the door opened, the light hit that face and Alice gasped in alarm. She stepped back involuntarily.

The resemblance was uncanny. Edgar surely knew it, surely relished it as he stepped up to the locked wire of the screen door between them and smiled into the living room.

"Grandma Alice?" he said.

Alice Lamp Corinth could think of nothing but the voice. *It was the same voice.*

And then he said it. Just like his grandfather, just the same cadence, inflection, everything. Even with that same wild-monkey look in his eyes.

"The whole world wants a miracle . . ."

And then Alice Lamp Corinth shoved her husband aside and grabbed that door and slammed it shut in Edgar's face as hard as she could. She locked it. Double-locked it. Then stood there terrified before her confused husband—a little shaken himself—while through the door they could both hear Edgar's laugh. At first it was right there, still right on the porch. Then it began to fade as he moved across the yard, through the gate. He paused there, laughing a moment more, then went on out and down the road.

It was the last time Alice saw or heard Edgar until she came to sit and watch his trial in Los Angeles years later.

Nine

CHOLO MOVED through the darkened neighborhood with the silence of a virus. Here was Cholo the dark, Cholo the swift, he thought. His focus was complete as he moved toward the old woman's place.

Her family, crowded around her a few years ago—when she had offended Cholo for life with the humiliating incident of the baseball—had now left. Cholo knew that they, like everyone else, simply couldn't stand to be around her.

He had thought of little else since the night before, when King Shit had revealed his plan. The more he envisioned himself forcing the explosive device down the startled, gurgling old throat and then pressing the small electronic detonator device, the more he got the warm, crawling stomach rush of excitement.

Of pleasure.

Now he stopped a moment just outside her house, peering through a side window, eyes gravitating toward her TV light.

She was enveloped in *Ripley's Believe It or Not.*

Cholo smiled. Even he could see the joke. She would believe it before long.

This time his entry to the backyard was not like when he was a young boy. No fear of discovery made him hesitate. He sought contact. He hoped for her anger because he would take all the more pleasure from pushing it back onto her, turning it to fear and finally exacting his punishment.

There was only a moment or two in which Cholo realized and clearly saw that King Shit had brought these thoughts out in him, encouraged them and made them grow far stronger than Cholo himself would ever have allowed them.

Sure, for years Cholo had kept the boyhood idea of punishing old Carlotta Rodríguez alive and festering. It was a dream, like owning a Cadillac or living in a Malibu beach house.

But King Shit made him step forward and bring it to reality.

Cholo knew that gave King Shit power, but somehow he didn't care just now. Maybe he would tomorrow, maybe he would even hate what he had done, especially when he saw Frito's pain and hate.

But that would be tomorrow. Tonight was for showing King Shit that Cholo and only Cholo could be the right-hand man he had talked about.

He couldn't help thinking less of her for the way she didn't even put a light on in the backyard. His irritation ticked up another notch. Who could blame a man for killing a foolish old hag like this? He checked once more to make sure the small plastic glob of explosive was still in his pocket, still attached to the wire, still hooked to the little electronic detonator button. All tucked neatly into the front handwarmer pocket of his sweatshirt. He kept the hood up while he was on the street, but now he pulled it down and felt the cool air on his scalp and the back of his neck.

He tested the screen door in back. Incredible. She'd left it unlocked. The woman was making it far too simple. All he would have to do would be to jimmy the lock of the kitchen door behind it. She'd never hear it over the show she was watching.

He bent to pick it with the tools he always carried.

But as he did, he looked up and found himself staring straight into the righteously indignant eyes of the old woman herself, glaring back at him through the glass of her back door.

"What the hell are you doing here?" she screamed.

And as he stepped back on reflex for a moment, amazed, he saw that in her anger she was truly a fool. She was reaching for the doorknob.

And holding a baseball bat in her other hand.

She took a swing at him as she came out and nearly broke the glass on the door herself. He ducked as the bat hammered into the wood of the door. His hand was quickly on the barrel of the Louisville Slugger, and for a second they grappled over it. He shoved her hard and the bat was his without question. Smiling at her as she backed into the kitchen and away from him, he slung the bat into the backyard behind him and followed her.

"Grandma's gonna die, ol' lady." His young whisper had a little laugh in it.

Carlotta Rodríguez knew at that moment that she'd made a terrible mistake. This wasn't one of the little kids in her neighborhood, the ones who'd been giving her such fits in the last couple weeks.

This was another kid from the neighborhood. From before. One of those stupid friends of her useless grandson.

This was like so many of the human garbage heaps her three daughters had raised.

A bad one.

Cholo would've only laughed to have heard such thoughts. He watched her while he ripped out the telephone she'd been thinking of trying for. He circled around her as she moved through to the living room, the two of them standing now in the blue light of the set as Jack Palance stared out and whispered and ooohed and aaaahed about something really amazing, so incredible that many people even now refused to accept it as the truth, but you could see for yourself and you could believe it or not . . .

Carlotta Rodríguez would never have to believe anything again. She crossed herself in fear as Cholo suddenly overtook her and descended like a whippet on a rat.

The crack of his fist on her cheekbone shocked them both, but color blotches exploding in her consciousness kept her thoughts from focusing. He had pinned her to the floor. His knees on her shoulders hurt and increased her alarm, bringing back clarity of thought with pain.

She was vaguely aware of him pulling something out of the pouchlike pocket of his sweatshirt as she struggled in vain, unused to tests of strength.

Outside, the neighborhood went about its quiet night business, unaware that inside her house Carlotta Rodríguez was being forced to submit to this lean, angry intruder. He punched her twice more with his fists, then forced her mouth open to cram the small glob of plastic into her.

The knife he put to her ribs seemed to come out of nowhere.

"Swallow, *vieja*," he hissed.

She noticed that he was sweating. The blue light revealed that his face and arms were drenched. She thought he too might be afraid, so after a second's thought, she shook her head, no.

The knife prodded, forcing its way a millimeter or so into her middle, then back out again.

"Swallow, you fucking pig!" His shout had not been planned. He couldn't restrain it.

The sweat was excitement, not fear.

Carlotta Rodríguez swallowed.

"Swallow more."

She did, getting the thing down, though it wasn't easy, though it gagged her and the wire attached to it filled her with dread and confused her even more deeply.

Cholo wondered if the damn thing was far enough into her belly for it to work right. For a few moments he didn't know what to do. The advertisement on the television blared and chattered at him about traveling to Australia and a young woman with huge breasts jouncing in her bathing suit walked toward him on the screen. Suddenly his rage flared and he kicked across her prone, shivering body and shattered the television screen, which popped and smoked acrid electric smell into the small, hot living room. The old woman flinched away from the set as this happened and he kicked her back to where she had been lying.

Suddenly he didn't give a shit whether he'd waited long enough, whether the explosive was far enough into her system. He stepped back under her watching, bugging eyes and viciously jabbed at the button on the detonator.

■ ■ ■ ■ ■

At almost exactly the same moment, in five other places around the far-flung Los Angeles area, Multiple Grandmas was going down.

120

All six old ladies met their rupturous end within three minutes of each other. This made Edgar Lamp happy.

The only member of the Assholes who encountered trouble was Frito. His perennial nerves left him with hands that shook so terribly he couldn't force the explosive down the old woman's throat against her struggle. In a dimly lit alley behind the Ralph's in Buena Park, Frito beat her to death first, then rammed the contraption far, far down past her by now broken jaw and into the esophageal passageway with his fingers.

He forced it farther still with the butt end of his large belt knife. By the time he finally blew her up he was desperate to get back to his car and get the hell away.

He kept driving the freeways, back and forth, wanting to make sure it would be impossible for the police to know where the killer had gone.

■　■　■　■　■

Husky looked at his little handwritten list of murder locations for the hundredth time.

> Pico Rivera
> Van Nuys
> Pacific Palisades
> Buena Park
> Long Beach
> West Hollywood

All the same m.o. All confirmed between eight-ten and eight-fifteen that night.

"I've never been to a morgue before," Garth said softly from the chair beside Husky's. They were in the waiting room outside the autopsy theater.

"You don't have to go in."

"No, I'd rather, actually . . ."

Garth was pushing, making himself stick his nose in it and take a good long smell. Husky looked at his watch. Sillitoe, the coroner, had been writing his reports for over an hour now.

It had given Husky time to think, to question.

There was no way Lamp could've performed all the murders himself. This stunt was meant to leave Husky grasping at how one man could travel around the city, gutting this succession of biddies while he went.

It was aimed at least as much at Husky as at the victims. Probably more.

From the moment the full complement of murder reports came in, Husky had experienced rage and more rage. He knew this was the wrong reaction even as he felt it.

The little shit was taunting, grinning through his ugly message.

Garth was scared. He'd done a lot of headshaking, trying to sound hard while muttering things about this guy being the devil and how nobody from *this* planet could possibly concoct such synchronized profanity.

"Spare me the soap opera," Husky had snapped, acutely aware of his own fury while somehow managing to sound cold, world-weary, heartfelt.

Sillitoe came out the door with his reports. Husky didn't give him a moment.

"I want a look."

"I know my fucking job." Sillitoe's eyes sent irritation.

"I had a thought . . ."

"You know what time it is?"

"I don't give a shit, Dale. There will be something different about one of those bodies. I'm not leaving till I find out what."

"The killer's signature . . ."

"Something . . ."

122

"Six old bats had their goddamn chests blown out. *That's* a fucking signature."

"I want a look."

"Bring your medical degree?"

"Kiss my ass."

Sillitoe sighed. He'd been expecting this.

"I had the boys leave 'em on the tables. C'mon."

Garth hadn't conceived of the throat-constricting reek.

"It's not the bodies, it's all the stuff they work with in here," Husky told him.

But Garth was riveted. Drains below tables. Glistening liquids lingering on too many surfaces, not yet wiped away. He hung near the door, safer there if he should suddenly just *have* to leave.

He marveled at Husky and Sillitoe walking around the corpses. Especially Husky, almost as far from his own element as Garth himself, peering at terribly frail faces on ravaged, betrayed bodies.

They look like children, Garth thought. Pale, still forms. Naked, toes tagged. Helpless, hopeless, forlorn.

Garth remembered his grandmother. His mother. Felt his blood pressure go up and the coldest sweat of his life suddenly cover his entire body. But he didn't move for the door. Possibly, he thought, because he couldn't.

Husky stood musing between Pacific Palisades and Buena Park.

"Beaten," he said, pointing to Buena Park.

"Fists. Before the trauma to the chest."

"Before . . ."

Husky looked at Sillitoe, who nodded, a little impatient.

"The others?"

"Only one not beaten was Pacific Palisades . . ."

Husky reviewed. Pacific Palisades was killed closing her shop. Small commercial center, three blocks from the

123

ocean. She'd had one of those little ceramics hobby joints. Sold the clay and the paints. What did they call the clay before you fired it? Greenware. It hovered in his thoughts for a few seconds, as if it could be a clue. Greenware.

Just a word.

He studied the face of Pacific Palisades for a few seconds. Why weren't you kicked around, Palisades? he wondered. Why no outer marks?

Then it hit him. Outer marks. The logical follow-up was . . .

"Any unrelated organ damage this time? That stress thing you wrote up?"

Sillitoe looked dour, shaking his head, no. Husky pondered this, sighing. Staring at the victims. Then he seemed to stiffen for a second, squinting as he looked at the face of Grandma West Hollywood.

"What about their throats?" He said it so quietly it didn't register to Sillitoe for a moment.

"Uh . . . no markings to indicate strangulation by hand . . ."

"Inside." Husky cut him off. "What about the insides of their throats?"

Sillitoe obviously didn't know. It had been late, he'd been tired, rushed, and the cause of death had been so plain.

"Check Miss Palisades' throat." It was a command.

Sillitoe put the gloves on, frowning.

■　■　■　■　■

Chief Nash had come to headquarters in the wee hours. He was in a four-letter mood as he closed the manila folder.

124

"What eternal wisdom am I supposed to snatch from this?"

"That there's a fucking major difference, Chief."

"Because only *five* of six get a severe bruising."

"And number six," Husky pointed out, "Pacific Palisades, had only an eruption of the abdominal cavity. Period. Plus *all* five others had severe blow-job scars."

The chief made the beginnings of a face. Husky didn't give a shit.

"Things were forced down them. Things that probably blew up, huh? See, Lamp doesn't have to beat you or stick anything down your throat, Chief."

"He doesn't."

"No, sir. Which brings up an important point. There's one facet of this case we haven't personally discussed, you and I, sir."

Nash looked quickly at Husky, then over at Garth.

"He know about this . . . facet you're going to tell me about?"

Husky nodded.

"All right," sighed the chief. "I get the feeling this is going to be high-grade bullshit, so let me have it mixed in with at least a certain amount of common sense, please."

"I'd love to, Chief. But it doesn't sound like common sense. Edgar Lamp, as we all know very well by now, is a sociopathic killer. He's done a lot of very strange things for a very long time, but beginning with the murder of El Chocolate Grande a couple nights ago, and continuing with the elderly female victim in Pacific Palisades, Edgar Lamp has proved to us . . . to *me* . . . that he is capable of killing"—Husky shored himself for the reaction to come—"telekinetically."

Chief Nash looked closely at his investigator.

"Could you clarify what that means?"

"He does it with his mind."

125

Nash just looked at Husky, blinking once or twice, thinking hard.

"It may shock the shit out of you, Martin, but I happen to know something about this kind of stuff. I read about it, sort of as a hobby, and I'm not uninformed on the subject."

Garth listened with greater interest.

"You mean you could . . . believe my theory?"

"If you can back it up. I personally see nothing particularly difficult in attributing certain abilities to the human mind that we have previously been unable to pinpoint. Yes."

Garth and only Garth could appreciate the dilemma into which this thrust Husky Martin. Husky had expected Chief Nash to call him an idiot and possibly fire him on the spot. Now that the chief seemed to want to side with him, Husky had to deal with an authority that might, incredibly, take him seriously in this matter.

"Well, sir." Husky collected his thoughts to deal with this new, unexpected situation. "We've got an eyewitness to the first murder. We know Edgar Lamp used no murder weapon, and El Chocolate Grande was seen by everyone in Tilly Taco's to . . . erupt . . . to turn inside out."

"And autopsy findings on him bear out such an occurrence?"

"Completely."

"How about this woman . . . Pacific Palisades?"

"Same . . . No skin bruises of the sort normally linked to beating, strangulation, any kind of brutality. And like I said, no . . ."

"Damage to the inside of the throat," the chief finished for him.

"Right. The point is, Lamp's messing with our brains here. He's got his buddies out there killing these other

126

women purely to drive us to think he can be six places at once. To think he's indestructible."

"Which he's probably believing he really is by now." Chief Nash sighed. Then he looked Husky in the eye. "You and I don't agree very often, Husky. And for the record, there's no way in hell I ever possibly said I concur with your . . . analysis of the Edgar Lamp case as it stands right now. But everything true doesn't quite fit on the record, you know?" Chief Nash looked at Garth. "Doesn't fit in books, either." Back to Husky. "If all this mind-over-matter shit wants to come out in court, then it will. Although personally I've got a feeling Edgar Lamp's never gonna let himself live to see the inside of a courtroom again."

"How do you figure that, Chief?"

Nash allowed himself a faint smile. "Prescience," he said.

■　■　■　■　■

Now and then it amazed Husky that a rambling organism like the LAPD could ever piece together a thing. But at other times, parts to puzzles would seem to simply descend from the heavens, needing only to be put into logical order on earth.

It had been a long day and looked to be getting downright marathon. They'd come back to Parker Center and the now assembled piles of data. They'd phoned Marge Glass, Husky intoning simply the word "Help," to elicit a "Be right there, just gotta find my face." The fluorescents got to your eyes after a while.

"Scav and the three other survivors of Tilly's who were willing to talk all said the accomplices were Chicano," Husky told Garth as he went over the reports.

127

"So he managed to hire out a gang?" Garth rubbed his face in weariness.

"Looks like." Husky nodded. "All the Chicanos wore gray pants, white button-front short-sleeved shirts over white T-shirts. They had short haircuts, less than one inch long, no sideburns or facial hair."

"How do people notice shit like that?" Garth wondered.

"They use their imaginations." Husky smiled. "And they also realize little things that're absolutely correct. Like all these Chicanos were probably kids."

Both men were silent for a moment. They knew perfectly well they could've described half the gangs in L.A.

"What else?" Garth finally asked.

"Pico Rivera," said Husky. "Pico Rivera's one of the old ladies who got killed, and Pico Rivera's also gang central. High likelihood of a hit in their own neighborhood."

"All right." Garth took a piece of chalk and wrote on the small board in Husky's office: CHICANOS—PICO RIVERA VICTIM.

"Okay . . ." Husky went on. "Now the fingerprints . . ." He looked for the file, frowning till he found it. "The victim's fingerprints tell us the lady's name was Carlotta Rodríguez. The perpetrator's . . . we haven't confirmed yet. He may have no record."

Husky looked at the woman's name, thinking. Without another word, he rose from his chair and went out to Marge Glass's desk.

"Carlotta Rodríguez," he said.

"Wrong," she said. "Marge Glass. I've worked here for years."

"I need to see the names of everybody in her family. She's one of the old ladies."

"Ahh." Marge nodded, getting on the phone as Husky headed back for his office. He started talking to Garth as he entered.

128

"If somebody in her family is in a gang, which you can pretty much assume in that neighborhood, then we start looking into that gang because there could be a rivalry within it. Then we check gangs currently hostile to that gang, for obvious reasons." Husky sat down when he finished. "And hopefully the killer's prints will help us bolt that down."

"This is very damn weird," Garth said, looking off. "Edgar Lamp has never, not once in his whole life that I know of, been hooked up with anything even remotely resembling a gang of any kind."

"Don't worry about it. He's never had to blow three deputies to hell to get his freedom back, either. He's doing plenty of things he's never done before, but he's still the same sweetheart of a guy."

■ ■ ■ ■ ■

Edgar knew Frito would be walking the big Glendale train yard that services Union Station. The Demon Viejo Dukes told him that's where Frito would always go hang when there was major shit to deal with.

Dead Grandma Carlotta would be major shit. It took twenty minutes for Edgar to sneak back through the yard, winding deep into the maze of cars and tracks. He walked far, far in, past the actives, freights, and few and far between sleepers sitting idle.

Frito would haunt the dead cars. Dusty, empty, stock-still. Way out in some neglected corner where he could think without worrying about being found by some railroad employee. Sure enough, Edgar spotted him ambling between these long, silent rows.

Frito had a right to be pissed. He'd put the Demon Viejo Dukes together with King Shit. He'd known where

129

they could rip the stuff for the plastic explosives, which was much better than the old-fashioned little bombs Edgar had thought they'd have to use. And Frito was the one with all the enthusiasm.

And now he'd be feeling like the one who'd been fucked.

Edgar spoke to him.

"I wish you'd've come and bitched to me instead of walkin' off like this, man."

Frito whirled. His eyes were coke crazy, jumping around. He drilled Edgar with them, then darted them all over to be sure Edgar was alone. They scanned everything. Searched the outline of Edgar's body for weapons; secret death. Frito wasn't anybody who needed to be coked, but right now he was launching eyebrow hairs with the stuff.

"What the fuck am I supposed to do when I see my ol' man and my ol' lady, huh?" Frito sounded whiny.

Still, it was more articulate than Edgar would've expected. He felt his usual rising contempt for other people's emotions. He thought they seemed childish, preoccupied with little shit.

Edgar advanced his program.

"Nobody else knew, man. I guess Cholo just didn't think, you know?"

"Cholo?" Frito's features twisted like he couldn't believe it. Even though he'd known it had to be one of them.

"Well, you kinda knew it couldn't've been me, right? We all knew where I went . . . we knew where everybody went. Did you forget or something?"

"I . . . I guess I just didn't hear where other guys were goin' after you told me where I was supposed to be. I just started thinkin' about that. How I should do it. I never even heard anybody *say* Pico Rivera, man . . ."

Edgar gave Frito a little laugh. Sort of your basic

friendly, geez-brother-it's-the-pits laugh nobody could get mad about.

"Pico Rivera had to be on the list, Frito. So nobody'd think it was you guys."

Somewhere in Frito's mind he knew that statement was nonsense. He knew gangs always fucking hit in their own areas. Still, he couldn't make his brain put the words in line to say it. He felt gagged, muted. He just stared at King Shit, who looked so relaxed. So patient. Suddenly, Frito felt exhausted, but the coke wasn't letting him crash like he so desperately wanted to. He put out a hand and leaned on the railroad car, looking down and shaking his head.

"It's fuckin' bad, man."

Edgar frowned. The guy was boring the shit out of him. Probably about ready to start sobbing. Time to move the moment on.

"Look. I wanted to tell you. I don't think a whole hell of a lot of what ol' Cholo did, okay?"

Frito's head snapped up; alert as he could manage.

"I mean . . . guy'd have to be a complete 'ron to go blow the shit outta another gang member's grandma."

Frito nodded, right with him, real serious, unaware how stupid it sounded. How stupid he was being.

"So I was thinkin', since we all decided for ourselves what ol' lady we were gonna do and everything, that this is kinda between you and Cholo and nobody else. And I wouldn't ruin you or anything if you had to go lookin' out for your family . . ."

Frito stared at him, his mouth just slightly open.

"You followin' me on this, Frito?"

Frito was in seventy-five places at once. He was plunging a knife into Cholo's heart. He was sitting in a max-and-dangerous wire cage down at County Central Visiting with a deputy right behind him and his mother crying at him over the phone and through the glass. He was trying to tell her what had happened . . . trying to figure out how all this had started.

Edgar grabbed Frito's shirt and shook him, bringing their faces close. Frito cleared right up, looking into Edgar's bodaciously weird eyes and putting his hands on Edgar's wrists for balance.

"I'm tellin' you I don't give a large shit if you bounce on the little fuckin' monkey's windpipe, Frito. In fact I'd take it as a special favor you were doin' for me, 'cause I personally don't trust the little birdshit."

Frito sighed, looked down, spat between his arms and watched it sop the ground an inch from his own shoes. He nodded, still looking down at the rocky dirt.

"I'd love to cut the dude, man . . ."

"You *can* . . ." Edgar cooed at him. "Any damn way you like. But do it quick. Tonight. I don't *like* him, and I don't *want* him there."

Frito nodded more. He didn't look back up for a while as he hung on to Edgar for support. But he nodded a great deal.

■ ■ ■ ■ ■

Carlotta Rodríguez was the jackpot. Out of the twenty-eight known relatives that popped up around her name in the computer, the one that gave the machine the biggest buzz was Fred Zito, alias Frito, alias Freet da Man, alias Bad Fritito.

"Alias the family jerk," said Husky as he read the data. "Guy's got one helluva résumé of minor crimes."

He also had a major asterisk by his name. He was not a gang member, at least not confirmed by any street sources or reliable talkers. But he was frequently seen in the company of one particular gang.

They were called the Demon Viejo Dukes.

Of Pico Rivera.

"You're sure about that?" Garth asked, feeling wary from his fatigue.

"You go someplace where there's a gang, then you don't know it but you're someplace where we've got all kinds of eyes. Any report we get that doesn't say the world is flat, we salt away in the electronic bowels of the crypt. Sometimes, like *this* time, fingers form. And they point at people."

He smiled at Garth, turning the page.

"Now, you wanna know about the Demon Viejo Dukes?"

Garth nodded.

"Old gang. Third generation, same neighborhood, thought to be almost exclusively family-passed membership. Plenty of great candidates according to high school records of kids in several of the families who've had members over the years."

"Do you know where they might hang out? Like a headquarters or something?" Garth was taking out his notepad now, jotting stuff.

"You mean, like where's the tree house?"

"That's . . . about what I mean." Garth was picking up on Husky's enjoyment of the moment.

There was something to go on. Husky went to the door and he had that little smile on his face that Marge knew so well.

"Let's put a little field trip together, huh, teach?"

"Sit by your phone," she said. "RSVPs to come."

■　■　■　■　■

The warehouse was steamy.

Everybody standing in the main room was animal taut and watchful of everyone else.

The main attraction, Frito and Cholo, faced each other now that accusations had been thrown.

Frito's aggravated jumpiness was still sustained by a combination of fair-quality coke and more than a little understandable human outrage. He watched Cholo closely. His eyes didn't dart now.

The others had been caught off guard by the flare-up, but they'd noticed King Shit quickly producing a flat black .44, complete with silencer.

The dude knew.

Cholo only looked at the heat for a moment. He couldn't afford taking his eyes off Frito, who might unravel anytime.

"Frito . . . I wasn't into that shit with your grandma by myself." Cholo knew it wouldn't mean shit to Frito, but hoped the other Dukes would side with him. He was talking for them to hear.

"King Shit knew. He told me, go get the old cunt."

"Bullshit," Edgar Lamp said very softly.

"He's the only reason I did your granny, man. Just like he's the only reason we all went out. He says to me, you the right-hand man, Cholo. All you got to do is prove it. And you know how he sets you up? He says killing the old cunt will make Frito fucking drop his beans so then we got no choice. We got to get rid of Frito, too, 'cause he's a last-place dude . . ." Cholo watched Frito, watched his fury as he kept up his rap. "See, King Shit says he wants us to be real stark, man. Real *above* wormy guys like Frito . . ."

Frito's eyes never left Cholo. The whole rap made zero sense to him. All he knew was the old lady was dead.

134

Cholo had done it. All he cared about was playing get-even.

But the other Demon Viejo Dukes were taking lots of long looks at the bullshit they'd been buying, and they weren't all falling the same way.

Cholo's little brother, Mr. Yogie, was of course ready to knife Frito from behind if he got the chance. He was also computing the odds of hitting King Shit from the blind side. You just didn't want to let those eyes go to work on you.

But the others, the very dudes Mr. Yogie had known well enough to soothe into taking the ride with him and Cholo on this little side trip . . . they were slipping.

The way Quiet Carlos was reading it, King Shit was setting everybody up from every direction. He probably had pushed Cholo to off that disgusting old bitch. Then he'd sat there and helped Frito work himself to the point of revenge.

And now who shows up with the gun? Who was the *only* motherfucker in the room with anything besides his dick hanging down?

Quiet Carlos wondered if he could grab a tire iron fast enough to throw it across the room and get lucky on King Shit's shiny forehead.

Zero and Spider Lobo were thinking most clearly of all. They wanted to do whatever was needed to stay alive in here—because everybody knew it was coming down to that—and get to the doorway and the dark street.

Frito, head on fire and sweat pouring, finally moved on Cholo. Frito wanted to kill him bare-handed. Cholo wasn't letting it happen that way.

The same knife was out again, this time going more than a millimeter into his adversary.

Frito screamed. Everything in the half-lit room went slo-mo as scream turned to cry. Cholo turned the blade.

135

He cut guts and flesh and muscle with several sudden jerks.

It was time to overthrow King Shit. Quiet Carlos moved on the tire iron as Mr. Yogie took Edgar's blind side with his own blade.

But King Shit had seen everything. Trusted nothing.

Tonight had been the night he'd be leaving the Demon Viejo Dukes anyway. He'd known it all day, scrapping any notions of hanging in.

The silenced .44 painted the corrugated-metal wall behind Quiet Carlos with brain and blood.

The tire iron was never touched.

Yogie swerved from his path while King Shit was turning on him and blowing a grapefruit-sized hole in the wall, a second too late to kill.

It was in the space of those seconds that Zero and Spider Lobo were into one of the primered Demon-mobiles. It charged forward right through the closed-tight doors and screamed into the night. As it did, the warehouse went dark.

King Shit had pumped two more shells into the car, shattering windows with one, puncturing aged metal Plymouth body with the second.

Neither struck Zero or Spider Lobo, who said not one word to each other as the car shot into the night, lights off. The two were desperately watching behind them for any sign of how King Shit might miraculously, terrifyingly follow.

Nothing followed.

King Shit was busy with Cholo and Yogie.

The brothers had discussed the betrayal of Frito before it had gone down because Cholo had been afraid and uncertain how the other Demon Viejo Dukes would take to it. Yogie had been sure Spider Lobo and Zero would not care. He had also been convinced Frito would come unstuck, so they'd decided to put something on ice in the little room just off the warehouse.

That was the room Mr. Yogie ducked into when King Shit pivoted to fire on him. The gun was behind a couple boxes, not that easy to get to. He had to work fast. Cholo was giving him a few moments outside, being ballsier than Yogie could ever remember.

"You a fucking fraud, King Shit," Cholo hissed out. He hid behind his own car, acutely aware that Edgar Lamp, with a large gun and the ability to kill with his mind, was just on the other side of it.

Cholo prayed his brother would hurry. Find the gun, he was thinking.

When Edgar started to move toward the door to get Yogie, Cholo again spoke from behind him.

"Where's my knife, King Shit? Where's your back, dude? Maybe I put them together?"

Cholo was creeping to the rear of his car as he spoke. He could see the vague outline of Edgar Lamp by the front of the vehicle. Edgar wasn't moving, trying to see where Cholo might be. Cholo knew it was giving Yogie time, if Yogie would only hurry.

Yogie had the gun. He was inches from the door, wondering in the dark little room where the fuck King Shit was. He hesitated.

So did Cholo, who could've thrown his knife and possibly killed. Edgar knew Cholo could see him, and had decided he must be at the back of the car. But he couldn't be positive. When that damn Plymouth had crashed out of the building, the impact had torn out some wall and ripped the wiring. So everyone moved in shadows.

Not far off, the police were moving in shadows as well. Even as they'd been sealing off the area, they'd received reports of the car crashing through the doors and something very wrong in the warehouse *before* their arrival. Husky Martin stared down the street toward that low, curved metal roof and wondered while they moved quickly, without sirens, maximizing their surprise.

"I really *want* this motherfucker," he'd told the SWAT leader. "Living and breathing."

The officer made no comment. Husky knew there couldn't be promises.

Edgar knew the cops must be sending plenty of blue suits after the crash. He had to off the greaser brothers quick or it was pig iron city.

He moved around the front of the car, forgetting Mr. Yogie in the little room for a moment. The door was shut there. To open it would make noise and give warning.

Edgar got to the passenger side of the old car. He was certain Cholo hadn't moved.

"Where's your knife, Cholo?" Edgar taunted back. "Didn't wanna throw that thing, did you? Huh, live-at-home boy? Huh?"

In that moment, he heard the doorknob rolling and knew Mr. Yogie was coming out. Edgar ducked down and opened the car door before him, which turned on the interior light. It threw faint illumination onto Cholo, behind the car, making him a shadowy but visible form.

Yogie, holding the gun and scared shitless, saw the form and fired as Cholo realized and shouted out. But the trigger was pulled. The room was dense with the loud bang of the gun. Yogie realized immediately what he had done.

Before he could tear his eyes away from his slumping brother, he was thrown back crash dummy style by the brute concussion of the .44 bullet hitting him high in the chest.

Yogie met the wall, dazed but still alive. His own gun had dropped to the floor.

Edgar moved to Mr. Yogie quickly, the two eyeing one

another for a moment. Without a word, Edgar shot him in the face.

It was very much time to get the hell out of the warehouse. There was another primered chopped Chevy sitting in the dim, indirect light from the street. As Edgar moved toward it, though, he sensed something very wrong.

He'd overstayed. There was a presence in the street, something watching him right now.

The four klieg lights went on across the street and bathed everything in the warehouse with a cobalt glow. Edgar saw what was out there.

Twenty SWAT guns aimed right at him.

At the same moment, a window behind Edgar shattered. Five more gun barrels poked into the warehouse.

He was at the eye of the gauntlet. He held his hands out before him and dropped the .44 as he looked into the blinding candlepower.

"Martin?" he called.

"Right here," came the answer.

Cops were moving on him now, taking him down on his face in the warehouse, double-cuffing him.

"You're an asshole, Martin . . ." Edgar yelled out as they got him back up. "Shoulda had 'em shoot me." He was grinning.

Husky Martin, standing now in the doorway . . . or what was left of it . . . watched without expression.

He had come very close to having everybody open up on the guy; have done with it. Now he was getting laughed at because he'd chosen to spare instead of destroy.

Did the other cops here agree with Lamp? Probably. They'd captured the guy, but somehow Husky still felt like the loser at this moment. Maybe Edgar was right. Maybe *Husky* agreed with him. Maybe he was an asshole.

Ten

"How come you had 'em keep me in this thing?" Edgar Lamp strained at the straitjacket uncomfortably.

" 'Cause you're fuckin' crazy." Husky spoke without even looking at his captive just yet.

They were in a little grilling room off Main Booking at Parker Center. Husky would just as soon have had them take him straight back to jail, but there were plenty of new charges.

"You don't think I'm crazy." Edgar kept looking right at him.

Husky could feel those eyes. He hadn't even let Garth in to hear this conversation, telling him it was something he had to handle privately. Garth had urged him to take care . . . and take a gun.

"I said you don't think that," Edgar repeated.

Now Husky looked over at him.

"You read minds, too?"

For a moment Edgar showed his confusion. Husky grinned, having caught him a little flat-footed on the mental stuff.

"When does it happen? Full moon?"

"I wanna get out of the straitjacket."

"No way. So maybe it's when the weather's real humid? That it?"

"You make very little sense for a big-shit cop, you know that?"

Husky held the gaze now, wondering what it would be like if Lamp suddenly decided to put the Evil Eye Fleegle shit on him right now, right here. Would it be painful, hypnotic, transcendent . . . what?

"This thing with the old ladies . . ."

"What ol' ladies?"

"Right. The old ladies you and your pals the Demon Viejos murdered. . . . That was very personal, wasn't it?"

Edgar kept cool, kept looking back.

"That was along the lines of a little card you'd send me, right? The card might say something like: 'You are hereby challenged . . .' or 'Catch me if you can . . .' Am I right?"

Edgar Lamp sat death-still. His message had been received, but perhaps not yet decoded. He was taking the policeman a great deal more seriously than ever before.

"I mean, to have several of 'em just die around town at the same moment . . . you were lookin' to blow my mind, right? And the way you hid the fact that Pacific Palisades was the genuine article . . . that was very sneaky, very smart." Husky smiled. Then his voice went a little colder. "But you've got a really resourceful, unusual . . . mind . . . don't you, Edgar? Yeah, you do. And now I'm onto it. So what the fuck you gonna do about that?"

141

"I will come back to haunt you." Edgar's words were barely audible.

Husky just watched him a moment, the words staying in his mind like a bad smell. The guy was nearly in a trance right in front of him, and going deeper. Husky wanted, more than he could ever have predicted, to just reach under his coat, pull out his gun, and resurface the walls with this guy.

"That's pretty personal, right there." Husky gave a little smile.

Edgar's face had become a blotchy red-and-white mask of pure poison. His lips somehow seemed thinner, his eyes going almost coal black. But even in his rage at Husky Martin, he knew he had to wait.

Husky knew it, too, though he was half expecting the beginnings of some ripping from within as capillaries and muscle tissue would start to come apart. But above that fear he, too, understood that even for a child-beast like Edgar Lamp, this was the wrong time.

Wrong because they were alone, because just outside the door were hundreds of policemen who would demolish Edgar instantly . . . and most importantly because it was not a moment Edgar himself had planned, staged, orchestrated, and calculated.

"My grandpa used to say the whole world wants a miracle, Martin. I will come back to haunt you. I'm gonna give you one."

"You're gonna be charged, booked, processed . . . and then you're gonna be taken down to that airport again."

"You and me, sooner or later," Lamp said.

"We put you on a jet, we fly you to Texas, and *they* prosecute your ass."

"You know what I can do." It was as if Edgar hadn't heard a word Husky said. "You're the one who finds them."

"Are you confessing?"

"Whole world wants a miracle. The next Proving is for you."

The smile, the taunt.

"You give me your little chant all you want."

"Whole world wants a miracle."

Husky could feel himself lose perspective and control as he leaned in real close, looking straight into Edgar's unyielding pitch-colored eyes. He was sick of this little shit. Something inside just couldn't leave it alone, couldn't hold the words back any longer.

"You do me a favor, Edgar . . . you go through what you've gotta go through. Then if you survive . . . if you can manage it . . . you bust your ass out, I fuckin' throw it down to you: do it if you've got the balls. Then you keep both eyes open . . . don't even sleep. 'Cause I'll be right out there. And it'll be you and me, sooner or later, just like you said. All you gotta do is give us the chance."

■ ■ ■ ■ ■

The entire body of the TWA 747 quivered in the chilly Los Angeles night.

Inside, sitting midway in the fuselage, Edgar Lamp seemed extraordinarily withdrawn.

"The whole world wants a miracle," he said matter-of-factly to the man beside him.

That man was Detective Stuart Johnson, a forty-year-old cop Husky Martin trusted completely. Johnson thought Lamp's black eyes were unbelievably cool and calm. He wondered what his partner, Clay Terrance, thought of this man. Johnson and Terrance were finally getting to transport their prisoner, having been left at the altar on the day Edgar had killed the deputies and escaped.

143

Now each detective had one of his arms manacled to one of Edgar's. They had simply shaken their heads when the prisoner had remarked how much more he liked these metal manacles than the plastic variety.

The wind on the runway was twenty miles per hour. Bennett Chen, the pilot, looked at the stat on his checklist and read on. Chen took a flight like most guys took a piss.

Workmen on the tarmac moved suitcases, mail, cargo, and rolling stainless-steel food modules all over the place. People watched from the plane and thought how detached it seemed. How different the course of lives.

"The whole world wants a miracle," repeated Lamp.

"The whole world wants you to shut up," said Terrance. Johnson looked over at him, wondering why this guy got on Clay's nerves. Neither smiled. Very few guys got on Clay's nerves, but Clay had admitted in the car coming down here, looking right at Lamp, that if given the slightest excuse he would happily marbleize the inside of the car with the guy's brains.

Just now, Edgar stared down the aisle of the 747 toward the cockpit, a football field away.

"You think so?" he replied softly.

They barely heard him, but both were surprised. Neither saw or felt his wrists momentarily test the manacles.

A few rows ahead of Lamp, Johnson, and Terrance, Garth Cheesbro sat jotting notes and disguising the jitters he felt every time he flew. He'd gotten over the resentment toward Husky for shutting him out of the interrogation room. He could even understand his friend's refusal to discuss what had gone on in there.

The murders of the old women had been a direct outgrowth of allowing Edgar to get away. Even though that had been the Sheriff's Department's fault, Husky would surely take heat for that at LAPD, and the captor-captive relationship would just as surely have turned personal. So

144

Garth expected to hear details after Texas—unless he got them from Edgar.

And you never knew what you'd get from Edgar.

The jet shuddered and rolled backward with a smooth, sickening glide from its stationary berth. Away from the boarding ramp that now yawned into the night like a severed, bloodless limb The bird was packed, thought Johnson. The cabin was warmer, less comfortable . . . close

Edgar was aware of all around him, but still stared down the aisle. Johnson guessed he was trying to somehow see out the pilot's windshield, though he knew it was physically impossible from where Edgar sat.

Captain Bennett Chen was feeling tired, though the coffee was starting to kick in by the time the 747 gleamed at the head of the runway, engine pitch climbing with a steady, escalating urgency. He yawned, shook his head, and complained about his wife's insomnia and her insistence on sharing it.

The crew liked Bennett Chen. He wasn't one of your holier-than-thou "doctor pilot" pilots. There were enough of those guys, the ones who made you feel like you were going into open-heart surgery when what you were really doing was far simpler: defying gravity for limited but intense little spaces of time.

When they got the go-ahead, they all felt the usual tightening in their abdomens, the customary blast of blood pressure.

"Time to make zoom-zoom," cracked Chen.

The engines screamed unholy harmonies as the crew watched lights blink before them and away for over a mile.

Chen ticked off the timing, building his power surge for takeoff till it felt exactly right.

Edgar Lamp was relaxed, settled in his seat, still staring down the aisle. Johnson and Terrance did the same, takeoff limbo having come between the policemen and their charge. Lights went down in the cabin. People waited to watch the city drop away. Garth put his pen in his pocket. Yes, as usual, he was scared on takeoff.

The brakes were released. Rolling. Picking up speed . . . seconds ticking as the rumble grew and the plane's body rattled, clattering and straining to remain earthbound.

Edgar leaned forward slightly, as if interested. Johnson watched him, because Johnson was a watcher. Terrance looked out the window.

Edgar was concentrating now . . . his face showed it. Johnson knew it, but couldn't pinpoint the object of all this attention. The lips moved slightly; muttering.

"The whole world wants a miracle, the whole world wants a miracle . . ."

Edgar was thinking of Bennett Chen. He'd never seen the man, but he knew just what he looked like. He had him, tightly locked, in his mind. This would be better than anything. Edgar didn't know how he could do this, didn't question it, didn't care. You never tried to fix what was broken, you never asked how you got the pilot in your mind . . . As he became more excited, Edgar didn't waver in his concentration.

Chen was engrossed deeply in his work now, not yawning at all. He was well down the runway, nearly to the point of takeoff. He began to nose the jet up, now past the point where he could safely stop, when the icicle of pain ripped through his head. His hands left the controls, flying to his face. The scream he let out was completely beyond his control as he twisted around on his seat in the unbelievable, total surprise of brain fire.

Everything in the cockpit stopped dead. The crew gaped. This was the worst possible moment.

"Bennett?" somebody said.

146

But the pilot was beyond hearing. A second after the pain in his head erupted, a far greater disturbance took place in his chest. Not just a corner or one side. His whole chest seemed to be *swelling* as if he couldn't stop inhaling but he realized . . . if there was real thought going on in there . . . that he wasn't inhaling at all. He was simply *expanding.* It dug at him, forcing his mouth open into a howl for which he lacked the air. He sat there, hands clutching and eyes bulging, mouth yanked as far open as it would go in a soundless scream, chest feeling as if it would explode.

Edgar Lamp, concentrating, saw it all as clearly as if he was there. He nodded his head ever so slightly forward.

Bennett Chen, knowing incredulity amid his fear and helplessness, realized that his hands were flying from his forehead and onto the control. They began, to his amazement, to push it forward. To guide the jet back down.

Everyone in the cockpit seemed to shout "NO" at once. Chen, awash in his own spontaneous sweat, now gaped through his frantic eyes at *them,* but what he saw made no sense. He was looking at the faces not of his crew but of loved ones he had lost. The dead. But they were not friendly, didn't seem to know him . . . they were only curious, judgmental. He knew it was impossible. He thought he was going mad. He tried to say something to them but only moaned. And drooled.

The plane was definitely going down now, having risen only a few hundred feet. People knew what was happening. They realized they were going to die. Garth Cheesbro forgot all about Edgar Lamp and Husky Martin and everything but the one all-devouring fact before him.

"A miracle," Lamp said. Or thought. Johnson and Terrance heard, or knew. But didn't care.

Bennett Chen's chest exploded at the moment of impact.

The giant bulb-nosed body of the 747 burrowed through the sand on the beach above El Segundo, brutally carving a path toward the dark water. On impact, the top of the fuselage split open like a rotting highway cat, shooting the flailing forms of passengers and crew, many already dead, into the black night air and onto the hard-packed sand or the surface of the water beyond it.

As this happened, the plane kept on, inexorably forward, until the first third was submerged and wave-washed.

Almost instantly, bright fires scorched the two outer wing-mounted engines.

There wasn't a scream from the suddenly immobile carcass of the giant plane. There wasn't a moan or shriek or gasp. Any left alive had all they could do to breathe. The entire world seemed, for the longest sagging span of moments, to have lost its voice. It stood in collective slack-jawed wonder at the snarled, bent monster that lay dead on its shore.

It ignored the monster that swam, then walked away.

Gradually, faintly at first, police sirens could be heard in the distance as tiny metal compartments with even tinier humans inside shot through streets to convene around this elongated, ungainly corpse. They brought papers and pens and orderly minds to lift reason from the physical chaos of great collision. They began to sort and categorize and bag and fold.

They cried and vomited and finally sat on the beach in exhaustion, but still it would not be finished. God knew what they would find, the deeper they went.

■　■　■　■　■

The drive from downtown was a quiet, desperate dash for Husky. One moment he couldn't believe his shit luck

148

with Edgar Lamp, even when he died. The next he couldn't keep his thoughts away from the terrible fact that not only had Johnson and Terrance probably died with him, but so, in all likelihood, had Garth.

The brutality of the scene he *might* find was enough to take his breath away and leave him with a cold, rolling emptiness in the pit of his gut.

The first unit on the scene had simply radioed; "God, it's awful bad."

Even with his desperate fear of personal loss, however, Husky decided to go to the scene. Friends or not, there were probably *hundreds* of victims. It was standard for Homicide to appear at such scenes, ask a few questions, cover the department's large blue ass when a jet sat somewhere like Playa del Rey with a full load of cadavers.

He broke out in a sweat at the thought of what waited for his once-over in the ocean air.

Despite every fragmented, tumbling thought, Husky kept his siren on as he high-laned it along the Santa Monica Freeway from City Center. The idea of Garth, poor innocent goddamned Garth, being dead on the beach simply would not give him a second's peace. With all the bodies Husky had seen, he didn't know if he could bear to see Garth's. Not in one of the unnatural poses struck at the scene of an honest-to-God catastrophe like this.

He was nearing the beach. From the Santa Monica he shifted to the wide, busy San Diego Freeway, built more recently and equipped to handle much more traffic. He took it to Century Boulevard, the off ramp leading to the Los Angeles International Airport. Traffic there wasn't too bad and the trip west on Century only took about ten minutes before he was zagging over, then continuing west to the beach near El Segundo.

The closer he got, the more police and fire vehicles Husky saw. They were all heading the same way he was.

149

His anticipation mounted. He reached a roadblock and the cop who signaled him to stop came around. Husky flashed his badge and was quickly waved on. Now traffic was non-existent here past the frontier and into the war zone. Beirut. The DMZ. As he neared the beach road he could see incredibly bright light from just over the next rise.

The crash site was ringed now by the bright gas lamps used late at night on freeway construction jobs. Brighter than those that had lit Edgar's warehouse capture. Husky couldn't remember whether or not they were called cobalt lamps. Something like that. The place was brighter than noon. The sand looked bluish white under the glare. Everything looked bluish white, in fact, including the busted-open fuselage of the giant jet.

From where Husky parked the car, he could see down into it. A moment of desperate, unrealistic hope came and went. Many seats were still in place, little rows oblivious in the cooling beach air. But clearly, the occupants of those seats hadn't fared so well. The twenty or so who had been catapulted out onto the sand made a nasty panorama. There were doubtless also plenty in the water. Somewhere. Three stretchers with living victims were off to one side. They were being put into ambulances just now.

Husky began his fearful, gut-churning walk toward the plane.

■ ■ ■ ■

"We can't find him." The worried blue eyes of the young officer looked as if they expected Husky Martin to strike a deathblow at the news.

But Husky, thoughts so fixed on his good friend, thought at first the young officer meant Garth. Then he realized. It was Edgar Lamp he was talking about. "Keep looking," came the answer. Immediately, Husky had an entirely new dread.

"We've done a pretty thorough search, Captain. Found Johnson and Terrance right where they were supposed to be. Still strapped in and everything."

"Maybe he got thrown."

Husky tried not to linger on the unbelievable carnage all around them as they stood inside the main cabin. *Broken bodies*, he thought. You heard the term. You never really visualized it.

"They're right over here."

The officer showed Husky where Johnson and Terrance were. Unlike those of many of the other passengers, their seat belts had held, resulting in collapsed chests, broken necks, and God knew what else. Blood had erupted from their mouths, their faces had been smashed against the seat before them. Or maybe on the floor. Or maybe on each other. They had dents in their heads, the way semi-deflated footballs carry dents. It all left them staring grotesquely ahead.

Johnson was purple; something out of a traffic-school shock film. Some guy who'd French-kissed a telephone pole in his Chevy at sixty-five.

The seat between them was empty. The strap had not broken because it had been undone.

Undone.

Husky looked at it. He also looked at the handcuffs still on Johnson's and Terrance's wrists. Undone. He felt his blood pressure go up noticeably. He looked down. Then he shifted his gaze to the young cop, standing by.

"Keep looking, son. Everybody's gotta be someplace."

The cop's expression didn't change, and Husky now realized his tension wasn't due to fear of any captain. It was because he couldn't understand what the fuck had happened here with Edgar and his captors any more than Husky could. There was no possible way Johnson and Terrance had allowed Lamp to undo those bindings . . . especially the cuffs. Yet they were detached, plain as hell.

And even though Husky was growing increasingly disturbed, frustrated, and baffled at everything here, he couldn't keep from making the Good Cop's comparison: in the car with those deputies, Edgar had been manacled, too. And he'd escaped.

"Why would those . . ." the young officer started, pointing at the manacles.

"I don't know," Husky said quietly.

They exchanged looks. Husky had the feeling the kid was fighting to keep his dinner down.

"You wanna get out of here?"

The young officer shook his head. Husky gave him a pat on the arm.

"Don't be a hero. We're all only human."

Garth had been one of those the giant plane had convulsively shot out onto the hard sand. When Husky finally found him he'd been covered with a blanket and tagged, based on his ID and the airline passenger list.

Garth would have gasped at how similar he now seemed to the fragile, openmouthed old ladies he'd seen at the medical examiner's.

His back had been broken so that he could not lie flat on it now, so they put him on his side.

The cigar Husky had given him as a parting gift was still in his inside jacket pocket, unharmed.

Husky looked down at his friend and then sat back in the sand, sighing and shutting his eyes. When he reopened them minutes later, he realized for the first time that the stars were out.

152

■   ■   ■   ■

Edgar Lamp walked along, staring at the moon for a moment before resuming his constant scan of the area around him.

He was cranked. He had an on-again-off-again hard-on and his whole body buzzed right to the fingertips. He couldn't stop thinking about it. He'd never, ever, done anything like *that* before.

He couldn't remember exactly what had gone down right after the big hit. It had all been a rushing, roaring succession of sounds and wind and cool all over. The sky had opened up. No, it had been the roof, with a great screaming blast of giving metal. He had looked up into stars and it was like he was moving, he guessed.

He'd been thrown into the water, clear of the plane, like it had all been planned out. He didn't feel terribly comfortable with that one, but he couldn't get away from it. He'd managed to get the cuffs off, the belt off, knowing he wouldn't want to be tied down with those two detectives when it hit. Making them sit still for it had been simple. No tougher than the deputies or that business with the pilot. But quicker. Maybe his adrenaline had been pumping, he guessed. But for a second he frowned. Could adrenaline help you with something like that? Who knew.

The water had been hard, hurting his back a little, but he'd welcomed it. He popped back up quickly, seeing he was beyond the waves. He watched the plane behind him, the fires on the outer engines. Pretty soon he'd started to swim along parallel with the shoreline, and then after he was well clear of all that, he swam in to the sand and sat there for a minute. He couldn't take his eyes off the plane at first, but pretty soon the idea that people would be com-

153

ing filtered through his excitement and forced him to his feet.

That's when he'd started this walk.

About now he was getting to the first apartment houses along the shore in El Segundo. These were old; beaten by years of sand and wind. They had a nice view, but they still looked like shit to Edgar Lamp.

There was a man standing on the balcony of the first house. The man hadn't seen Edgar yet. He was staring down the beach at the growing activity and sounds of the crash site. Then suddenly the man's eyes swung over when they caught something, a form, moving through the shadowy darkness on the sand.

The man on the balcony and Edgar Lamp looked right at each other as Edgar walked by.

Could the man have seen that Edgar was wet? Edgar peered at him, the two pairs of eyes locking over fifty yards of sand. Edgar kept walking, kept looking at the man. Could he possibly add two and two . . . get the idea that Edgar was *from* that place down the beach? That he had driven it into the sand?

Edgar knew he could do this man, too, and he was toying with the idea. He was feeling magnanimous, generous, confident. There was no way the man could guess. So Edgar just looked back. And kept walking down the beach.

The man watching from his apartment balcony was named Chris Bixby. He was alone in his place, and this staring contest with the guy on the beach had left him sweat-soaked and rattled. Maybe it was because it came right after that horrible noise and seeing what it was when he ran to the balcony to look. Seeing that plane out there . . . that carcass of a thing. Chris was a TV writer . . . he'd been sitting in his den trying to figure out the beats to an episode he was pitching tomorrow at Lorimar, and he'd been off in that dreamy alpha place he loved so much. He loved it more than anything because there everything worked out the way he figured it.

Control World, he called it.

And then, boom. And this guy on the beach, walking by and just looking at him. Not making a sound, not calling out about how weird that fucking plane down there looked and how everybody in it was probably dead or something.

Chris thought about that one for a moment. Everybody down there really could be dead. Right on his beach. He might never look down that way and feel the same again.

But his thoughts brought him back to the look that guy had given him. Even from the beach, even in the dark, you could tell it was a fucking bizarre look. Maybe the guy had been coked out of his skull, going down the beach, and all of a sudden this plane had dropped down right behind him and the whole thing had permanently turned his brain to cottage cheese. Chris lingered for a moment—just a moment—on what a bizarre idea for an episode of *something* that would make.

But as he turned to go back into his apartment, after the guy had gone by, his shadowy figure finally lost in darkness down the beach, Chris came back to the other feeling. The look of that guy had scared the shit out of him. But not just that. It had *chilled* him. Like a physical blast of cold air in a bad place. A place you wanted to get out of, but you didn't know how.

Chris mulled it. He had wanted to get off that balcony out there. He realized that now. But he couldn't. Total leg lock. They wouldn't work. He'd been unable to turn away and conceal himself behind the curtain he'd thought of pulling. Could somebody make you freeze like that? Make you stand there and look at them while they sized you up?

Chris had an open bottle of wine, and he drank from it, never mind the glass, still thinking about this.

155

Probably all these feelings came from his own perverse fascination, he reasoned. Probably after hearing that crash and then looking down the beach and seeing it, like a dog pitched over dead on the sand, to see some guy strolling down along here had hooked him. The more he considered it, the more he liked the humanness of his own fascination. Like peeping through a keyhole at Mom and Dad going at it when you were a kid. Just bizarre enough to hold your attention even though you knew it was somehow out of sync with what was *right*.

He took another swig.

Bullshit. That had been fucking weird. He hadn't wanted to stay at the peephole just now. He'd wanted to come inside, close the curtain, lock every lock he owned, and sit there with a butcher knife waiting for an unusual sound. Fight-or-flight reaction when you had no place to run resulted in a combination of both. And when you put it together you told yourself it was a pragmatic response. Don't get mixed up with that clown out there heading this way from the direction of a mother of a crash in his soaking-wet clothes . . .

My God, thought Chris Bixby, realizing. The guy had been *wet!* But how could he know that? Not rationally, that's for sure . . . not from, what, at least forty yards? Fifty?

But he did know it. It had been information passed, somehow. He closed his eyes and tried to verify the idea of that wet cloth . . . he could see it in his mind's eye . . . and even though the figure he saw was too far away to be reasonably certain about, he again *was* certain. The clothing had been wet. He would swear on it. In court. In the guiltifying presence of his mother . . . on his very deathbed he would swear that the man's clothes had been wet.

Chris put down the wine and grabbed the phone. He dialed "0" and asked for the police.

■ ■ ■ ■ ■

Chief Nash found Husky still sitting beside Garth's body, and got him to walk back toward the cars as they took Garth away. It was one of the few times Nash had ever felt anything other than irritation toward Husky. But plainly the big cop was stricken to his soul on this one.

"I know you two've been friends a very long time . . ."

Husky nodded, looking a bit wide-eyed at the sand before him while they walked.

"I think you should get out of here, go home for a couple days."

"They don't know where Lamp is, Chief." It sounded like somebody else's voice. Lamp seemed unimportant. He was only the reason, and the reason didn't hold a candle to the loss.

"We'll find him. He can't be doing too well, if he's lived through it at all."

Husky looked at Chief Nash with a moment of hope. The idea that Edgar Lamp was also dead hadn't really occurred to him. In a moment, he realized why.

"I think he did this, Chief."

Nash put a hand on his shoulder; sounded condescending but firm.

"Like I said, you ought to go home, have a good stiff drink, and try to sleep a while. I'm always yelling for more cops in this town, and the mayor just gave me a whole slew of new ones, so we've got a lot of boys on the force right now. I think if we all get together, and believe me we will, we can let you take some time off."

"But nobody else knows this guy . . ." Husky knew he was on automatic. He knew he couldn't really carry it off anymore.

157

He finally nodded.

"You're right."

"Glad to hear you say that. I'm going to have somebody drive you home. We'll let you know as soon as anything shakes loose. You've got my word."

Husky nodded, looking again into the chief's eyes. He never believed the chief's word about anything, but just now he would settle for it. Just now he didn't fucking care.

■ ■ ■ ■ ■

Officers Skakel and Purdue, back in their blues after the Tilly Taco's massacre, listened intently to Chris Bixby's story. They sat in his living room taking notes, asking every question they could think of.

It was hardly the glamour side of the investigative process. Here they'd just come from a mind-fogging plane-crash reality to sit through the ramblings of some half-crocked beach dweller.

Still, the guy was damned insistent. He swore over and over he'd seen something relevant.

And Chief Nash—fucking Chief fucking Nash himself —had personally shoved this assignment up their snoots.

So here they were in Chris Bixby's living room.

Chris Bixby was pretty agitated, and most of what he said had the ring of hysteria. People got worked up when jets fell out of the sky near their houses.

So did chiefs of police.

Skakel kept trying to bring Chris Bixby to the point. Could he make out clearly the features of the man he'd seen on the beach?

No.

Could he possibly have seen that the clothes were torn

158

or wet or anything like that from the distance that he'd seen the man?

Well, not actually, not physically. But he just knew it for sure.

The two cops had done a lot of sighing and talking in calm tones. They weren't lost on Chris Bixby.

"Look, I know you're thinking I'm talking like a fruit-cake here."

"You'd have every reason in the world to be worked up, Mr. Bixby. Plane crashes traumatize the people on the ground, too."

"I'm telling you I've never had feelings like this before. I don't like to tell people I just somehow divine something is either this or that. I like to sound like I'm rational."

"But the fact is he was too far away."

"Yeah, but I could see his eyes. We were staring right at each other. Like a contest to see who'd blink."

"And you still say he was wet."

"Soaked."

"Came out of the shadows and just looked at you as he walked by."

"And I couldn't move. Like I said. I was rooted to that fucking deck out there."

"You know you might be seen as somebody with an overactive imagination, being a television writer and all. People might say you're sort of writing this in your mind to make it more dramatic."

Chris Bixby smiled and looked a little sad.

"Television writers don't get accused of having imaginations all that often, Officers."

"Well, we're not putting down what anyone does for a living but you *probably* just had a staring contest with a vagrant, Mr. Bixby. You know that."

"A vagrant with flawless timing."

"Lots of 'em have it. And your own mind probably did

159

the rest. What I'd suggest you do is have a little more of that wine you've got there and go to sleep."

"You're going to ignore what I've told you."

"No. We're going to file it under 'interesting but hard to lean on for solid help.' That bother you?"

"That's about what I figured. No, it doesn't bother me. Least I got it off my chest."

Skakel and Purdue managed smiles.

When they heard the radio call about the dog farther down the beach, their smiles vanished.

■　■　■　■　■

Purdue and Skakel met the woman who'd called the police just outside her front door. The beachfront house she lived in was far nicer than Chris Bixby's, and in the middle of the Hermosa Beach strip. Money Incorpored.

As she led them toward the sand she said she hadn't been able to tell at first if the squeal of pain she'd heard was animal or human. Only after she'd gone to take a look with a couple of her neighbors—who had not chosen to hang around to talk with the policemen—had she found the poor dog.

It had been a German shepherd, good-sized and fairly young.

Now it was simply dead.

Purdue and Skakel exchanged loaded looks when they saw the animal. Both were grimly silent as they examined the remains and found that the internal organs of the chest cavity had been somehow yanked out. Both remembered how El Chocolate Grande had looked just after his death. Both had read the general departmental reports on the old ladies. "Only one squeal?" Purdue looked at her.

"That's all I heard. And I was in my front yard talking

with my neighbors about that airplane crash, so I heard all there was to hear."

The woman looked beyond scared. She looked spooked. Skakel, the older of the two police officers, knew the expression. Scared was when something happened but you could understand exactly how. Spooked came when there didn't seem to be a real great explanation.

He could understand the feeling just now.

"Well, I don't really see how . . ." Skakel began to try to steer the woman away from anything even remotely like the truth.

"I don't care if you can't see how." Irritation flashed across the lady's face. "I'm telling you what we all heard. Then we found him right here, just like this."

"I'd like to have the scene looked at just like it is before we move him," Purdue said, looking to Skakel for agreement, which he got.

"Absolutely." Skakel nodded. Then he looked to the woman again. "Real fast, huh?"

She nodded. Her impatience with these two dumb cops was plain as day on her features.

"You've gotta forgive us, lady," Purdue started, "but see, if it was slow and there was lots of yelping here, then it'd make a whole lot more sense."

"No shit." Her face didn't change.

"We're just as hard put to figure it out as you are, ma'am." Skakel tried to sound as soothing as he could.

"Don't be condescending with me, Officer. I don't need your reassurance. I know I'm not crazy, here. I'm a psychiatrist myself, and I understand hysteria. That's not what I'm feeling right now."

"Fine." Skakel nodded. "Glad to hear it. But if it was as fast as you say, then I'd sure like to know how the hell all those insides got outside that way. I mean, take a look at it.

161

One great big wound, just like that, about two feet long, broke all those ribs."

"What you're trying to say is that it looks like the poor dog exploded, Officer. Isn't that right?"

They looked at her for a moment, realizing. She was right. That's exactly what it looked like.

No sooner had Skakel and Purdue reached their car than they got another call. A *human* murder victim had just been found about a quarter of a mile farther down the beach in a parking lot.

"Jesus," muttered Purdue, "this is turning into your basic bright red midnight."

As Skakel put on the sirens and lights and peeled out of dead dog territory, Purdue put in a call of his own to headquarters. It took the operator two repeats to get it, but a bunch of lab boys would be heading down to check out the shepherd on the sand. The angry lady shrink had promised them she'd keep an eye on it and not let anybody move anything.

"She'll probably kick any stray sea gulls away," Skakel had groused.

They spent the next few blocks bitching to each other about the lady shrink and her razor-sharp tongue, trying not to discuss what they were both afraid of. When they got to the parking lot they forgot all about everything. For a little while, at least.

The guy was sprawled across the hood of a three-year-old Chevy, his blood all over the windshield.

His guts were all over it, too.

His chest was wide open. One clean, simple wound about two and a half feet long, complete with snapped ribs pointing straight up to the sky and an absolutely amazed expression of pain on his mug.

Skakel and Purdue stood and stared for the longest time.

162

The small crowd was waiting for them to act like cops and do something. They were both remembering the dog, the lady shrink, and El Chocolate Grande.

"I'd say we've got us a survivor from a plane crash," Skakel said quietly.

Purdue nodded, then turned to the people.

"Did anybody hear anything?" Purdue asked. He felt instantly stupid. They all looked at him like he was bats.

"We found him like this. We were having a party down there on the beach . . ."

"Where?" Skakel looked toward the beach.

"There . . ." The same kid who'd spoken up pointed. It wasn't in the direction of the exploded dog. Skakel and Purdue swapped looks. Shit. "We were . . . drinking a couple beers, you know . . . and then that plane went down over there and we sorta watched it all for a little while . . ."

"So when did you find this?" Purdue was taking out his pad.

"We were getting ready to split, you know . . . I mean, parties and plane crashes don't exactly go together, you know?"

They looked at the guy again. The kid was pretty upset.

"Listen, this is my old man's car . . . you think maybe we could get it cleaned off for him or something?"

The body had been "cleaned" of wallet, coins, keys. There was fresh oil in the parking slot next to the kid's old man's bloodied Chevy, which led Purdue and Skakel to assume the murder had occurred while the victim tried to get into his own car, which had then been boosted along with the guy's belongings. This didn't take a genius to deduce, but then they weren't geniuses. The cops talked between themselves.

"Are we agreed?" Skakel asked.

163

"Gotta be, I'd say."

"Then he's survived the crash, killed the dog, and killed this poor guy."

"*And* taken off with a set of wheels, some money that might've been in his wallet, and God knows what else." Purdue sighed. "One shepherd, one schmuck."

Skakel looked at his partner.

"You wake up thinking shit like that?"

"Don't worry about me. Worry about where our boy's headed."

Eleven

HE'D LEFT THE LIGHT ON in the bedroom when he'd gone in to change clothes. Now that light was a dimness from the other end of the house. It was all right, he didn't want to see too much just now. He'd seen enough in the last few days.

Garth had said once that houses where guys lived alone were like rough drafts. Women were great at redrafts and polishes.

Most of the married guys Husky knew lived in their wives' houses, it was true.

He looked out the window into the backyard. He was avoiding the issue but it seemed like every other thought he entertained would bring him back to something Garth had said or done or influenced.

Another brace of hooch, Husky decided.

He'd been throwing them back ever since getting home. He'd even offered one to the young lieutenant—couldn't

165

remember his name now—who'd been so concerned and solicitous. Offered to stick around and shoot the bull all night if that's what Husky'd wanted. Offered to put a guard outside in case he thought this guy might have his number or something. Offered to even take Husky over to his place, for God's sake, and put him up in the guest room.

Even Chief Nash had been somber back on the beach, aware of Husky's feelings. All that stuff about going home, resting up, remembering nobody was an iron man.

"You can't push yourself past breaking, Husky," was maybe the chief's all-time best line. Not a great line, to be sure, but it'd do.

But he'd been concerned, Husky knew, and he'd probably been holding back a good dose of anger, too.

Husky wouldn't have been surprised to hear he was *completely* off the case, busted down to lecturing school kids, and asked never to publicly admit he was a cop.

The drink was good. They were starting to feel smoother now, after . . . shit, he didn't know how many.

Fred hovered near his master just as he'd done all evening.

"Sensing something's fallen off the ol' boss's neatly regulated track?" Husky asked him. Smiling sadly, he reached down and patted the safe, comforting mat of fur on the big dog's back. Fred stood there, patient, letting the hand knead the pliant, healthy muscle and skin around the shoulder blades. The relentless pant of Big Dog was the only sound in the house just then to Husky. The brown eyes with their funny questioning little brows would be peering up, but he couldn't find them in the darkness.

They stood before the window to the backyard like that for a couple minutes; man and dog bonded.

Until man's mind started to wander back.

Guilt was a funny one. Every day of his life, Husky

166

dealt with guilt. He got paid to go chasing after men and women, pointing his finger and performing the function of Guilt's Unholy Messenger.

He was extremely good at proving guilt. At sensing where it hid.

But now he realized that until this moment he had not even begun to understand what guilt felt like.

Husky believed Garth's death to be Husky's own fault. It had been impossibly stupid to have him involved all along. Impossibly self-aggrandizing, unsafe . . . and just plain bush.

Sure, Garth loved doing the book, loved the excitement . . . but he'd been in almost constant danger. As a responsible cop, Husky should never have allowed him so terribly near.

He'd not only failed to do his job right, he'd failed his friend.

Edgar Lamp had indeed come back to haunt Husky Martin.

Edgar had of course not been responsible for Garth's flying on that plane, but Husky was sure Edgar must've enjoyed the chance to make good his threat through Garth.

Husky tapped his glass idly with his fingernail, nodding at nothing. He was convinced Edgar had forced the plane down. Nothing could ever make him change his mind.

And he would bet the next day would bring news of Edgar's apparent survival.

He'd known it the moment that young cop told him: "We can't find him."

As he shuffled down his hall, back toward the bedroom, the Tireless Question again reared its head. What the fuck, really, was a sane person doing this for?

As usual, there was no answer forthcoming from the

Martinian brain. This time there wasn't even much of the feeling that usually responded.

Garth Cheesbro, his most trusted, complete, total friend since their second year at UCLA, had followed him into the hell of Edgar Lamp's reality and had not come back. Sure, Garth had been curious. He'd wanted to see what Husky's shoes felt like, wanted to get involved and know about the life his friend lived. Maybe it was an exhilarating personal drive to salvage a fading ego, too. Garth was proving to be a real journalist who got out there and risked and dug and scrambled, instead of one who simply listened to the radio and commented.

Husky hated himself because he hadn't protected the man; because he hadn't been able to see shadows in shadows. So now he felt and appeared truly defeated. An aging blunderer in his dark house. He knew of course that *nobody* could see shadows in shadows . . . not really . . . but rational truths like that didn't matter when it was Garth, for Christ's sake, who'd been killed. Not if Husky was the man's friend, not if he wanted more than anything for the man to be alive, well, and safe. Then there was no excuse, anywhere in his heart or head, for normal failings.

Husky reached the bedroom. More dishevelment. It struck him with photographic clarity: this was not the bedroom of a hero. He'd always wanted to be one. Hence writer turns cop, chooses real man tests over imagined. Hence old friend *assumes* he somehow will high-wire the Edgar Lamps of this world when they cut the Garth Cheesbros from the pack and move for their kills.

He wanted another drink, but he'd left the bottle back at the far end of the house. He dimly hoped for alcohol poisoning and the easy solution of simply not waking up. Bullshit, he thought. No commuted sentences for despondent cops.

He felt a little short of breath as he hit the bed. Sweaty, achy, unable to find comfort even in his own familiar sheets. His eyes wanted to be open. Here, as in his office, he scanned familiar ceiling fissures for the millionth time, playing automatic little eyeball games from unconscious habit, regardless of mood. He found he couldn't do it so well intoxicated; he lost focus as the cracks neared the walls and came together.

The expected, comforting rocking of the bed happened just as it always did. Fred had lumbered in with him, sniffed around the room making sure no space cats had dropped from another dimension while he was out, and now joined the boss on the bed. Husky waited while the ritual finished itself. Fred turned a few times, picked his spot, and settled with an epic dog sigh.

With that sigh, Husky was remembering it again. For the thousandth time since he'd actually lived it that night, his mind went over the confusion and anger he'd felt there on the sand. First, the realization that the body under the blanket was Garth.

Then the increasing awareness and feeling that everything was even more oddly out of control than first look would imply.

After all, Husky had personally allowed so much of it to happen.

He sagged physically under the realization of his own responsibility.

He'd felt a sudden, nagging urge to hurry up and get back to the car. Envisioned himself running for it so he could drive away, denying he'd been such a towering *fool*.

Somewhere in these memories, recollections flowed seamlessly into dream time. Even then, Husky's awareness that Edgar Lamp had humiliated him did not leave. Garth had been used as a terrible weapon.

But finally, in Husky's dream, Garth had come back

from death, miraculously able to carry on life despite his shattering injuries. In the dream, Husky threw his arms around his old friend, cried boy's tears with him and promised never to let it happen again. Never, never, never. He would always see shadows in shadows and know where the evil lay.

Dreams are short, but paths the subconscious then follows during sleep last the night. They expand, change, and twist simple dreams to elongated confusions.

But Husky's didn't change. The boy's tears remained, the sworn promise of protection, and the oath of never, never, never.

He slept, with brief periods of waking, until late afternoon the next day. Fred slept, too, between periods of watching his master's sleep-changing face.

Twelve

"SHAKE 'EM LOOSE, Husky, c'mon . . ."

The voice was familiar. It soothed while it commanded.

He wanted to be asleep and not hear this. He wasn't ready to face anybody. This would've been a good time to simply withdraw, mysteriously leave town. Send a kiss-off letter to the office from a remote cabin in the Ozarks, from which he would never return.

"You can't bullshit me, Husky. You never could. I know damn well you're wide awake and hoping I'll give up."

His lids still didn't open, but he was now certain it was Marge Glass. She'd come to reassemble her shattered boss.

"How'd you get in?" he asked, eyes still shut. His voice sounded like he'd been on a year-long drunk instead of one lousy night.

"You gave me keys a year and a half ago."

Now his eyes opened. He couldn't remember why he'd ever done such a thing.

She read his mind.

"You had a slight case of pneumonia, which you played for all it was worth. I got keys to come and go and bring you my bad soup. I didn't give 'em back."

"Why didn't you just follow your instincts? Become a full-fledged Salvation Army colonel or something?" He sounded more snappish than he'd really intended as he sat up. His head felt like it was decomposing before death.

"The outfits make me look fatter," she said.

"They're supposed to, so nobody wants to jump your salvating bones. Jesus, is there a spear in my skull?"

"I couldn't find one."

He scowled.

"It's good we can have these talks, Marge. Makes it worth waking up. Did you think I'd gone out and killed myself?"

For a moment there was real concern, real love in her eyes. Neither of them could stand that for very long.

"I kind of hoped you'd stayed in to do it. You know, Roman bathtub job. Stuff runs down the drain, easy cleanup."

"How 'bout if I just promise to keep it in mind?"

She sat on the bed beside him and put a hand on his forearm. This seemed odd. Was she going to do something incredibly uncomfortable like confess how much she'd always cared about him?

"Took this blow pretty low, didn't you?"

"Oh . . ." He wasn't ready for the direct approach, "Yeah. You know, it was . . . probably lower than the belt."

"I'm sorry, Husky. Anybody could understand . . . you felt like hell and you got tanked. I would, too. And then I'd expect you to come over to my house and kick my butt out of bed."

It crept up on his face, but he had to smile. She held her

172

arms out for him. It seemed just right, just fine that he should accept her hug. They held one another a long time, attended only by Fred, who had opted for the rug in front of the closet.

"Thanks," he said softly, still hugging, feeling a little better.

He didn't even mind when she patted his back. Not when he owed her this much.

"I don't know if I can go back to the office, Marge. I don't know if I'm ever gonna see that place the same way now."

They broke the hug. She took a long, searching look at him. He was surprised to see his star cynic of the Investigatory Typing Pool could tear up a little bit herself.

"Put the decision off."

"Until what?"

"I don't know . . ." She looked away, shrugging, vague. He watched, unable to read her thoughts.

"You've heard something," he said, finally.

This brought her eyes back to his.

"I just think I might've come too soon. You probably need a lot of time and I got all caught up."

"I don't need more time." He smiled, looking at his bedside clock. It read six.

"Is that six as in the next night?"

She nodded, still not opening up.

"Tell me. What happened to get you . . . caught up so completely?"

She looked at him, making up her mind to get on with it.

"Skakel and Purdue."

"What about 'em?"

"They're in your living room. Chief had 'em follow up on a couple things and it pretty much locked down the fact that Lamp lived through it."

173

Husky started to climb out of bed, slowed only slightly by the fact that his head felt like a balloon.

"Make 'em some coffee. Make me some coffee, too, while you're at it."

She was watching him with a faint smile.

"What?" he asked.

And only then did he realize he was wearing just his shorts.

"I must've been pretty drunk. I usually remember to take 'em off."

She got up and started toward the door, smiling back over her shoulder.

"Probably for the best. Considering it's our first date."

"Hey," he said. "It got pretty shitty last night, Marge. It's a lot easier with somebody around the next morning. I'm glad it's you."

He watched after her as she smiled, avoided his eyes, and closed the door. He was alone now with Fred, who seemed utterly bored.

"This gets in the police newsletter, Freddy, I know who I'm coming after."

He started for the bathroom, marveling at the elasticity of the human mood muscle. He was deeply depressed about Garth, yet he'd just shared his first semi-warmth with Marge Glass. He could even have seen himself coming on to her.

The oddest feeling of all was the gallows humor. Cops relied on death-scene laughter as a fair feint around the tall, dark faceless guy with the hood. Husky'd never been overly big on it personally, yet now he made flirty quips with a lady he'd known since Christ was a busboy. Not twenty-four hours after his best friend had been murdered, like everybody else who died on that plane.

The bathroom mirror showed him a rumpled, gray, unshaven translation of the Guy Inside. He looked like a car

174

wreck, searching his own eyes for some reply to his feelings of guilt.

No reply. Just a disquieting conclusion: you're better off than Garth.

That was survival talking. He fumbled for razor and foam. Husky Martin, survivor. Fact was he would've returned to the office sooner or later, and he'd known it all along. You get friends, you lose them, same as your family. Your walls get knocked down but you come back to do your business. There was no other choice, unless you wanted to be like those guys pushing shopping carts down Hollywood Boulevard. They wore batting helmets to fend off falling meteor particles. They wrecked the view for sightseers. Husky was never gonna be one of those guys. Never gonna wind up a ragman or a cardboard hoarder or a sleeper in that little park along Franklin with the modern free-form concrete statuary benches. No sidewalk mattress for this boy.

He started to shave.

He never considered cutting a little deeper to solve his problems.

■ ■ ■ ■ ■

Skakel and Purdue sat with Marge in Husky's living room, staring at the floor and feeling uneasy.

"What do we say to him?" Purdue wanted to know.

Skakel looked at his partner, shrugged. "What you say to anybody, I guess."

"He'll be all right," Marge said quietly, not sounding entirely like she believed her own assurance.

Husky came out with a somewhat sheepish smile on his face, spotting the coffeepot and moving right for it. Marge poured while he held his cup.

"Sorry you guys had to come down here . . ."

"Don't give it another thought, sir . . ." Purdue felt like a bonehead the moment he started talking, and his words sort of hung there.

Husky knew exactly what he was feeling, and smiled at the young officer.

"Thanks." He sat down in an easy chair and took a sip. Smiled. The room was mortuary quiet, and he finally sighed. "C'mon, guys, if I didn't break last night I'm not gonna start now."

"We got this call from some guy saw a very strange white male walking down the beach away from the crash last night. Says the guy stared at him, scared the hell out of him." Skakel was red-faced as he spoke.

"Could've been a traumatized witness."

"Possible. But the guy in the apartment said he felt like he couldn't move to get out of this guy's sight."

Husky frowned. "What the hell's that mean?"

"Take your pick, sir," said Purdue. "We were inclined to write it off till we got to the next call, which was a German shepherd a little farther down south along the beach."

Now Husky just listened. Playing devil's advocate had just about run its course of practicality. Skakel picked up for Purdue.

"The animal had wounds that looked a whole lot like the old ladies and that guy up in the Hollywood Hills."

"El Chocolate Grande . . ."

"Yeah. Chest cavity wide open, internal organs gone."

"He did this to an animal?" Marge couldn't believe it. Skakel went on.

"Then we get back to the car and get a call down to Redondo, where we find this guy sprawled across a Chevy and *he's* got his torso pried open, too."

"ID on the victim?" Husky asked.

176

"None yet." Purdue shook his head. "He was cleaned and there were no eyewitnesses. Guy who owned the Chevy had no idea what kind of car was in the next slot."

"What about prints?"

"Lab's on the guy's clothes and the car he was laying on."

"They won't get shit." Husky looked away, tapping fingers on the arm of his chair. He was thinking, mind racing, trying to come up with some reason *not* to believe all this was Edgar Lamp in action. "What about powder burns? Powder burns around either the dog or the guy?"

"Sorry." Skakel sighed. "Looked like the guy exploded out, just like the dog."

Husky just looked back at them, but he wasn't seeing them. He was seeing Garth on the sand last night.

And now he could add a mental image: Edgar Lamp walking away.

Husky looked at Marge. "Musta been thrown through the roof into the water, huh?"

She could only look sympathetic to his pain.

"Sir, if you've got any kind of idea what all this is . . . that Lamp's doing, I mean"—Purdue was trying to be forthright without being callous—"could you tell us just what the hell goes on with the guy?"

Husky stared at the young cop for a moment, then finally nodded as he rose from the chair to get another cup of coffee.

"We think he does it with his mind, Officers." He looked over at their confusion. "How's that? Make it any easier to understand?"

"No, sir." Skakel's reply was flat. "You wouldn't be shitting us at a time like this, would you, sir?"

Husky sadly shook his head. He took a sip.

"Here it is. Whatever else Lamp is, he's a highly active homicidal sociopath. He runs in phases just like any of those guys. When he gets tired he might lay low. He might just melt into the framework and go normal on us for months, become fucking impossible to find. While he's resting up, he could have a sudden attack of brains and get the hell out of town, which means we lose him and somebody else has to figure him out all over again." Husky came a bit closer to Skakel and Purdue. "I really don't *want* to lose him, guys."

"Draw him out," said Skakel.

"Very good. Man's on his way to detective ranking . . . written all over his mug." Husky slapped Skakel on the shoulder, actually grinning, but with an almost insane intensity in his eyes. "And you know how we do it? We use Garth."

"Husky . . ." Marge couldn't help herself. The sadness in her tone said it all.

"You think I'm nuts? I'm not nuts. I'm not avoiding here, I accept that he's dead. I'm talking about his *book*. I know what's in there, and I know how to grab Edgar Lamp right by the gonads. You do it with his screwball grandmother." Husky smiled at the ceiling. "Thank you, Garth."

"What can you do with the old lady?" Marge asked, almost afraid to hear.

"Fly her out here. In fact, Marge, I want you to get down to the office and get on the phone. Work it out so she's got a plane in and a plane out, same day, tomorrow."

"Will she cooperate?" Skakel wanted to know.

"All the way. She's scared to death of him, hates like hell having him in the family. Said so in Garth's notes." He smiled. "You know, when all this shit's over, I'm gonna move fucking heaven and earth to get that thing printed just the same."

"What do I tell her?"

"Tell her we'll protect her start to finish. She'll be out of

178

town and back on the plane so fast she won't believe it. We'll make him think she's staying in L.A. awhile. Once that happens, we keep ourselves on close watch, just like we have been."

■　■　■　■　■

Skakel and Purdue had promised Husky they'd sit on their knowledge of how Lamp seemed to work. This didn't keep them from enjoying a relatively good existence the day after their discoveries of the dog and the body on the Chevy hood.

Their report had started one of the department's finer betting pools, dealing with how the fuck this guy Lamp did his stuff. They'd been treated pretty well around the station. Give 'em a bet, they loved you.

As night fell, big money was sitting in the death-by-crowbar column, but the chain-saw theory was doing brisk business.

Skakel and Purdue had opted to remain above the betting, though they could've gone for "none of the above" without betraying Husky's confidence. But both decided they were just too damn close to the investigation and the truth was probably *too* ugly.

This was harder for Purdue, a single man known to haunt racetracks on weekends.

Skakel, however, was married with a daughter in college and a son halfway through high school. Any old betting temptations had long since given way to fear of wifely reprisal. She'd've been right, too. Kids really did tend to run up costs, plus the outside of the house was due for painting this summer. And sooner or later they'd better put something aside to give the pension he was building a little booster shot.

He was talking about how anemic those police pensions were in this town when the call came over the radio.

Their black-and-white rolled to a stop behind the Safeway. About six people stood around the dumpster. These people lived in houses bordering the supermarket parking lot and in an apartment house nearby.

"It's in the dumpster, Officers." The voice was a young girl.

"What's that?" Skakel knew it was a body from the call, but when you got out, you let people answer. Answers could lead to somebody saying too much.

"The dead girl, Laura Rumph," she said.

"You know her personally or you find her ID?" Purdue looked at the girl.

"I live a couple apartments down from her. We're in that building over there." She pointed.

Purdue nodded. "Your name?"

"Cathy Marcus."

"You last saw her when?"

"I don't know . . . last weekend maybe? We talk Saturdays 'cause she works nights and I'm days."

Skakel had gone to check the dumpster. Laura Rumph was in a green trash bag. She was a small girl, but a quick look through the violent rips in the plastic told him she was lighter now than usual.

A man who told them he was Carl Furillo, no relation to the ballplayer, said he'd heard two dogs having a death match out here by the dumpster. His house was the one just on the other side of the cinder-block wall, right across from it. He said the only time he'd ever heard dogs go at it like that was over meat or something.

"Is that what they were doing?" Cathy Marcus asked. "Eating her body?"

"Probably starting to," Purdue said, looking grim.

180

Skakel's look told him this was no dog's dinner. They managed to get the bag out of the dumpster. Carl Furillo was right with them, watching everything.

"We called you guys first, then we called the emergency number they post on the front of the market. Night manager oughta be here pretty quick."

Skakel scoped his watch. Four-thirty. Even night managers were sleeping at this time.

The two police officers took everybody's statement about how the dogs had been chased away with hoses and rocks. The funny thing was nobody'd noticed the body until they'd all gone home and the two animals had come back to start their battle all over again. Couple great big Labs or something, Furillo told them. It had been then that he looked to see what they wanted so bad. He'd only done it because he suspected meat, and thought it was against some kind of law for supermarkets to leave meat out like that.

"The bag was ripped like that when you found her?"

"Wide open. One of 'em got here first I guess, then the other must've showed up and challenged him." Furillo was shaken by what he'd seen before, and by the better look he had at Laura Rumph's bagged body now, lying on the pavement. "I've seen a lotta dead people, but I never saw anybody half eaten, you know?"

After the coroner's buggy came and carted the remains away, complete with now familiar oddly bent ribs, Skakel and Purdue went with Cathy Marcus back to her apartment. She offered hot chocolate. They passed, preferring a look at Laura Rumph's apartment, car, anything that could turn out to be the death scene.

There hadn't been enough blood in that dumpster.

It turned out to be the parking stall. Cathy Marcus gasped when their flashlights hit the empty slot. There was a wash of crimson on the next car, as well as all over

181

the padlocked storage unit where Laura Rumph kept her extra belongings.

"What did he shoot her with, a cannon?"

Neither cop answered. It was just like the scene at the beach. Lamp had done it here, then obviously decided it would be better to bag her and dump her across the road. Probably figured it'd take longer to trace back.

"You wouldn't know her license number, would you?"

"What?"

"He took her car, miss."

Cathy Marcus stared at the empty space. Of course he did. She tried to remember. Come on, she told herself, you know her license plate, you've seen it ten thousand times. Cathy was the assistant manager here, she made it a practice to know numbers, faces, names. Then she got it.

"One bedroom, six twenty-five."

"Excuse me?" Skakel said. Maybe the girl was buckling on them.

"That's how I remember numbers. I make little words and sentences out of them. One bedroom six twenty-five is her license. One, B-D-R, six-two-five."

■ ■ ■ ■ ■

Husky wanted nothing more than to personally kill Edgar Lamp, but he knew when to put aside emotions and play the ball as it was hit.

The suspect was driving around in a Honda Accord, license number 1BDR625, color something like metallic tan or gold. It went on the computer, went out to every unit rolling in the city. He wanted particularly intense scrutiny on the hobo circuit, places like the freeway underpass where he and Garth had been directed toward Skidrow Scav.

182

Laura Rumph had been found two hours after her estimated time of death, according to Sillitoe over at the coroner's office. Sillitoe was starting to cooperate, having seen enough emptied abdomens and chest cavities. He'd also found this latest victim particularly upsetting since she bore a mild resemblance to his own daughter.

Marge found Husky staring at his office clock as she was heading home.

"Doing okay?"

He nodded at her; a tired smile.

"Make you some dinner if you want."

"Best offer I've had in a helluva long time, Marge." He thought for a moment. "Might be over real late, if you don't mind."

She didn't.

"Don't forget to watch the news," he told her.

"Faithfully. Just tell me you'll call if you need anything." Was she making a fool of herself? Snappy banter had gotten real old, real fast. Garth's death and Husky's reaction had unmasked the dishonesty of her cynical "normal" relations with Husky. It forced her real feelings.

"I'll call," he finally said. "Either way, I'll call."

With a slightly awkward smile, she left. For reasons she couldn't quite pin down, she hurried home.

■ ■ ■ ■ ■

After Alice Lamp Corinth was picked up at the Los Angeles International Airport, she was brought to Husky Martin's office at Parker Center in downtown L.A.

"You're sure you'll be willing to do this to your own grandson?" he asked.

"Mister," she said in East Texas tones, "I got plenty of

183

reason to take blame for that boy, and plenty of reason to hate his guts. Blood or no."

It was good enough for Husky, who ushered her down to his own car. He was taking her to a television studio.

As he drove, he tried to place her. Alice Lamp Corinth looked so familiar it drove him crazy at first. Finally, memory broke through.

Queen Victoria. Round face, nose line, severely back-pulled hair and small, missionary's eyes. All that with the severe long-sleeved, high-necked, buttoned-up aura of farm women getting heavy after condemning themselves to Red Cross shoes and light-resistant stockings. This woman had tossed in her cards in the femininity game.

"Jesus don't plan for babies to grow up like Edgar. I know Edgar, saw him real clear from when he first lived with me and Harper. There was no possible peace 'tween him and his grandpa." She looked over at Husky with a stare that commanded response. "That boy drove a grown man from his own home. He drove him out, hunted after him, and just plain terrified him to death."

Husky didn't know what to say . . . didn't know that she wanted him to say anything. How the hell did anybody endure this woman? Finally, Husky picked up the conversation.

"Y'know . . . it's always bothered me that nobody could prove a hand was ever laid on Harper Lamp . . ."

"I told you. He terrified the man. Edgar can do that to most people. Except me."

"Really?"

She nodded.

"Always been just the other way 'round. Edgar isn't scared of a single soul on this earth except his grandma, Mr. Martin."

"Is that why you're willing to come out here? Because you think he's afraid of you and he'd never hurt you?"

184

"Partly. Other part's I know the only way to catch Edgar. And I figure he's about humiliated his family and mankind in general long enough."

Husky wondered just what brand of loonball he was driving to the TV station. She was still on her own train of thought.

"The way to catch that boy, Mr. Martin, is through *me.*"

"Mrs. Corinth . . . that's why I sent for you. That's why I'm having you flown right back out of here and home again just as soon as we're done this evening."

"*No!*" she shouted, surprising the hell out of him. "I wanna be around when he's caught."

"That's suicidal."

"That's your opinion," she snapped back. "When he was eight years old he told me, 'Grandma, I think you should die, but I'm scared to do it myself.' Now, you really think after a thing like that, I don't want to stay here and see him caught with my own eyes?"

"He's been *caught* before." Husky stared at the road, sighed, and said it: "What's got to happen is a good deal more final than that."

He felt her gaze.

"Y'know, you're the first policeman's come right out and said what I've known for years. Only way anyone . . . *anyone* gets rid of Edgar's by killing him just as sure as I'm sitting here."

"You talk mighty tough for somebody's grandma."

"You oughta talk just as tough." She almost smiled.

Husky shook his head.

"Look, I know what I'm up against here. You might not. He's not the boy you knew. He's the smartest damn killer I've ever heard of. He lives for nothing else, he has no sense of wrongdoing. It's like his victims are playing pieces in some kind of game he's playing against us."

"Against *you,* Mr. Martin. Don't be bashful. It's you

185

personally. Which is *why* I said you oughta talk tough, too."

"Because I caught him . . ."

"Damn right. See, in a whole lotta ways right now, you and me're the same thing to him. And after that business with the plane, I don't see how you can do anything but chase him till he's dead."

"Funny, I thought that's what I was doing . . ."

She wasn't laughing.

"So you believe Edgar caused that crash outright?"

This just made her mad.

"Mr. Martin, you ain't nobody's idiot. You know Edgar's beyond the whys and wherefores of some fool with a six-shooter."

"He's done a lot of shooting."

"Throwin' you a change-up. He ain't the biggest problem in this city 'cause he uses a gun."

"How the hell do you know *that?*"

" 'Cause I know him. And like I *told* you, my first husband was *terrified to death.* I don't know what *you* call it, but I call it the *mind.* I can feel it in my own . . . I don't really know how, but it's there. I *know* when he kills. You understand? I have the knowledge that it's happened. I sense it. I die a little bit inside myself every time and I'm damn *sick* of it!"

She was leaning closer to Husky now in the car, her voice a tremulous, foggy whisper of emotion and conviction.

"Does he know this?"

She shook her head; no.

"I still can't let you stay."

It was a stalemate, which meant Husky was the winner. She'd come into town on his ticket, his invitation and bidding. She was being transported by the police department, and as such was a cooperating witness. If she quit cooperating, he could take her into custody and simply *eject* her from the city.

"It's a shame, Mr. Martin. I was pretty much convinced that I would like you . . ."

■ ■ ■ ■ ■

When Alice Lamp Corinth saw the television cameras before her, she was intimidated. She shook visibly. Her voice had a tremble in it, but her eyes showed steely on the monitors. Three local stations would carry her message to Edgar.

"I'm using this chance to talk personally to my grandson, Edgar Lamp. Edgar, I hope you hear me sayin' this. If there's any harm you want to do to someone, you come do it to your grandmother. You never did have much use for me or your grandpa, but we both know you were scared to death of me when you were little. Now you're a great big bad man and you shouldn't have any such fear." She paused a moment as flashbulbs chattered. "If you think about it, you know you've got to come lookin' for me. I'm down at the Hilton Ho-tel in the middle of Los Angeles. You can call, or you can just show. I won't tell you there's no police, 'cause you know they'll be around. But the fight's ours, Edgar. Any way you want to set it up when you phone. Any time, any place, any conditions. I'm not afraid of you, though I may look old and frail and foolish."

And with a nod to the cameras, she stepped down.

While the videotape was sent to the three local stations for showing later—though all three had agreed to call it live—Alice Lamp Corinth, scowling and refusing to speak to any police officer about anything, was rushed to the airport.

187

Her plane was off the ground before the tape was ever shown. Husky breathed a sigh. He'd kept her clear of the monster. Now all he had to do was hope the bastard would try and show his face somewhere near the Hilton.

Of course, he didn't believe it for a moment.

That Honda with the 1BDR625 license plate was a far better bet.

Thirteen

EDGAR LAMP was holed up in San Pedro. He didn't like this shitbag room in this shitbag hotel, but it was easier to get lost down here.

He looked out his window. The docks started two blocks away. Everything in the area was longshoremen's halls, union local offices, and fishermen's bullshit. Equipment businesses, groups of mumbling Italians, Greeks, and Mexicans hanging around waiting for some boat to crew up or unload.

It bored him. Small-time. But maybe going to sea a while wouldn't be that bad. There must be somebody around here willing to take a guy with no union card. There always was. But in a funny way Edgar would've felt trapped out there walking around the decks of one little boat. Like a helicopter could swoop down, out comes the sharpshooter's barrel and scope, and pop-pop. He imagined himself hitting the water, over the side, never knowing a thing by the time he was wet.

189

Then there was the cop, Martin. Suppose Martin somehow found out he was on some boat. It wouldn't be that hard. There were people who might know his face, might tell a cop anything to make a deal. Then when the boat checked in someplace, Edgar would step ashore and into the last scene of a bad crime movie.

No, the thing to do was sit tight in this hotel about twenty-four hours, maybe less, then take the car he'd gotten from that girl he bagged and drive right the fuck out of L.A.

Maybe it'd even be better to change cars again before he made the move. Cover his ass on the license plate. Thinking this over, he turned on the TV set.

They were playing the tape of Edgar's grandmother on the news. She was just stepping up to the microphones. He watched wide-eyed, not breathing at first, feeling that same old cold creep over his skin.

He hunkered into a catcher's squat and stared at the screen, inches away as she talked, looking earnestly out at him. Talking right to him.

Right away, he started thinking it was a cop trap. They could be doing it any number of ways. They could figure he'd show up at the hotel and of course *she* wouldn't be there, only cops. If he called her at the number of the hotel they'd trace it. They could figure damn near anything.

There was no doubt, she was here to end him. To get her vengeance.

He had to think clearly because it would mean his life.

Still, he couldn't stop watching her. Couldn't stop getting angrier and angrier. That bitch, back in his reality, playing with his brain! And right now, just when he was feeling his power. Just when he was running that cop all over town like a dog after a Tampax!

"Shit!" he shouted, and snapped off the set, glaring at it.

He stomped back and forth in the room. The cops, he

reminded himself. Think about *them*. He knew cops never slept, never gave up on you when you were hot shit. He assumed Martin planned the whole thing. Again he tried to think—should he just haul ass now, or what?

The Honda had been sitting along the curb almost nine hours. When the first officers spotted it, they quietly questioned people up and down the street. In the ugly green hotel directly across the street from the car, they found out about a scraggly young man. Fairly tall and thin, by himself, no suitcases, belongings, or much of anything. He'd checked in the night before. The manager wasn't sure he'd been driving the Honda, but then she hadn't seen the car on this street before, and yes, it'd been there quite a while now. It felt like a good maybe.

San Pedro put out the word, which jolted everybody back at headquarters. Husky Martin heard it and was moving for the door, coat in hand, before the sentence was out of Detective Patton's mouth. Patton just watched him, worrying. He turned to another cop nearby.

"Hair of the dog," Patton said.

Husky felt the same way. It wasn't all that bad going out again so soon after Garth. Maybe it was just the idea of seeing fifty SWAT guns validate the last of Edgar's Green Stamps. Maybe it was just for this one last time.

"Bullshit," he said to himself aloud.

Back inside, Patton remembered calling Husky at Dr. Beerey's office in the middle of the root canal. Husky hadn't given much of a shit then. Maybe he'd been bored with Edgar Lamp. Or scared of him.

But now the fact was Edgar Lamp somehow invigorated Husky Martin. Not a point cops often admit, but Patton recognized the syndrome. He'd gone through it. You almost wanted to thank the fucking perpetrator for putting you back on your game, getting your blood pumping for the job again.

Almost.

It was about six-forty now. Edgar was feeling the cramp again. He got it, though he didn't know how, every time something bad was about to go down. Suddenly the room would shrink around him. It would get hard to breathe. Maybe the feeling was related to being able to do Provings, he didn't know. Maybe he had powers other people just didn't have—this he figured was probably true. Right now he wasn't dwelling on it. He was simply realizing he'd better pay attention.

His fear that cops were figuring out his hiding place had been growing in his belly for a little while now. He'd checked the window several times. He didn't like the Plymouth parked right behind the Honda he'd taken. He didn't like the two guys in real casual jackets and jeans— too casual—who'd gotten out of the Plymouth to start walking the neighborhood.

At first he'd thought they were salesmen going door to door, or collection guys. Then again maybe they were a couple of those preachers who stood out in your hallway telling you real loud through the door, "We've got the word out here."

Yeah, thought Edgar, and I got something for you in here.

But the other possibility, that they were cops looking for him, had welled up to supersede everything.

When you're playing halfback against the Man, somebody had warned him in county jail, you *always* assume it's him outside the door. You figure every car behind you on the freeway for a pigmobile. You do it all the time, maybe you never get caught.

Why the fuck had he waited so long? He could walk out

192

of here into a *worse* pork jam than he'd envisioned coming off some boat!

He pulled the gun out from between his spring and mattress and opened the door. One of the two guys he'd seen walking around was now standing at the end of the hallway, by the front door. The other wasn't around; at least not visible.

The cop had made a mistake. He was framed from behind by the early evening daylight-savings-time sun, standing out like a motherfucker. He crouched a little in surprise to actually look down the hall and *see* Edgar Lamp, King Shit himself, with a gun aimed at him.

Nobody in any of the rooms heard a thing because of the silencer. Edgar thought it was like a Charlie Chaplin movie as he watched the left side of the cop's body splatter the wall beside him, bright crimson on the dull green. The guy jerked right back out through the open archway and down the steps, tumbling onto the walk. All silent.

There was no way Edgar would go out that front door. There was a staircase a couple steps away, and he took it. As he did, he noticed how the hall smelled like ten thousand drunken tuna fishermen had pissed in it for a hundred years. The banister was rickety when he grabbed it. He wished he was already on the road.

Down and behind him he heard a voice call out. It said, "Wes?" That would be the second cop finding the first on the walk outside. Edgar was on the second-floor landing now. He picked a door and silently blew the knob off it.

Inside a young Chicana was nursing her child, alone in the room. The unexpected glimpse of her breasts amused Edgar. It also got him instantly hard, but there was no time to pursue the matter. The woman stood up, still holding the baby to her breast, outraged and unashamed of her half nakedness. She didn't seem to care that he had a gun

193

as big as a Pontiac. She glared back as he looked at her milk-enlarged breasts.

Finally he said, "You got a car?"

"What the fuck do you think you're doing?" Her English was without accent, which surprised him. He took another look at her face. Intelligent, pissed off. He smiled.

"You know, I might come back for you," he told her. Then he said, "I asked if you had a car." He raised the gun toward the baby. "It'd help if you did."

"My husband took it to work," she said, eyes on the gun.

Edgar could tell it was the truth. He looked out the window of her apartment, which was roughly above his own. Now there were more cars, several just pulling up, some even your outright black-and-whites. The plainclothes cop who had called out "Wes" was talking to other, uniformed cops. Edgar realized this was not the room he should be in. This was *facing* the street, giving them the advantage. He left the room without another word, but he winked at the still staring, still nursing woman.

He bolted down the second-floor hallway of the rotting old building. God, he hated it here. The place shook when he ran. He shot off another knob, this one to an apartment at the very back. It would face out on the alley and the parking places, such as they were, for long-term tenants.

Oscar Navarette, a squat little man living at the hotel until he could persuade his wife to accept him back into their North Hollywood apartment, had been sound asleep.

Oscar thought this was punishment. Maybe his wife had finally made good her threat to hire a killer. You could never understand women, Oscar had long ago decided. All he wanted was a little side action from her son's wife. Surely the son, Raúl, would have understood. But not Oscar's wife, the big shot cleaning lady with her high morals

194

and all the secret money she saved from the side jobs she never told him about.

So Oscar, rising up in his T-shirt and pathetic baggy Jockey shorts, shouted in Spanish that this was ridiculous, that a man should not have to live in fear and die in his bed just because he had wanted to put his dick maybe in the wrong place. He was just a goddamn man like any other, wasn't he?

The question, for Oscar, was answered in a way he hadn't expected. The intruder, Edgar Lamp, moved even as Oscar protested, to the key chain on the gritty dinette at the other end of the room. One of the keys had GM imprinted on it. That was all Edgar needed.

"You speak English?" he demanded.

Oscar stopped. Questions on being bilingual weren't what he'd anticipated.

"I . . . am a man of the world."

Edgar didn't smile, though he thought it was pretty funny. He stepped quickly up to Oscar, the gun aiming at those T-shirted ribs, and reached down.

Oscar gasped as he felt Edgar's fingers go inside the waistband of his shorts to pull it wide open. Then he closed his eyes as Edgar pointed the gun right down into his open shorts, until the smooth nose of the silencer pressed directly against Oscar's right testicle.

"You don't do exactly what I want, you won't be a man at *all*."

Oscar looked into Edgar's face and waited. He would follow every instruction.

"Just tell me what you want."

What Edgar wanted was to open the window over the parking slots. Then he made Oscar, still in his T-shirt and shorts, jump down into the back of a pickup and wait while Edgar did the same. "Move it," he whispered with a wave of the gun.

Oscar did, his balls still aching from the mere idea. That awful pressure.

Edgar had known it; the guy drove a five-year-old Impala. He ordered Oscar behind the wheel. Edgar would hide in back with his gun aimed right through the seat at Oscar. All he wanted was to be driven out of this place. Then he wanted one hour on the freeway in any direction, after which he would get out and walk out of Oscar's life. Oscar nodded enthusiastically, wondering if his eagerness betrayed how much he wanted to be rid of this asshole with the ball-killing gun.

"Let's go." Edgar cut off his thoughts. "But remember, I know what you're thinking, motherfucker."

Oscar put the car into reverse to pull out. What did that mean? He didn't have time to mull it over. The first and hardest part became immediately clear. He would have to drive past a growing cluster of police. But a quick look around told him they hadn't cordoned anything off. He saw a left turn would take him past fewer of them, so he went that way.

"Good boy," Edgar said from behind.

But Oscar knew Edgar couldn't see from his vantage below the seat back. So how did he know? It wasn't a good idea to inquire.

The Impala passed within twenty feet of Husky Martin, who had just parked and was heading toward the shitbag hotel, which was about to be completely surrounded. Husky was focused on the building, figuring it for escapes and defenses, but he noticed the Impala.

"Who's that?"

"Some Mexican," said the young detective who'd found Wes on the walk.

"Sure?"

The young detective was sure. He'd gotten a good look.

196

"One more greaser in one more dirty white T-shirt going out for a drive in his chopped Chebby."

"Shut up, son," said Husky.

In the Impala, Edgar stayed low. He said, "Get on the freeway, head downtown." It would be easier to melt in down there. He would make Oscar park someplace, climb into the front seat with the guy, and do one more belly-rooter job in L.A.

One for the road.

Then he remembered what had triggered all this. He felt sure the cops had set it up with Grandma Alice. They must've known where he was and wanted him glued to his TV while they got him in their sights. Well—he smiled—King Shit didn't catch easy and now they'd be getting the point.

But so would Grandma. She wanted him to come settle with her, she could damn well bet she had a deal. What did she figure to do, hit him with a fucking switch? He suddenly knew just what to do. He was going back home. All the way back. Go down there, wait her out till she came home and she was all alone, figuring he'd never show. Then he'd step out of a shadow to watch her ugly fat face shake and her mean-bitch eyes just bust their sockets.

Maybe he would even *make* them bust their sockets. For a moment, he wondered if he could. Shit, of course he could. He'd just never tried. There were reams of things he'd never tried.

He'd get to them.

Fourteen

"You're sure it was Lamp in that place . . ." Marge knew damn well it was Lamp, just on her gut feeling. The thing was, she didn't want Husky going after him.

"Gimme a break, course we're sure."

"Couldn't've been some coke mule? Maybe he was laying low at the harbor till somebody he stiffed got sick of looking for him?"

He shook his head.

"Descriptions up the wazoo. The woman nursing her child practically got him to a T. She said she thought he used Mennen deodorant from the way he smelled. No shit, she really said that."

"Well, how exactly did he get away from the place with all those blues down there?"

"Forced some guy at gunpoint to drive out while he hid, I guess. We found the guy's doorknob blown off, and there was no car in his stall. Pretty standard, considering how brilliant Edgar's supposed to be."

198

"It worked," she said.

He nodded agreement.

There was uneasy silence in Marge's kitchen dinette. Husky sipped coffee; she just stared at the yellow vinyl floor.

"So when do you take off?"

"I drive."

"Where?" She looked at him now.

He thought about it first. "Texas."

"*Back* to Texas? Why should he do that? How do you know?"

"I just know," he told her. "It's the old lady. He didn't try downtown at the Hilton at all."

"No, he was busy with you." She laughed.

"He was hiding," Husky said. "The TV was warm in his room, tuned to one of the channels that ran the tape of his grandmother." He smiled. "He watched her. Do I know my assholes, or what?"

"What does that mean?"

His smile faded a little. "Means he hates her, he wanted to kill her, but he doesn't think for one second she's where she *said* she'd be."

Marge fiddled with her now empty cup. She'd downed it too quickly. Her stomach was knotting between it and the tension she felt.

"Wouldn't you think the guy's too smart to fall right into going after her to Texas?"

"No, I wouldn't. She's an emotional hook for him. Maybe the *only* emotional hook. So my gut tells me he's gonna snap back too quick, be out of control, maybe get caught with his ass hanging out."

"You wouldn't wanna get caught like that yourself, Husky. He's still the smart guy you've been talking about. He still pulls surprises out of his back pockets. You told me yourself."

"So, he figures I'm coming after him. But he won't know when." His smile tried to be apologetic. "I can't take a pass on this, Marge. Just can't."

"Why're you driving? Why don't you fly?"

" 'Cause he'll drive. No way he'll go near an airport 'cause he's number one on the surveillance hit parade and he's gotta know it. And if I drive I might catch him *before* he gets near Granny." He smiled. "I'd rather do it that way."

"It's so easy to lie in wait for some cop who's supposed to be following. Maybe *he'd* rather you do it that way, too."

"If I didn't know a whole lot better, Marge, I'd swear . . ."

"Don't swear. Just listen."

"No, you listen. I really might be able to catch him where he didn't figure he'd have to hide." He was talking serious; talking softly and quickly. "And who knows how many impulse victims he's gonna splatter just to give the trip a little topspin? Maybe I can keep him off their backs."

"Husky, I'm being selfish, okay? I don't wanna hear how they found you someplace. You understand?"

"I understand."

He was looking at her now. Closer than he'd ever had the nerve to before. She'd broken the ice, he thought. Can't blame me, it's her opening gambit. Now he knew he could follow up with any brazen asshole's line he wanted. He could always say he'd gotten the wrong impression because of what she'd said.

"You know, I didn't come down here to find out if the way I was handling the case earned your approval, Marge."

"Yeah?" She looked at him close now, too. Especially his eyes, which weren't ducking hers at all.

200

Something was going on.

"I came down here to thank you for pulling my ass out of the sling over at my house."

"Well, I didn't mind . . ."

"And for keeping quiet about when you heard . . . about Lamp and all that."

"Don't remind me."

"Okay."

And he moved forward across the table, this guy in his mid-fifties, and took Marge Glass's face in his hands, her face in her mid-forties, and kissed her like he was some college kid. Kissed her so it stuck, he thought to himself. Then he managed to stop thinking and just kiss. They hung over the table like that for several seconds. When they broke it off, she kept her eyes shut a few moments longer.

He was still looking at her that way when she opened them again.

Then she got up and moved to him, stood close to his still sitting body, and pressed him to her in one of those hang-on-let's-drown-together clutches. When he clutched back she let out the kind of involuntary sigh people are ashamed of unless they're just feeling and forgetting how to judge.

■　■　■　■　■

Downtown, Husky got himself a shitload of maps and road guides and sat hunched over his desk until he'd come up with what he thought was the best route to the little town of Gullickson, Texas.

He was worried about his dog, Fred. The family that normally looked after him didn't seem to be home. Then he remembered this was the week they were going up to Sequoia. Shit, now what?

For a second he thought maybe Garth could do it. The reflex was so automatic, so natural, it made the realization and memory a moment later that much more painful. You got into habits . . .

His next thought was Marge, but after the way they'd parted it would be ludicrous anticlimax to show up with his dog and ask her to baby-sit. No, Husky told himself, even the Great Lover Martin is more romantic than to undercut a success with good ol' Fred.

No, he'd think of some damn thing to do with Fred.

The chief's voice startled him from his doorway.

"Plotting your course, Martin?"

Husky just looked at him for a moment. What the fuck, give him the straight answer.

"I'm goin' after Lamp."

"Nice of you to let the department know."

"I would've. Just wanted to get myself prepared first. Should be leaving pretty quick."

"Gonna use your . . . clairvoyant abilities on this particular chase?"

Husky smiled. Nash watched him a moment, then nodded.

"You know where he went, don't you?"

"Well, Chief, I had the advantage of sitting in the interrogation room with Edgar quite a few times. I also had the advantage of knowing everything Garth managed to wheedle out of him, which was quite a lot."

"You're an officer of this department, Martin."

"I remember. And believe it or not, I'm loyal as hell."

Husky and Nash looked each other in the eye. Each weighed the other's sincerity.

"All right," Husky finally sighed. "He was always telling us how he'd make tracks up to Canada if he got the chance. Figured all that wide-open land would be easier to hide in."

"So you're assuming he's making a beeline up toward the border."

"Right now." Husky nodded. "And I'd love like hell to chase him, sir."

"I don't mind telling you I think you've gone a little bit nuts on this, Husky, I know you lost your friend. You think I'm immune to things like that, but I'm not."

"Damn sure could've fooled me sometimes." Husky figured he'd start slugging back.

"You wanna slice me up, you better cut deeper. I didn't make chief 'cause I cry over shit you hand out. What I was getting to is maybe you're more than a little nuts here, and maybe I'm pulling your ass off the case."

"The fuck you are!" Husky shouted.

"You're making a damn fool . . ."

"Who you gonna put on it? Skakel and Purdue? I know where the goddamn furniture is in the dark. Rest of this department doesn't know this case for shit."

"You're undoing your career." Nash had taken just about enough.

"Fuck my career." Husky was ready to go to the wall. He truly didn't give a shit. It became liberating when that happened. "You take me off the case, I save you the rest of the trouble. I'll walk my ass off the damn force and you have a good time finding the guy to take this office. I'll drive to Canada as a private citizen and do whatever I want."

The chief gaped at him for a moment. Then he did something Husky hadn't expected. He laughed. Not a bullshit laugh, a laugh of real amazement at how far the guy would go.

"All right," he finally said, amused but not friendly, "you wanna do your manhunt, I can stall forty-eight hours. Then I let the dogs loose. If you can do it faster than that, congratulations."

"Don't bullshit me, Chief."

"I wouldn't."

The guy was being straight. Husky looked closely at the chief, who gazed evenly back.

"You're gonna do it no matter what. I don't want the papers picking up some shit story of how a detective on my force quits to go kill America's number one homicidal maniac in cold blood as a free agent. I want the credit to come to *my* force, same as any damn chief." Nash saw Husky waking to the reality of who-gets-the-credit. "That's right, pal. You blow his ass right over the Canadian border. Then you show your LAPD badge when they come take pictures."

When he slapped Husky on the shoulder, Nash had no idea how close Husky came to belting him.

"You're on special assignment." The chief smiled, not trying to hide his opportunism or love of the game. "Follow that suspect north. Follow him to fucking hell. But get a dead-positive kill. You understand?"

Fifteen

HUSKY'S CAR bored through the sun-blasted air of the California desert, headed for Texas in his chase after Edgar Lamp.

Less than an hour after he left, Husky's radio told him that authorities believed Lamp to be bound for Canada, a place he had often told police he'd like to take refuge in. Husky had smiled and clicked off the radio.

Nice to know a fella could trust his chief.

And it'd be just as nice for the chief to know he could trust his ace homicide dick, too.

"Tough shit," he muttered to nobody, and kept driving.

Fred sighed from the passenger seat as cacti whirred past. Husky reached over and patted his ol' buddy on the back. There'd been nobody to leave him with, so Husky had allowed himself Fred's company. It was a self-indulgence no cop in pursuit could afford. It took his mind off the chase. It was also bush league since it made him emotionally vulnerable and slightly fatter, as targets go.

He cussed himself for such a mistake. Though he was glad for the company, he knew he had to be diligent.

Cruising heat-scarred hostility flats, where any cactus could hide Edgar Lamp or a "bottomless cup" roadside diner could lull you into sitting with your back to the windows, you needed to think of Just One Thing.

Old predator feelings returned. Not for centuries had Husky known them this strongly.

He'd always worked best alone. Having no one to jaw with, he became scared of his own stupid tangents. He paid more attention to staying alive. It'd worked well for years; it'd help him now.

When you did the Hunt, sidekickism always resulted in anger or sadness, anyhow.

Look at Garth. Look at others, too. He'd cried at too many funerals while rows of blue uniforms stood stock-still to watch a casket lowered and a widow led away.

The damn funny thing was the guys getting buried were usually the smart cops. Better cops. Or maybe those were just the funerals he remembered most clearly because the loss and waste seemed greater.

The "four D's," as somebody had called them once, always seemed to hold true: "Dumb Dicks Don't Die."

Fred suddenly leaned over and licked Husky's face, whining and whimpering. Big brown dog eyes watching him under oddly expressive brows. Definitely the pee signal.

They'd driven in plenty of cars over the years, this man and this dog. The lick, the whimper, followed by that particular look, with head cocked slightly to the left, meant an imminent episode of the bladder.

"For real this time," Husky warned, pulling off the road onto the shoulder.

Fred had been playful last time; going through the entire ritual for the hell of it, for attention. Not a drop pro-

206

duced. Husky hadn't been happy. He had too much time to make up. God knew how many hours of driving lay between here and Gullickson, Texas.

He grabbed the leash out of the back and fastened it to Fred's collar. Next came the .38 Police Special, out of the glove compartment, into the waiting cup of his shoulder holster.

A quick check reassured him: the shotgun was still snugly in place between driver's seat and door. It'd stay put till he pulled it out of there.

For all this precaution, Fred still made Husky grin. They walked a little until, with a meaningful look, Fred dispatched a worthy piss.

"So what is it, Freddy? We got the right road here?"

Walking back to the car, Husky stared down the blacktop ahead, then swung his gaze back where they'd just been.

Fred strained at the heavy leather leash, wanting to get back to the passenger seat.

"All right, all right." Husky's voice was soft.

He opened the passenger door. The window had been left down the customary eight to ten inches so Fred could stick his entire head out into the wind and blink happily as the car roared down the highway. Why dogs loved dirt in their eyes, God knew.

Pretty soon they were moving again, Fred nose first into the stiff breeze, sticking out almost to the shoulder. Husky looked over for a moment, afraid he'd opened it too far, then deciding not.

His thoughts returned to business at hand. They'd probably know something by now back in L.A. He would stop at the next phone booth.

Miles later he realized he hadn't unholstered the .38, but he decided to leave it there. It had begun to feel better close to his body.

The idea that this could be the wrong direction to follow Edgar Lamp now seemed ludicrous. There was no proof, no surprised traveler left by the road with ribs pointing skyward, but somehow the smell of the man permeated this rail of rock and tar as it rose and dipped through the inexhaustible heat.

Eventually there *was* going to be some signal. Something besides his own conviction that the old woman, Alice Lamp Corinth, had indeed hooked her grandson.

Even as he thought this, Husky felt the red rush of embarrassment wash over his face. The master cop, he told himself, as he stole a quick glance of self-appraisal in the rearview. Following his hunch halfway to hell with nobody to talk to but his fucking dog.

And now he's expecting *signals*.

Husky laughed aloud. He tried the radio, which gave him static and a faint country station that floated in and out like some weepy ghost. There would be a lick or two of steel guitar, then nothing but crackle. He wanted to hear some news out here. Something concrete, factual, designed to take him out of the wavering off ramps his thoughts offered. Thoughts about the trouble you could run across in places like this. People could hide here, watch you drift by and close their traps. Victims didn't sense such shutting jaws till much later, when they stopped to rest or shit or gas it up. And the desert people often figured you were just one more city prick, so who gave a damn if you died or managed to crawl away? Traps could be simple in the desert. Quiet, inevitable, gila slow, so all the cop instinct in the world became worthless.

Husky Martin straightened up in his seat just a bit and confronted the fact that yes, there was a part of him that was scared. He could face that, live with it, possibly even *use* the fear to do his job better. He'd wanted this particular chase. Now he'd better turn it around and make it his ball game.

Which wasn't a bad way to think of it.

Edgar Lamp, however many miles ahead he might be, could very well be spending most of his time worrying about how far behind the cops were. He'd never know it was only one single solitary slightly overweight snoop. He might even laugh if he found out it was Husky Martin.

But the laugh wouldn't last god-awful long. It had been Martin who'd found him before. Martin pumping a shitload of tear gas into that Truckworld Rent-A-Space joint by the highway outside San Bernardino when they first caught him.

Lamp had almost slipped him that time. Big Bear Lake would never have been the same if Edgar had made it up the mountain in the back of somebody's pickup. He'd have raised hell, and he'd've been impossible to pin down in those mountains.

But he'd never reached them. He'd gone to jail and to trial . . . and then to the airport.

The owner of Truckworld had said he'd never seen so many cops in one place at one time.

You oughta see cop funerals, Husky had thought, but he'd held his tongue.

Husky finally found the news on the radio, but it was in Spanish.

■ ■ ■ ■

He called from Arizona. She could hear the tension and fatigue in his voice.

"You oughta hit some motel, get a couple hours' sack time." She tried to hide her alarm. He didn't sound right. He sounded . . . out there.

"Pretty soon," he came back. "First I gotta get in a good chunk of distance."

He was watching the road that ran past the dust-caked phone booth. He scanned the flat land around him, more confused about whether he was hunting or being hunted than he'd been a few hours before. The mind went through cycles and reruns of cycles when you took it off alone in a car like this.

She told him about the two Chicano boys who'd turned themselves in as friends of Edgar Lamp. How they'd been at the warehouse before the police arrived and how he'd wanted them to steal cars and guns for him. They said he'd been talking a bad game.

Meanwhile, the fingerprint boys quietly checked Styrofoam cups they'd sipped water out of at the station. The prints came in dead ringers for those on two of the old-lady bodies from the night the boys said Edgar Lamp called Multiple Grandmas.

Once the two were separated and squeezed on their prints, they started blaming each other. They blamed the dead boys, Cholo and Mr. Yogie. And the one they said was Quiet Carlos. This was the first hint on who he was, since his face had been seriously scrambled in the shooting and he carried no ID.

Quiet Carlos had never actually been booked for anything, so there weren't even prints to run his fingers against in the files.

Husky just stared off, looking now and then at Fred, who watched him with perked ears from the car, while Marge went through the full scope of information.

Edgar Lamp had turned his herd against itself.

Zero and Spider Lobo had finally begun to talk about how one of the dead women from Multiple Grandmas, which they kept calling it, had been Frito's grandma. Piece by piece, Skakel and Purdue questioned the two until they had it all. Lamp had discovered how the one called Cholo hated Frito's grandmother, and he'd exploited that hatred.

"He knew what he was getting to," Husky said softly.

"Yeah, that's what the boys said they thought, too."

"What're we doing with them?"

She hesitated. He could tell she thought he wasn't going to like this.

"I won't break," he finally said.

"They got a hotshot p.d., Husky. Guy really wanted to carve a deep one on the system."

"Anybody ever tell you you talk like a cop?"

"Only at the office." Her laugh was refreshing. It brought her closer to him. For a moment he closed his eyes and let it fortify him. "So you wanna hear this or not?" she went on.

"Sure," he laughed, too.

"Okay. The p.d. figures if Lamp gets caught and dragged in, there's still the whole schedule of charges against him for the Demon Viejo activities. So these two boys start to figure as major material witnesses."

"Gotcha. He's doin' his job, Marge. And he'd be right, ordinarily . . ."

But angling for that bargain made the big assumption Edgar Lamp would make it back to L.A. alive. And the defender was a good long way from the center ring.

"You think he's blowing smoke?" She sounded anxious.

"Not for his purposes, no. But he's never met Edgar Lamp, right?"

Her silence hung on the wire. He smiled uncomfortably as he stared at his feet in the hot desert sun.

"Don't worry," he finally said.

"You really think that's gonna do it? Tell me not to worry?"

"It's all I've got right now."

211

"You're a jackass, Husky."

He considered braying. He decided against it.

"Will you at least promise me you'll drag the local sheriff into it when you get to Gullickson?" She didn't like her own tone. It was whiny. She hated whiny.

"No," he finally said.

She'd expected as much.

"So you got anything else on Lamp before I get back on the road?"

She thought a minute.

"Yeah. Remember he forced some guy to drive him out of the hotel where he was hiding? They found him by a dumpster, too."

"Really. He's gettin' in a rut, huh?"

"You tell me. The dumpster was in back of a police station out of Reseda. Borders right on this park. He took the guy to the other side of town, did his business with him, and left him for some jogger to find at about eight that night. Guy said he was running and he all of a sudden hits some mud and goes flying and slides in it."

"Jesus," Husky said, "only it wasn't mud?"

"Right. It was the guy, Oscar Navarette. The jogger went sliding in this guy." She was getting madder at him as she was saying all this. Then she couldn't stop herself. "Have a real *great* drive out there, Husky," and she hung up.

She knew that out there in the desert, he would be staring at the phone with that bemused half-smile on his mug, knowing it upset her no end and not being able or willing to do shit about it.

She could've killed him for that. He was just being a good cop, right? Just avenging his dead friend, too.

She felt like a fool. Getting involved, after years, with this guy of all guys was her all-time self-destructive prize-winning stunt. Why was she doing this? And why now,

212

when he was chasing that walking butcher shop like it was his personal thing to prove to the entire world?

It made him look like an idiot to anybody who knew the full history.

It made her look worse, biting her nails over it.

She loved the idiot.

■　■　■　■　■

Husky ambled back to the car, picking up a can of Diet Dr Pepper from the machine in the gas station concession room.

He considered giving up the fucking chase completely, turning back to L.A. and retiring from the force, but that didn't even last till he got out of the air-cooled vendorama and back into the hot, dry sun.

Do that, and you've got an incurable tension between the Man and the Woman. She'd be convinced he'd done it only for her, which would be absolutely right. She'd be equally sure he was holding it against her, gritting his teeth and resenting the fact that she'd deballed him while he was trying to make things right.

This could also be correct, but probably wouldn't seem so when his head cleared and he thought about how stupid the whole thing was.

Still, he was here.

He didn't turn the car back toward L.A. Even as he thought about it, he kept moving southeast.

Talking to Marge had regrounded him, reminded him who he was and what he was doing. She'd kick herself if she ever heard such a thing. The artificial sweetener made the soft-drink taste dull and he wanted to throw it out. There was the moment of true policeman's break-any-law guilt before he went ahead and littered the highway with his little bit of colored metal and brown liquid.

He'd been doing this all wrong. The whole point of coming out here after Edgar Lamp was to be a bigger monster, just once, than the monster himself. Chief Nash had at least known *that* much when he said get a dead-positive kill. Nobody wanted the man brought back, tried, and jailed.

Least of all Husky.

He remembered talking to Garth, seemingly a century before, about making some kind of mark. Now he smiled. The mark he wanted to make would be a small, dark, round mark directly in the center of Edgar Lamp's forehead. It didn't bother him that he was smiling about this.

He imagined how it would look, probably in some field someplace. Maybe in Alice Lamp Corinth's barn, if she had a barn. He liked the picture his mind conjured, liked the thought of having the first look at dead Edgar Lamp, face down with cheeks dirty, pale skin getting paler. It would be good old-fashioned justice, for once. Justice that was a rarity, if you asked Husky. Law and lawyers and courts and judges had made it that way; taken it right out of common experience and replaced it with plea bargains and budget-minded paroles to save public coffers from the weight of long sentences. In that way Husky was like most cops, wondering a good deal of the time why he was laying life, limb, ass, and experience out there. After all, what prick with a gun and an armful of something that soothed and burned ever gave a thought to letting *him* off easy?

He drove a little faster. This was his locker-room scene before the big game. He was the bug-eyed linebacker getting himself cranked on hate, slamming his locker till his hand bled. Building artificial but effective righteousness to bludgeon and murder.

But he was into it. He began to estimate the situation

214

differently; size his odds with the goal of destroying instead of merely surviving. Out here there was no reason the quiet, irresistible jaws couldn't close on the *other* fool if *your* mind was in the right place. If you were the prowler instead of the prowlee. Husky slapped the steering wheel and Fred looked up at him.

Husky didn't notice. He was looking for a radio station again. This time he found one and he got the news. In English. A check of his watch and he decided to give it another three or four hours before pulling in someplace to sleep. When he did, he'd be halfway to Gullickson. Even Edgar Lamp would have to be sleeping by then. But Edgar would sleep longer, lacking discipline and never imagining that behind him, coming down the road like a button man instead of a cop, was his long-overdue payback.

Sixteen

Edgar Lamp wasn't a guy who got off on running. On this highway across California, Arizona, and New Mexico and into Texas, he was doing a marathon.

Just now he was ready to drop Oscar Navarette's car out of the picture, but he'd have to pick a suitable replacement. Then he'd leave this overheating taco wagon to cook in the sun forever.

Shit, it was hot. He'd forgotten true sun-belt heat since being in California. Heat like this made you feel mean. It made the shitty red cloth upholstery in Oscar's car, which smelled anyhow, take on the hot, dusty reek old fabric gets when it's dying of sun. It was the smell of Grandma Alice's old cars back in Texas.

He hadn't been twenty miles into desert before realizing he'd be doing lots of radiator watching. He'd lost count of the water refills, but everything was slowing him down, adding tension.

He kept looking back.

He thought he'd wear out the rearview.

He felt stupid worrying about one damn cop. It'd be Martin himself. Edgar was sure. Martin was obsessed.

The only thing Edgar didn't like about all this was how he was now playing the cop's game by the cop's rules. Edgar was leaving the scene, running out. He tried to tell himself this was okay because he knew how cops worked now. Really knew. He'd been busted, booked, tried, processed. All that time he'd watched cops, listened to their bullshit. He knew what they smiled at and what shook them. They weren't so tough to figure.

That's why he'd thought Multiple Grandmas, the great plane crash . . . the whole thing . . . had been so perfect. He'd turned their game on them like he'd been cop and they'd been running.

They hadn't been able to find their own dicks that whole time back in L.A.

But fugitives didn't have the offensive. Edgar could kick himself now. The minute he'd run at all, it was like admitting they'd catch him.

Now and then he'd considered cranking the wheel oneeighty and slipping back into L.A. He'd easily bop right on by Martin, who'd never think to watch the cars going *west*.

But his better judgment kept pushing him back home. He had to have the last round with his grandmother.

He remembered her distinctive smell, her perfume and stale sweat. The old gagging panic of boyhood hit him all over again. He'd never told her about it, not even when he was little and too fucking honest for his own good. Not even when he'd told her how he wished she was dead but he was scared to do it.

She never knew how the very goddamn close-up smell of her jammed his nostrils with a reek it took hours to shake, or how he'd run outside, gasping for fresh air to replace her stench. But he could never run fast enough to escape the feeling, and he would vomit from the coughing he would begin to do. Just thinking of it now he coughed . . . but stopped, fighting the sudden rise in his gut.

This also worried Edgar. If simply thinking of her made him feel this way, how the hell could he confront her in person?

He slapped the steering wheel in frustration. How the fuck did it get like this? How did King Shit, smokin' down the road from L.A., the darkest fear in the heart of any soulless scumbag prick in this whole damn wasteland, ever wind up letting him*self* feel weak or scared?

Easy. He knew: it was all this running away. It was making him *think* scared. Right now he was thinking they might've traced the spic who owned this car. They might be watching for his plates over the next hill.

He decided to cure *that* worry. There was a sign advertising the next Denny's just four miles ahead. Cure it there.

He felt better right away.

Maybe he'd even generate a little miracle action up here at Denny's. He smiled; laughed to himself. Shit, haven't *been* too fucking many miracles at Denny's, he thought.

The doubt was still there, but he was overpowering it.

"Whole world wants a miracle, just like every other day," he said aloud.

And he checked the rearview.

Nothing in it but road, like before.

"Whole world wants a miracle, right now."

The Impala labored down the highway. Nobody going the other way could tell the dirty-haired, pale-faced driver was enduring a mild anxiety attack. Nobody knew he watched the rearview as much as the road ahead.

And no one would *ever* have believed this jumpy driver

fought to keep his mind off a little old woman still hundreds of miles away. A little old woman who feared him for his cruelty, but who also terrified him simply by continuing to exist.

Grandma Alice just had to die. It was down to that. Edgar was willing to puke till Christmas to get it done.

■　■　■　■　■

The girl in the Denny's watched the dirty gray Impala park just outside the window.

She was cooling her jets here, soothing a slight sore throat with quarts of Denny's coffee and a couple scoops of vanilla. She never ate chocolate since somebody told her chocolate was just all the other kinds of ice cream that'd been sitting around the freezer too long put together and dyed brown.

The sore throat was probably from being up all night a couple nights straight and all the driving she'd been putting in.

She watched the guy getting out of the Impala and decided he had a nice butt. Not real well dressed, but big deal.

She got the feeling from the way he looked carefully around the parking lot that he could be a little risky, a little dangerous. Like he was expecting to be expected. Maybe he'd robbed somebody. Maybe some pissed-off husband wanted to cut his balls off. The idea dug a divot in her consciousness and kept rolling around. She could imagine that butt moving up and down over some Phoenix housewife. Maybe he was the gardener. Maybe her son. He was definitely on the lookout for something. Or somebody. He came with a story, possibly one that would make him jumpy and unpredictable. That wasn't too bad

219

to break her monotony on the long drive from L.A. to Houston.

Personally, she was way ahead of schedule. The Scorpions wouldn't hit Texas for a couple, three days yet. She'd been antsy to get away from her father and his endless droning.

The guy from the Impala sat down three seats from her at the counter. He'd definitely noticed her as he came in, checked her out, and plunked it medium close to see what came up.

"Come from the coast?" she asked, friendly.

He looked over, real distinct gaze. "Yeah, all in one shot, too." He was measuring her, she thought, satisfied. She did well when men measured her.

"Long haul." She put lots of sympathy into it, eyes locking on his a moment. Strange eyes.

"Well, when you need to be someplace . . ." Then he smiled.

"I'm Dee Dee." She put up the best smile she had, thinking about being a Phoenix housewife with a garden and deciding to go for it.

She told him about herself. About how she was basically not into doing much in your normal constructive sense, such as the junior college bullshit her father was laying on her. Instead she followed around one or two really good— exceptional, if you asked her—bands.

He asked what kind of bands. She sighed. She knew this was where they could part company. They were strictly metal, as if he couldn't tell from her clothes, right? The black leather and studs and shit? Metal was basically her religion, her passion, her world. Anyway, maybe there was some kind of book she could write. Like *I watched the boys on the road,* or something. She wasn't sure about it, but then it was basically a new idea.

220

"You get fucked by the boys on the road, too," he said, and she saw he also had a smile that *wasn't* really so nice.

But she figured she was fair game for that kind of remark since it was true and she didn't give a large shit who knew.

"Play an instrument?" she finally came back.

He laughed, looked at the menu and opened it. She moved one stool closer.

She didn't tell him how guys in bands knew her on sight and figured a guaranteed fuck when she was around. Which was pretty nearly all the time. They called her Dee Dee the Slutgirl, which she also didn't tell him.

She filled his ears with enough, though. Like her real name was Deette Bonnaro, she was twenty-seven and came from Palos Verdes, back in California. He said he knew about it, out by Marineland. She shook her head in disgust; that was all anyone ever knew. Like fish lived there instead of people. Actually, that wasn't too far off, if you knew her parents and their fucking department-store friends. The place was Money Incorporated. Her folks dumped cash on her all the time, but they always tied it to the same sermon. Her father, especially, was the most one-track asshole she'd ever known. At least twenty times now he'd said she could have a few thou if she'd just drop the black leather shit and make herself an understandable young woman. She couldn't believe he'd actually think she'd ever make herself understandable.

At least to him.

So whenever they came across with the bills, "just to prove we're serious," Dee Dee the Slutgirl would hop in her very nice Trans Am and book it down the freeways to wherever her faves were playing.

"Your old man sounds like a fucking feeb," Edgar Lamp told her. "You're twenty-seven, you won't change."

221

By now she was on the stool next to him, warmed to her story and checking him up close.

"He's not gonna notice. He's into his old shit, just like my mother." Dee Dee shook her head. "I mean, she keeps giving me grief about how I'll get my ass knocked, all right? Like I'm gonna feel obligated to go carry some little shiteater nine months and ruin my life once I dump it?" She looked at Edgar, who looked back, expressionless. "I mean, you believe her? The woman does not understand *dick* and she's preaching to me about *babies?*"

Edgar didn't like her, so therefore his considerations about whether to fuck her were entirely in the abstract.

He noticed the lack of one finger on the right hand as she babbled. She realized he'd spotted it and went right into a well-rehearsed spiel.

It had been the big stumbling block, that missing finger. It had shut doors on her, thanks to shallow, stupid modeling agencies or really *serious* dance academies.

"They're definitely not into deformity, which is what they called it. I mean, no one in my entire life called it a deformity till I tried to get work. You know, the face is good. The body works . . . huh? So then we get to the hands. What do they want me to do, stick my fingers up my nose for the camera? Is that why they can't fucking hire me with this hand?"

"Bitter," he observed, by now drinking a coffee. Exhaustion had washed over his shoulders. It made listening to her chatter harder.

"I'm not even a *little* bitter, man. It just showed me how fucking shallow the world is, that's all. I got wiser for it. Besides"—she gave him the coy smile, maybe with a little fuck-me eyes mixed in—"guys in bands like girls with a little difference, you know?"

Edgar Lamp did know. Since he'd noticed her missing finger, he couldn't shake the vision of that hand touching him. He looked her directly in the eye now, a look that reminded her of all those guys in all those bands. The power look. The look that would've driven her father to hire someone with a gun. The look that knew something she could never quite figure out about herself, like how she felt. It was pure confidence, especially from this guy, who was maybe a little more intense than she'd realized at first glance.

"You're an easy fuck, Dee Dee," said Edgar with a smile.

She just looked at him. She couldn't meet his challenge. She loved it when guys told her shit like that. She didn't know why, but it made her hot.

"See that?" he went on. "Grins when I tell her she's an easy fuck? Maybe the easiest. And me sitting here knowing we're both goin' to Texas and maybe it wouldn't be such a bad idea to caravan from here on, you know?"

"It'd be safer," she told him.

"Sure," he almost whispered.

"I mean, you hear about stuff all the time out on the road, don't you?"

"Daily." He touched her hand. The one without the finger. She spread thumb and forefinger. He put his own finger between them, hard and tight.

"You won't get pissed off in Texas? When I go my way and you go yours, or anything? . . . I mean . . . I'm goin' out there to see my boys in the band, all right?"

"I ain't your ol' man, Dee Dee."

"No, you sure ain't . . ." She said it with a laugh.

"In fact, the only problem we *do* have is how fucking tired out I am." He sounded serious.

"You did drive a long way in one shot."

He nodded. "I was thinking maybe a little snooze in a motel. Then I could do the rest of the way to Texas without any more stopping."

"I make this drive a lot," she told him. "There's a Sleepy

223

Bear six miles up the road in the right direction. I stopped there last year when I went out to Dallas to catch Van Halen at the convention center."

"Would you mind or anything?"

She laughed, a little dirtier and hornier than she wanted to sound. But what the fuck.

"I'm tired too, man. I'm always kinda tired, right?"

He didn't answer. He just motioned for their checks.

■　■　■　■　■

All the way over in the limping Impala, Edgar wondered how well he could maintain. Dee Dee had obviously been porked by all kinds of different guys. Performance in bed wasn't his greatest talent and he feared comparison. He wanted it to be perfect. The chance meeting in Denny's was a good start. Now he needed to overwhelm her. King Shit dominates in the hay. He pictured a wordless, intense encounter like the ones normally featured in his fantasies. Once he'd done that, he would do whatever he wanted with her. But the fucking had to be right. This had to go down just so. For some reason it was suddenly a test he had to pass. He fretted; bit a nail.

If only he'd fucked a little more before this. He even considered telling her she was getting a car with 'real low mileage,' but quickly threw the idea out. She would wonder why. He couldn't say they'd mostly been true scags, street shit, fleshbags old enough to be Dee Dee's old lady. He couldn't say they'd been unwilling. He might be odd with women, he thought, but no need to broadcast it.

The air-conditioned blast came out to them as they opened the door to room fifteen of the Sleepy Bear Motel. She didn't look up as she led the way inside. He felt his confidence coming back when he noticed how uptight she seemed. Almost shy. Until she shucked her leather shirt-vest with a little too much cool for his liking. She had a thin torso, so her fairly large breasts seemed even bigger, standing in contrast over ribs that showed a little. He guessed she was probably drug-bony. Like he gave a rat's ass.

When she dropped the leather pants and stepped out, bare-ass naked and sizing him up, she let herself smile.

"Gonna brush your teeth first?" She laughed.

He laughed back, not liking the slightly doofy sound he made. But she wasn't keeping track of what seemed dumb. She was moving in.

He never let on, but he felt trapped for a moment as he was aware of the hand without the finger, now probing just as he'd imagined, right down in there, grabbing while the other hand worked his zipper. But he couldn't shake feeling like times in childhood; cornered. Times when he would get tickled past the point where he had control. Into discomfort. A little panic.

But the panic passed.

He wasn't as tense as he'd imagined he might be. She talked too much, whispering shit and thrashing her head back and forth like this was a movie. Her movie. Ol' Dee Dee was definitely the star. He watched her from above as he moved inside her, breathing through his mouth but unaware of it.

She moved too much for him, that was basically it. It started that cornered feeling all over again, and this time he *really* recognized it. She was making him feel like his grandmother used to make him feel. The close, insistent presence. Her hot heavy breath was on him like perfume, mixed with her own particular extra-sweet aroma and the sweat of too many miles on the road in that Trans Am.

The skin of her arms draping over him clung and stuck slightly while her hands caressed, felt, pinched, and grabbed. This was the most irritating. The arms imprisoned.

She was startled slightly, then smiled, when he took her wrists and held them, pushing her hands down onto the mattress. Her arms were pinned. He looked a little out of it, but he was getting aggressive and she liked that. She couldn't get her arms back up off the sheets no matter how she tried. She arched her back as she pushed against his hands, and smiled a dirty little grin before she gave up.

Fucking turned to wrestling. She took what he was doing as a challenge. She strained to buck him off. He was surprised and irritated even more. With stunning speed his right hand slapped her across the face. She gave a little yelp and stopped struggling. For a moment, she wasn't sure. His hand was back on her wrist already. Then his movement into her resumed, a little faster, while his eyes never left her face. Now he looked just as out-there, but fascinated.

They went on in silence for a minute or two. He sank into living his wordless dream, but then she began whispering to him again. She told him she loved it when he held her down. How she wanted to be controlled, overpowered like this. She wanted him to do whatever he wanted with her, just like guys in bands did, but she told him they didn't do it like he did.

He just looked down at her as she went on, thinking that he could do one thing no one in *any* band could manage. He could really surprise her, he finally told her in a whisper. She loved that.

"God, surprise me," she said. "Surprise me . . ."

He picked up his tempo.

"Close your eyes," he told her.

She obeyed.

She wasn't aware of exactly when his gaze moved down

226

past her large, sweaty breasts and the pale red pimples on her rib cage to concentrate on the triangular area at the top of her solar plexus.

"Whole world wants a miracle, Dee Dee."

She just moaned, like she understood.

He said it again, and as he did, she began to feel something strange. It pulled at first, a bit like the tightness after too many sit-ups in an aerobics class. But it became intense, became pain.

Quickly, it became all she could think of.

She opened her eyes in amazement, gasped. Her look was the stabbing victim's look.

It was way too strange, but for a moment he looked to her like some kind of ape or something . . . then almost like her father.

She thought she was flashing back on some mushroom or something. She didn't know it, but tissue was on the verge of rupturing inside her.

"My God," she managed. "My stomach . . ."

And she saw he was looking there. That it was more than looking.

"*Stop* it," she said.

He didn't hear her. He didn't stop anything. Not the pummeling drive of his penetration, the soft slap of his skin against hers, or the Proving look.

"Stop what you're doing, *please!*"

But then her voice rose in a reedy note of amazed pain. His hand left one wrist, but the wrist didn't move. The hand covered her mouth, stifled the scream.

From Edgar's vantage, propped in half push-up, he watched Dee Dee come apart beneath him.

As she did, he had the most violent orgasm of his life.

When he was done, he opened his eyes again and got his bearings. He disengaged and pushed off the bed, standing for a moment beside it as he looked away and caught his breath.

He paid no attention to the sprawl of red across dingy sheets and cheap carpet. He noticed only the blood on himself. Irritation flared.

He'd suddenly become tremendously concerned with time.

Martin wouldn't give him leeway to fuck a path to Texas.

The shower was quick. Coming back to the bedroom for his clothes, he took a long look at her. He never stopped moving, getting into his things, but his eyes never left Dee Dee Bonnaro.

He'd never seen one so long after a kill.

She looked smaller than when she was alive. Like neighborhood cats did when found dead in the flower bed.

His grandmother's flower bed . . . the thought jarred him. Hurry, he thought, but he looked a moment more.

Her head was still turned to the side. He'd turned it there to hold her still.

Her open eyes were just as before. Both arms were bent, palms upraised, again just the way he'd pinned them.

He'd posed her.

An odd, feminine pose. Overpowered. The eruption in her chest beneath the serenity of that face struck even Edgar as jarring, but it made him smile.

With his clothes back on he slipped from the room. Taking her money and keys, taking her car, he left on screeching wide tires, a southeast mover, a wave of bad news with the radio loud.

He didn't need sleep. He was rejuvenated.

He wanted only to hurry, to get there, to stay ahead.

For her part, Dee Dee Bonnaro would lie waiting for several hours before an unsuspecting maid would find her.

Her pose would not change. Expression and upraised palms would beseech wordlessly, still wondering how and why.

A butcher-shop madonna, far short of Texas.

Seventeen

As HE PASSED the Denny's, there was no doubt Husky would have to get off this road, close his eyes, and seriously sleep. Everything was failing, from tricks like rolling down the windows and sucking up wind to slapping himself in the face and pinching behind the knee.

"It's a long way to Texas, Freddy." He smiled at the dog.

The dog, he noticed, was sound fucking asleep.

At first he'd considered pulling onto the shoulder and shutting his lids. Fred could probably bark the shit out of any intruder—even Edgar Lamp, God forbid.

But "probably" didn't cut it. A car could be a target, fat and sassy, from a helluva long way off. Optimum sneak-up.

A motel with plenty of rooms presented better odds, plus he'd still have Fred with him, ready to woof his deep, resonant, full-chest woof.

230

And finally, a nice fresh bed in an air-cooled cubicle of Late American Anonymous furniture represented comfort, avoidance, orderly interruption of mid-desert.

■ ■ ■ ■ ■

One sand-blasted, sun-baked highway patrol car sitting in front of the Sleepy Bear would've been bad enough to kick Husky's stomach over. Two of them made it almost a sure thing: this would be the first irrefutable proof he was on the right track.

The sheriff, an unlikely thin customer named Pascual DeMerrit, sized Husky Martin up with pissed-off steel-colored eyes. He removed his reflectors to scowl at the badge, read the ID that went with it, and then take a second or two to just look this intruder in the eye.

"Wanna see a California driver's license, too, Mr. Martin. We don't get a goddamn lotta freak killers out here. Mostly they shoot or stab each other or something like that. Whoever did this had something like a chain saw . . . maybe a pickax . . . I don't know yet."

"Who's the victim?"

"Young woman. Probably a traveler. Probably got picked up over at the Denny's. Couple people work back there said there was this girl went off with some guy rolled up in a gray Chevy low-rider."

The low-rider was sitting in plain sight, not fifteen feet from where the two men were talking. Husky looked at it.

"Run the registration?"

"Haven't actually jumped to check it out, Mr. Martin. I normally wait to quit pukin' before I get on the radio."

Husky looked disgusted. Fucking windblown geeks. How did they catch anybody?

The papers were untouched in the glove compartment.

Oscar Navarette, all neat and tidy. The guy the jogger stepped in.

Husky put them back, clicked the compartment door shut. The car didn't look tampered with, just driven. It smelled hot . . . a hint of radiator-rust perfume lingered inside. Lamp had probably worried about breaking down in the middle of nowhere and gone for the switch.

Husky shut the door and looked at the car a moment. When he turned away, the sheriff was watching him.

"Wanna check the room?"

Husky started toward the door, but the sheriff stepped in front of him. Pascual DeMerrit felt resentful, to be sure. Country boy getting his hackles up at the taciturn dick from the big city.

But this sheriff was also probably a good cop. He would ask everything to have all the pieces—or as many as he could find. Also, there might always be ass covering to be done.

And it was a fucking bizarre story to tell them down at the beer bar after he got off.

"Personal?" DeMerrit smiled, humorless.

"Not the girl."

"Any of it?"

"I've been . . . more detached, yeah."

DeMerrit's arm stayed in his way, hand on the jamb.

"You get yourself pissed off at a guy like the one did this shit, you get your stones mailed home in a jar."

Husky smiled.

"You ever worked as a city cop, you'd know my stones're long gone."

DeMerrit looked a little confused.

"I have tried to keep my balls, though."

Husky didn't get a laugh.

"You tryin' to be one fuckin' funny guy, huh, Martin?

You probably get decorator shit like this all the time back in L.A., right?"

Husky stood, waiting to be let in, uncomfortable but unwilling to back off. The face of Pascual DeMerrit was four, maybe five inches from his own, and glaring hard.

"You come in here, even a damn fool with shit on his sneakers like *me* knows you're *chasin'* this guy."

"That's real good. You probably watch Andy of Mayberry, huh?"

DeMerrit didn't miss a beat.

"This is that serial killer, am I right? Edgar Lamp? He did this bullshit in my county? He took this girl and pulled this crap?"

And with that, Pascual DeMerrit threw the door violently open, revealing the shitty, nauseating secret of room fifteen. He watched with only distant satisfaction as Husky winced a little—really just in the eyes—and involuntarily held his breath at the smell.

Two more officers were inside, trying not to look right at Dee Dee Bonnaro's eternal confusion. They took notes, making a record of where everything was.

Husky experienced a sudden surge of frustration. He turned to the two officers.

"Anything on the sheets besides blood?" he asked.

One of them nodded. "Looks like semen, but that's a helluva mess, you know?"

Husky turned toward the door. This was new. Until now, sex had never played a traceable part in Lamp's murders.

"Leaving so soon?"

Husky really could've lived his whole life without meeting Pascual DeMerrit, but he paused a moment.

"What kind of car did *she* drive when they left the Denny's? Anybody remember that?"

"Trans Am. This year's."

233

"And?"

"Ran a useless check all the way to the state border, both directions . . ."

"Only direction matters is toward Texas."

Eighteen

EDGAR LAMP parked the Trans Am about a mile from his grandmother's farm and walked the rest of the way. He'd done that same walk thousands of times. It hadn't changed, but somehow *everything* had changed.

Fields that had seemed to be without borders now looked confining. The men who worked them couldn't possibly be unfathomable, silent keepers of great secrets, either. Not here.

They were Texas dirt farmers with anonymous little checker squares of disagreeable land. They'd never been anyplace, they lived with pigs and chickens and all their ever-pouring shit, and from this, they believed, sprang wisdom or patience or country smarts.

Edgar walked his walk and hated them all. Maybe when he was through with his grandmother he would make the rounds of these places. Maybe he would take their children right before their eyes, pump them beyond capacity with his power, and leave them to die slowly. Not quite exploded but ruptured hopelessly within.

He was building to a good-sized, much-needed, blood-pumping howl of a rage. He stalked down the road, looking for his grandmother's house like a bad kid cruising for a fight. Maybe this was how Cholo and his mental-defective buddies had felt when he'd taken them up to Mulholland, if they had the collective brains to think about it. Edgar had a feeling they'd never thought about a thing.

This had been the way he used to come home from school, when they'd actually gotten him to go. With every yard, he would feel the urge to turn away and run. It had been his grandfather who'd made him feel that way at first, until Edgar realized how easily he could put fear into the old man.

But Grandma Alice was different. She didn't fear her husband, the God he ranted about, or anything.

She especially didn't fear Edgar. At least not back then. If she did now, it wasn't the same fear most people felt around him.

It had often been just about this time of day that he'd come home from school, too. Right around three-thirty, three forty-five in the afternoon.

The sun was in the right place and reminded him. He checked his watch. Three thirty-five. Bingo.

She'd be into the job of fixing dinner and he'd always try coming in the front door. The kitchen was nearer the back of the house, so sometimes he could sneak through the entry and upstairs without her knowing.

Good days, it would be better than an hour before she came looking.

He remembered his breathless dashes, his hopes that she wouldn't hear. Then there was the clutching feeling in his throat at the crucial moment—when he'd hit the stairs.

The thought of being questioned by that pasty, squishy-looking face had given the younger Edgar Lamp fits of anxiety more than once.

It had given him nightmares, too. Ones that continued into adulthood. They were his only moments of fear now. His only times of weakness.

For a few moments on his walk, Edgar couldn't shake the image of Grandma Alice looking down at him, speaking in that sharp cackle-bark of hers, the ever-present and unavoidable smell drifting into his nostrils.

He only forgot his thoughts when he first caught sight of the old house.

It had been repainted, probably more than once, but no change in color could ever alter the basic hopelessness it exuded for him. The mere sight of it stopped him in the road. For several moments he stood there, a lead weight in his belly, slack expression on his face.

The attic window.

Holy shit, he thought, the fucking attic window. How many times had he taken refuge up there to stare across the field and the road he was now standing on, looking into the distance at mountains and God knew what all else?

Always with the single desire to get the hell away.

The attic window was where he'd go whenever he managed to creep silently in after school.

The attic window was where the stairs ultimately took him. Up from the first floor to the second-floor landing. Through a thin little door hidden right in the wall and up a second, shorter set of steps in total darkness. Through another small door with a string pull instead of a handle and into the hot, compressed secrecy of the attic.

Edgar smiled, still standing in the road as he looked at it. No other memory of that house was good for him. But the attic was *his* part of the place. He'd never accepted her ownership of that tiny room. It was his domain from the moment he'd discovered it.

Now he walked again, faster than before, still staring at the attic window. He remembered that there were stronger boards and weaker boards up there. Time had taught him the places in the floor where he could walk without ever making a sound.

He wondered if he still knew where they were.

He wondered if the sound of her voice would still paralyze him with anger and terror like it used to. Since hearing it on television a couple days before, he'd thought about it almost constantly. He knew there was no way in hell he'd have come back to face her, to destroy her, if she hadn't asked for it—*ordered* it with that fucking display for the whole world to see.

Now he was almost to the spot where the old tar drive branched off from the county road, snaking back through the break in what Grandma Alice called the "road bushes" toward the house. His apprehension grew as he neared this point. When he got there, he could be spotted by watchful eyes in the kitchen window.

But once he got to the head of the tar drive it was obvious nobody was looking. The carport had just one car, an old Plymouth with Texas plates. He knew from looking at it that the car was hers, the same way he'd have known a certain coat would be her coat or Red Cross round-toes with thick old-lady heels would be her shoes.

He was struck by the sameness.

The voice of his dead Grandpa Harper, preaching tent-style full Gospel at the top of his lungs to a kitchen full of pots, pans, and Edgar, could have rolled out over the flat ground here just as naturally as anything. Nothing had changed from that time.

The terrible dead smell of his Grandma Alice, far

238

younger than today and hot on his heels to dole out farm justice, had never left this place either.

Not for Edgar Lamp it hadn't.

He stared long and hard at the old place. It must've been another ten minutes before he thought to move.

What if she was watching him? No, couldn't be. She'd've done something . . . said something. It wasn't like her to lie low.

Maybe she's asleep, he thought. In the same moment, he realized that if she was, he would have a tremendous advantage. He would never have to look her in the eye if he didn't want to. Never have to talk to her or listen to that voice . . . none of it.

He broke for the side door, the one to the kitchen, on a dead run. Suddenly he was out of breath, desperate and hurried.

He thundered up the steps, through the door, and into the kitchen. He stood there in sudden silence, feeling his entire being buzz. This was going to be the time for Grandma Alice. This was judgment.

"Grandma Alice!" He sounded like an animal, a madman, and he didn't give a shit. Moving with a lunge from the echoey old country kitchen out into the living room by way of the dining, he saw her just rising from her resting chair.

She looked like she was having trouble figuring out what was happening. She must've been sleeping after all!

He was shocked how old she looked. How tiny. Her gray-blue print dress was one of those light, straight-line jobs old women wear when all they want is comfort and to hell with looks. She seemed like a dwarf in it.

She blinked up at him, shaking a little, appearing terribly fragile. An old woman robbed of her chance to shore herself up and wear a steel face for an enemy.

Without the steel face, the expression Grandma Alice showed him was very familiar to Edgar Lamp.

It was fear.

He was fascinated. All his own worry blew away in this moment's reality. He stepped toward her slowly, savoring dominance, watching her seem to actually shrink back. He felt as though he was filling the room, taking her place, smashing her into a tiny corner.

"Look what turns around," he said softly.

She looked at him as though she didn't understand English. But what she didn't understand, he knew, was how this was happening. How it could be so out of her control. How he could so completely have grown past her, into something she couldn't even make a dent in.

"Look what happens to me and you, Grandma Alice . . ." He smiled.

In an effort to remain composed, she tried something that might have been a smile. Her chin quivered, her suddenly dry upper lip caught on her teeth, rendering her ridiculous.

Even as she grinned this idiot grin, even as she backed away, her right hand went to her apron pocket and came out with a small handgun.

He saw it immediately, saw she didn't have it gripped right. She would have difficulty firing it. Her process would take far too long. He never even felt threatened as his own hand shot out and caught her by the wrist, pointing the barrel toward the ceiling and away from him.

She caught her breath in surprise as her meticulously considered plan of defense crumbled. The little gun conked to the floor and lay there between them. He locked onto her eyes with his own.

It struck him just now that she didn't even seem to have the old smell. Maybe that had been boyhood, too. Maybe everything in boyhood was lies.

240

"It's not the same, Grandma. It's not even close." He came nearer. "You know, *I* do Provings. Better than Grandpa Harper ever even *hoped* for. Better than he talked about." And his voice fell into a cadence that mimicked the evangelical rhythms his grandfather used to favor. "I can lay down the facts and make you believe what you see . . . 'cause it's just nothing but the goddamn truth we're dealing with here . . . the goddamn truth . . . and you won't know what it is till it gets here, 'cause that's the way these things work . . . but when it does get here, you sure *can't* miss it . . ."

And he smiled down at her with such hate, such controlling, unstoppable menace that she could not summon an answer. She could only stare, eyes distorted through her thick glasses.

God, he hated her face.

Even as he realized that all over again, he was thinking how strong he felt.

How special this would be.

With his hands, he reached out and shoved her backwards against the wall. She hit near the fireplace, reacting to the pain as the stoking utensils clattered to the ground. He moved closer.

"I've got the Proving look," he said softly, and with a stare she could do nothing to stop, he lowered his gaze to her chest . . . her solar plexus.

The breath rushed out of her. She couldn't inhale, gasping. She clutched at the wall but found nowhere for fingers to take hold.

And no air to bring in.

It was as if all the air in the room had been sucked away from her as he continued his fixation upon her.

Finally, quarter inch by quarter inch, to her horror, her feet began lifting off the floor. Her body, now very much out of her control, was *rising*. Edgar never altered his look, never varied his concentration.

She felt things moving inside her. Vital organs lurched back and forth. Her chin snapped suddenly upward as her teeth clacked shut in a permanent jaw-vise. Her eyes stayed wide open, and an overwhelming hissing noise poured through her brain. She believed that she was passing out. But before she did, she felt . . . *motion*.

Though he never took his gaze off the initial spot; her solar plexus, it was as if he could look for the first time at someone's *entire* body with the Proving look.

He should have been surprised when she rose with wide eyes off the floor and seemed to slide up the wall . . . he should have been absolutely amazed when, finally, her body began turning toward the horizontal in the air . . . but all he felt was vague, detached satisfaction.

He never let up.

Just as she thought she would pass out, her body began to turn faster. When she was almost finally horizontal in midair, there was a sound of concussion and separation.

It was not a single rupture this time, not a question of merely the chest cavity.

Edgar Lamp let out a bellow of release, killing his grandmother like a pinwheel. She showered the living room of her old house, erupting from her middle, her limbs, and her head at once.

He stood alone, gasping in the aftermath, incredibly freed, full of his power. His arms were straight out to his sides, clenched tightly. Every muscle was taut. As his conscious mind began to return; to take control again, he turned and surveyed all around him. Ideas formed in rapid flow as his eyes traveled the room and its array of objects . . . some mundane, some triggering new ideas. Edgar couldn't hold a laugh. Martin was coming.

■ ■ ■ ■ ■

Husky rolled into Gullickson around eight that night. He found an open coffee shop along the Interstate and got some information from a waitress. Old lady Corinth lived not too far away. Down this road, up the next, then out in farm country. Just east of town proper. If alive, Garth could've taken him there.

Fred was up on forelegs to let cool night air brush through the partially opened passenger window and over his nose and face. Husky drove slowly down unlit back roads toward Alice Lamp Corinth's farm.

He'd double-checked his guns hours before; played the image of killing Edgar Lamp thousands of times in his mind. It seemed certain Edgar would already be there or hiding nearby.

The idea still bothered Husky when he reached the driveway. The mailbox bore the right address. He killed his lights and went up the thin strip of black toward the house.

There was a light on downstairs in what looked like a den. But that was all. Most of the house was abyss dark. Looking into windows yielded nothing: from the downstairs living-room glass with its bright blue flower box outside to the tiny lightless square looking blankly down from the attic above the second floor.

One car in the driveway. Texas plates. No Trans Am. Didn't have to be a cop to guess it was the old woman's.

But there was that *feeling*. He swallowed and felt dry. Gut knot forced him to pause a moment. Breathe deep; collect.

He'd known it often enough to pay close attention. A

243

pause in his heartbeat, brought on by a blinking chemical alarm unit in some cranny of the senses.

Instinct? Whatever.

One hand went to his holster; made sure the gun was there. The other closed around the shotgun, picked it up, held it across his lap. He took the flashlight from the map box between the two front seats. Fred sighed. Husky gave him a pat and got out slow, closing the door almost silently behind him.

Maybe she was just sitting in her TV room watching *Hotel.* Nice image, but it didn't fool his unconscious, animal side.

He'd been forced to snort a whole lot of cocaine once by a pusher with a sense of humor. The guy'd gotten the drop on him, taken him prisoner, and gone for the fun of seeing what happened when a cop got skull-juiced to the max. Husky didn't like to remember much about that night, but he remembered the adrenaline rush. Something like this moment.

He could *feel* Edgar Lamp's eyes but he couldn't find them. He knew they were out there. Or maybe *in* there. Watching him as closely as possible. It drove him quietly crazy. He wanted to scream Lamp's name, call him out here to try and do it to *him*, get it over with. Come on, motherfucker, go for *this* boy's ribs!

But silence was everywhere, coating like thick syrup. It had *weight*, clinging to the fabric of matter. Not even country crickets chirped. Husky felt like his ears had been plugged, like sudden and total deafness crushed in on his brain.

He *had* to force that feeling out of his head. He scratched at the dirt with his shoe, hearing the noise, reveling in it. Dimension! It released him, brought him down from his anxiety high, enough to start remembering things. Important things.

244

Watch your back.

If Edgar Lamp was here he certainly knew Husky was, so Edgar had an advantage. But Husky, in truth, had set all this up, beginning with Alice Lamp Corinth's press conference scam back in L.A. He'd expected it would come to this. He'd longed for it. For the memory of his friend, whose death rested heavy on the conscience, Husky had in a very real and direct way chosen this moment.

When he opened the kitchen door—he somehow had never even given a thought to trying the front entrance—there was another sound. A good old-fashioned hinge creak.

It was the last thing he noticed before his flashlight beam caught her face

The face had nothing behind it.

It was a visage; features with bone structure, ripped from the head by some incomprehensible tearing violence, separated from the rest of the body and thus utterly lacking expression.

Husky forced himself to analyze, as dispassionately as he could, what lay on the kitchen table before him. It was the front half of Alice Lamp Corinth's skull. No apparition. No thing of evil.

Connected to nothing, resting on the dinette.

God knew where her brains were.

He found it difficult to breathe. A sudden wash of fear forced him to move the flashlight beam, checking the rest of the room.

There was a left hand on the counter by the sink. A fragment of gray flesh, connected to a section of meat from what may have been abdomen or leg, was on the floor near the doorway to the dining and living area.

From the kitchen he could see into the living room, where a wash of red seemed to emanate from a central

245

point, fanning out in a sunburst circle over carpet, walls, furniture.

Disembodied parts and sections of Alice Lamp Corinth were scattered like chunks of a ruined doll.

When he stepped into the living room, Husky stood silently, staring at monstrosities his flashlight beam unveiled. With each revelation the smell grew stronger. An old body turned inside out, then left to ripen the air.

He turned on one of the lights, an old pole lamp with a blood-spattered shade.

He'd been to hundreds of murder scenes, examined untold numbers of victims, but only rarely had his hard-cop exterior crumbled away even slightly. Only once in a blue moon had true horror crept into his consciousness to leave him shaken.

In this room, he was appalled. Concentration left him entirely.

His mind wandered. He remembered Garth's agonized, quizzical expression on that beach. Now, staring into the crimson despair of the room where Alice Lamp Corinth had literally exploded with her grandson's hate, he again felt helpless, weak, lost. His head hung down, eyes drifting vacantly from point to point. His hunger for the hunt was obliterated.

Above him, in the pitch-black attic, Edgar's eyes were animal wide. His ears strained to pick up anything. Until this moment it had been easy, but silence disturbed him.

He'd watched the car come up the road from the attic window. Watched it pull into the drive with lights out, watched everything. The great care Husky Martin had taken had seemed comical, and Edgar had nearly laughed outright.

But he'd known the value of the attic. He held his tongue.

246

When Martin had entered the house, Edgar's vantage had become one of sound. He could hear everything from where he sat. The house was like a speaker: all sounds rising to where the two sides of the roof came together, just over Edgar's head.

He'd known no cop would try getting in through the front door. They never did it that way. They were naturally more careful than that. So he'd kept track as Martin had opened the kitchen door.

Its creaking hinge stood out like a road marker.

At that point Edgar had felt his excitement start to mount. Martin would've been seeing Grandma Alice's face! He'd been doubly sure because he *hadn't* heard the kitchen door close again behind Martin. *It wouldn't close by itself, you had to shut it by hand.* The cop had been so fucked up by what he'd seen that he'd forgotten all about it!

Taking the face out of the living room and putting it on the kitchen table had been perfect.

Kiss this, Husky.

But this silence was bothering him. Of course, not even Martin would've expected to find anything like what he'd done to Grandma Alice.

He'd done her very well.

In fact, he'd never done anybody else even remotely as well.

Old people were supposed to be more brittle. When they broke their bones it was supposed to be much worse. He remembered the old woman he'd popped as his part of Multiple Grandmas.

He'd been surprised how easily she'd given up, how the pain had straightened her back at first, making her actually seem taller than when she'd been okay.

Grandma Alice had been slightly different in the going-out phase. She'd clutched at his arm as he pushed her against the wall, sort of getting up on tiptoes when she hit it. He thought she'd muttered something at him in her pain, like she hated his fucking guts or something, right to the end. After that he'd ignored anything she might have to say. After that she was *his*.

Then it had been thirty seconds, at the most, before Granny pot pie.

Now, in the quiet, Edgar felt tension. He wasn't used to it, and decided he couldn't endure it. There was an absolute need to move, but he forced himself to think. Don't assume that cop down there has quit trying. He's standing stock-still in the living room, or wherever, taking an inventory of what's happening in this house right now.

Edgar smiled. It didn't matter. He still had the advantage of the house.

Now he was glad for all those times he'd come up to the attic to hide as a boy. His memory was crystal clear as he looked out across the attic floor before him. He knew exactly where the strong beams were. Edgar stood up, went over it in his mind, then took a first careful step.

Not a sound.

He moved quickly after that, increasingly certain and suddenly filled with the complete confidence he'd felt years before. His grandmother had known this house cold, but she'd never known it like Edgar.

Just before he reached the string-pull door that led to the secret stairs down from the attic, he stopped. His hand was on the string, ready to open it, but he was gripped by a fear of what might be on the other side. It was almost as if Martin had brought something more than himself to this house. Edgar closed his eyes and tried to understand why he was suddenly so worried, so timid. It must be the place, the old boyhood feelings plaguing him again.

But his grandmother was very dead, he reminded himself. That made him feel better and stronger. The string

248

was pulled, the door opened. Nothing waited on the other side.

The house was Edgar's ally now. The old, strong beams in the attic floor, the cramped dark stairs leading down to the second-floor landing. Even the perfect, oiled silence of the wall door at the bottom of the hidden stairway.

Edgar came out into the cooler air of the second-floor landing and stood absolutely still for almost a minute. He was listening for Husky Martin, who might very well be listening for him.

The light from the pole lamp in the living room below was an old, yellow light, making everything seem as if cast in candle glow.

After paying exhaustingly close attention to anything that might be alive on the landing near him or in any upstairs room, Edgar felt certain Husky Martin was still on the first floor. Probably still standing in the living room.

That would mean he was trying to understand.

Edgar loved this; it made him smile and relax.

From his place on the landing, just inches in front of the secret wall door, Edgar took a long step across the floor and rested his foot lightly, carefully, *right beside* the bottom runner of the handrail frame. As he did, he caught the rail with his hands, after which he could swing his weight . . . and his other leg . . . forward without making any sound at all.

This done, he was peering over the rail and down into the living room. He had come down from the attic with the silence of a ghost.

What Edgar saw was Husky Martin, motionless as his own death, standing exactly where he had been standing for several minutes.

Edgar's heart jumped. Martin had no idea he was standing here. In fact, Martin looked like he might even be in

249

some kind of stupor, posed there, face aimed at the red sunburst that spread on the carpet and thinned out as it tinted the entire room. What the fuck was he looking at? What the fuck was he thinking? Edgar wanted to yell, but he simply stood there above Husky and watched, fascinated.

Husky was watching, too.

He was watching Edgar Lamp.

He could see Edgar's reflection in a brass flower pot that rested on an end table not two feet away from his left hand. He saw the curious, meat-eating expression and the mounting disease in the shocking white bullets that were Edgar's widened eyes.

Husky felt like he'd won. He'd come into this man's trap and created a trap of his own, assuming Edgar Lamp could not have patience anymore. Not here.

Husky spun as rapidly as his body would allow, shotgun in motion even as his right foot pivoted on the toe and his left swung out of the way for the turn. The two shots shook the structure and filled the stale old air with more sound than it could hold.

Edgar had disappeared from his rail in the last fragment of a second that was his own to control. The shots moved through the space he'd just occupied and pierced the ceiling, then the attic air, then the roof; then the night.

The silence that followed the shots was so thick Husky winced. His ears rang. So did Edgar's, but Edgar didn't care. He was moving to the side, out of Husky's line of sight, and suddenly throwing himself over the banister several feet from where he had been, plummeting with madman's perfect aim to hit Husky at shoulder and ribs and trunk.

The older man gasped, taken down hard by the flying attack; wide-eyed with shock when he discovered his wind was gone, really gone, for several seconds.

And yet he had to fight in those seconds. Edgar wasn't giving him any time. The struggle for breath made it impossible for Husky to concentrate completely. Impossible to match the unreasoning thrashing intensity of his younger, lighter opponent.

Finally breath began to return. Husky realized he'd been battling desperately, but he'd also been *thinking* about it. Edgar thought of nothing but murder; a tremendous advantage. As he managed his first precious air in several seconds, Husky wondered how he could spend such unbelievably important brain time intellectualizing about Edgar's attack. Yet he felt oddly outside himself, distant from the savagery he had to contend with.

It was only at this moment that he realized the fight itself was over control of the shotgun. Suddenly newfound strength surged and Husky began reversing Edgar's early gains. His upper body hurt from the blow, but no doubt Edgar's did too.

The gun between them was at stalemate; neutralized.

Seconds passed. The two struggled for control of the wood-and-metal barrier dividing them with everything they had. Edgar just stared, expression dead, a machine of ruin. Husky knew the man's will was bottomless.

Edgar could feel the cop's arms weaken slightly, then tense again as the older man became aware of his sapping strength. Almost ready to be had. But the gaze Edgar returned was less impressed than any he'd ever encountered. Even El Chocolate Grande had not looked back into Edgar's Proving stare with anything approaching this level of cool. Edgar had to admire it.

And he had to destroy it.

Now he understood why Martin had been the one to catch him, and how he could keep the pressure going throughout their duel across and around L.A.

"Show it to me, Edgar! Show me the stuff!"

Edgar couldn't believe he was hearing this. Couldn't believe the cop would *bring it up!* He just stared as they continued to struggle over the shotgun; a little back, a little forward.

All Husky could think of was Garth. This had been the face that killed Garth. It brought fury into his body he hadn't known could possibly still be there. Husky was glad he'd come here alone to fight this way. He wanted this one.

But right after this surge, there came a slight wavering in Husky's efforts. It was what Edgar had been waiting for.

He lowered his eyes slightly and began to focus on the spot with the Proving stare.

At first Husky thought he'd somehow broken the sonofabitch, forced him to look down. But quickly, very quickly, he knew something had to be wrong. A dull pain was beginning in his solar plexus, getting to him, driving strength out of his arms and hands. He lost the battle for the gun.

Edgar threw the gun away; it smashed across the room.

"Right now, Martin . . ."

He shoved Husky back, and the cop went down hard, falling over a footrest in Alice Lamp Corinth's living room.

Edgar was right above him, right on him, pinning him. Husky's guts were on fire, but the fire had decreased. He groaned, trying to touch it with his hands, but Edgar wouldn't let him.

"Feel that?" Edgar grinned.

Husky stared up at him, fascinated even while he was desperate to think of something.

"It gets worse, pigshit. It gets to where you're pretty sure you can't take it. Which is the absolute fuckin' truth."

252

Edgar slugged Husky in the jaw with an alarming, cruel suddenness. He remembered the girl in the motel and how he'd hit her. This was nowhere near as much of a turn-on, but it was a different kind of fun.

He started again, lowering the eyes and holding the agonizing older man down. It was pretty easy until the pain began to build, then the struggle increased and Edgar had to really work to keep Husky where he wanted him. Edgar kept telling himself this was going to happen, going to happen just like all the others only in some ways a whole lot better because this guy was the one. *The* pig ass who had followed him and dogged his butt worse than the rest.

Edgar was blowing air hard out his nose and mouth, heaving like a miler, going into red and white splotches all through his face and neck. His veins stood out like a road map above Husky's straining body.

Edgar's mind kept feeding him: the whole world wants a miracle, the whole world wants a miracle . . .

Husky realized that the thought he was almost hearing, almost experiencing like physical, audible sound, was *Edgar's* thought. Like a chant.

The whole world wants a miracle.

Husky's eyes were open wide as he renewed his struggle against Edgar. Was that what this was? Was this a miracle?

Husky's hands had been locked around Edgar's throat for several seconds, but they could not, just as El Chocolate Grande's could not, do anything to speak of. Arm weariness seeped in. His shoulders were pure fire, nearly rivaling the pain in his middle as he felt the intensity of Edgar's effort building.

Demoralization swept. Husky knew he would lose whether he kept fighting or not. There was no resisting. No logical, physical way. But he couldn't stop. He shook his head, felt flying droplets of his drenching sweat, and

253

tried once more to close his fingers with force around Edgar's throat.

And the pain reached a new pinnacle. Husky's hands fell from Edgar as the final burst of concentration built the agony even more. Husky cried out, certain he must be coming apart in the blind consuming slash of heat that raged from his balls to his sternum.

It was an unending blast of time for both men, destroyer and victim, in which experience so enveloped that nothing could be heard, smelled, or sensed.

Not the chiming sound of Alice's clock as it turned the three-quarter-hour mark.

Not the sickeningly soured reek of the blood-drenched carpet upon which they writhed.

Not the sound of desperate, deep-chested breathing or frenzied feet clawing at glass as muscles pushed and twisted through small space.

Neither man heard the furious scurrying across hardwood or noticed the subtle give of floorboards under added weight.

Neither sensed the breathless final silence before Fred's bared teeth hit Edgar Lamp's reddened, straining throat.

Husky heard the strike-snarl and saw the clamping of the dog's jaws and knew they would not release as the eighty-pound projectile of enraged muscle and instinct swept its target off of Husky's body. He had never seen or imagined Fred like this. He watched transfixed.

Unwaveringly loyal and loving friend protected lifelong master.

Fred stayed with Edgar's throat after impact, just as Husky had seen his bite become a relentless hold in dogfights. But this was far easier and far more final. This prey had no chance. Fred ripped Edgar's throat wide in a spewing fountain of sudden, hot blood, then kept at him, tearing and ripping in a frenzy of vengeance. Husky did not move. Would not. It seemed to him entirely right and just as his dog dragged and threw Edgar Lamp around the room like a damp, dead thing.

Finally the dog relinquished his tireless grip, standing motionless and growling over the mauled form.

Seconds hung endless. At last, Fred was certain there would be no more movement. No more danger.

And in that second he relaxed, looked around, fixed on Husky. Curiosity appeared in Fred's eyes.

Husky held out a hand to his dog.

"Come here, Freddy . . ." Husky was alarmed at the weakness of his voice. Maybe the dog was, too, because he approached slowly, tail moving back and forth only with the gentlest motion. The lingering caution.

But then a familiar arm, tired as it was, came up to circle the strong, warm chest . . . and to hug . . . and cling.

Husky buried his face in the welcome, welcome fur, and cried. Fred stood patiently, knowing at last it was all right again. He moved to the sitting position Husky could never successfully order him to assume, posing patiently as this man he loved hung on, just now completely realizing he had kept his hold on life.

Through sobs, Husky knew he had lost the battle with Edgar Lamp.

He'd come here like a fool, attempting to rise to some idiot's moment of revenge. All his guile, all his well-planned moves and lethal knowledge had left him wanting.

Failed him utterly.

Staring at the floor through watering eyes, finally catching something that felt like a full breath again, Husky knew that the only reason he was alive just now was that for years . . . without question or condition . . . he had loved something and it had loved him in return.

There was nothing else in the entire scope of his life and experience that had come to his rescue.

Nothing but this complete innocence, this complete return of love and protection.

Fred licked him across the face, tail now wagging at normal tempo. And Husky could manage, in that sour corner of Edgar Lamp's hell, a laugh.